DODGE CITY™

JOSH TRUJILLO

CARA McGEE

BRITTANY PEER

GONÇALO LOPES

BOOM! BOX™

ROSS RICHIE CEO & Founder
MATT GAGNON Editor-In-Chief
FILIP SABLIK President, Publishing & Marketing
STEPHEN CHRISTY President, Development
LANCE KREITER Vice President, Licensing & Merchandising
PHIL BARBARO Vice President, Finance & Human Resources
ARUNE SINGH Vice President, Marketing
BRYCE CARLSON Vice President, Editorial & Creative Strategy
SCOTT NEWMAN Manager, Production Design
KATE HENNING Manager, Operations
SPENCER SIMPSON Manager, Sales
SIERRA HAHN Executive Editor
JEANINE SCHAEFER Executive Editor
DAFNA PLEBAN Senior Editor
SHANNON WATTERS Senior Editor
ERIC HARBURN Senior Editor
WHITNEY LEOPARD Editor
CAMERON CHITTOCK Editor
CHRIS ROSA Editor
MATTHEW LEVINE Editor

SOPHIE PHILIPS-ROBERTS Assistant Editor
GAVIN GRONENTHAL Assistant Editor
MICHAEL MOCCIO Assistant Editor
AMANDA LaFRANCO Executive Assistant
KATALINA HOLLAND Editorial Administrative Assistant
JILLIAN CRAB Design Coordinator
MICHELLE ANKLEY Design Coordinator
KARA LEOPARD Production Designer
MARIE KRUPINA Production Designer
GRACE PARK Production Design Assistant
CHELSEA ROBERTS Production Design Assistant
ELIZABETH LOUGHRIDGE Accounting Coordinator
STEPHANIE HOCUTT Social Media Coordinator
JOSÉ MEZA Event Coordinator
HOLLY AITCHISON Operations Coordinator
MEGAN CHRISTOPHER Operations Assistant
RODRIGO HERNANDEZ Mailroom Assistant
MORGAN PERRY Direct Market Representative
CAT O'GRADY Marketing Assistant
CORNELIA TZANA Publicity Assistant

DODGE CITY, October 2018. Published by BOOM! Box, a division of Boom Entertainment, Inc. Dodge City is ™ & © 2018 Josh Trujillo. Originally published in single magazine form as DODGE CITY No. 1-4. ™ & © 2018 Josh Trujillo. All rights reserved. BOOM! Box and the BOOM! Box logo are trademarks of Boom Entertainment, Inc., registered in various countries and categories. All characters, events, and institutions depicted herein are fictional. Any similarity between any of the names, characters, persons, events, and/or institutions in this publication to actual names, characters, and persons, whether living or dead, events, and/or institutions is unintended and purely coincidental. BOOM! Box does not read or accept unsolicited submissions of ideas, stories, or artwork.

BOOM! Studios, 5670 Wilshire Boulevard, Suite 400, Los Angeles, CA 90036-5679. Printed in China. First Printing.

ISBN: 978-1-68415-247-6, eISBN: 978-1-64144-109-4

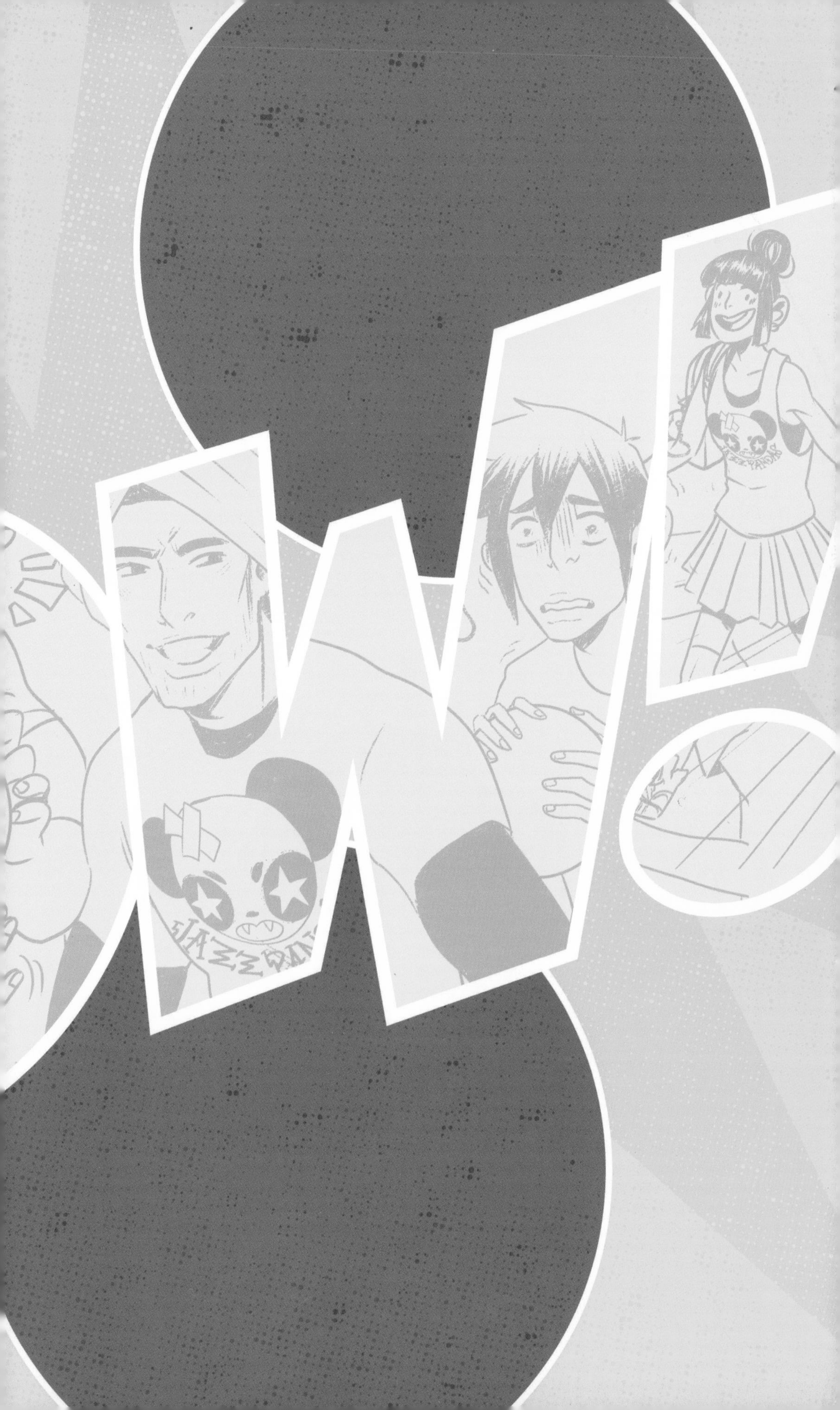

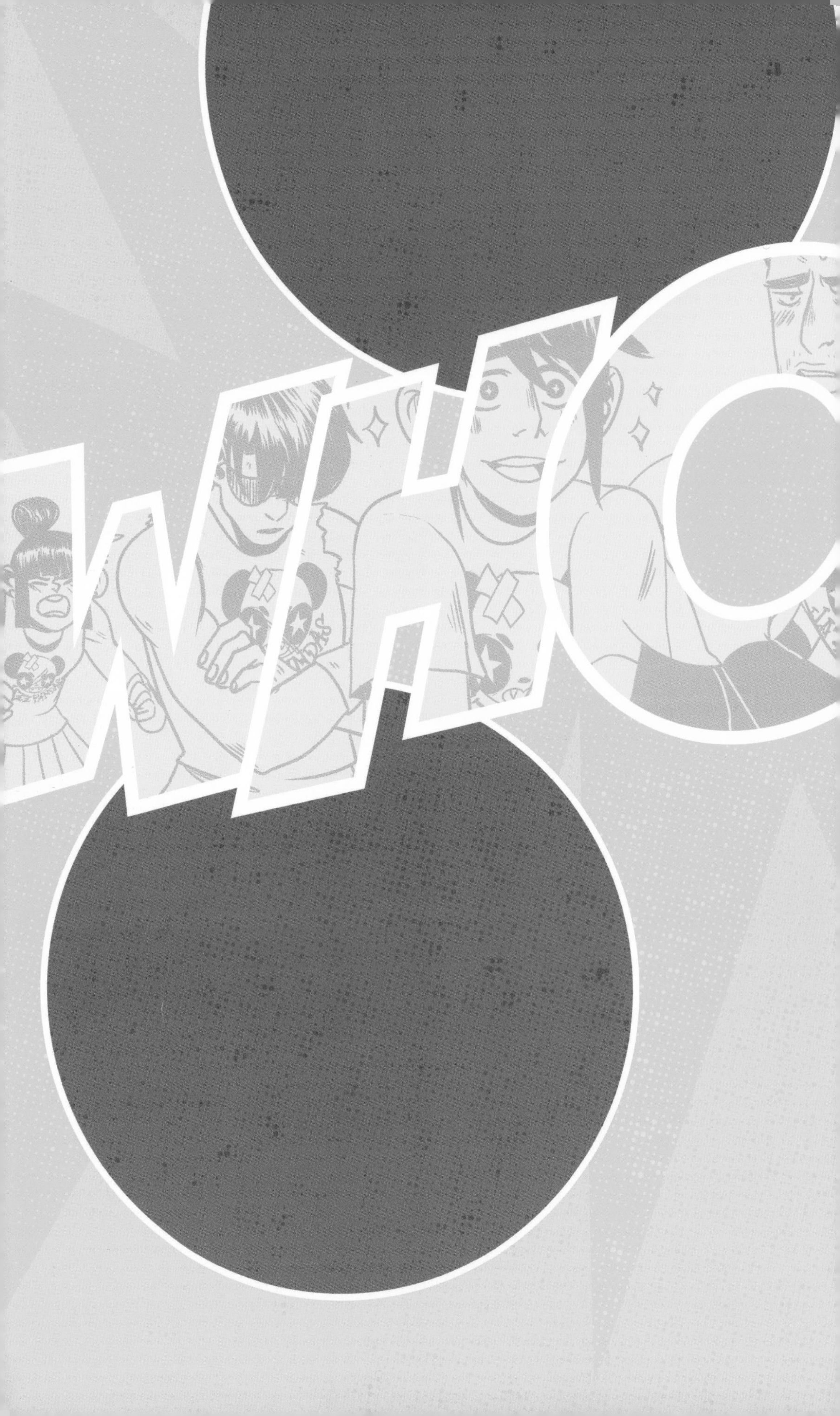
WHO

Created & Written by
JOSH TRUJILLO

Illustrated by
CARA McGEE

Colored by
BRITTANY PEER
(chapters 1, 3, and 4)

With GONÇALO LOPES (chapter 2) and CARA McGEE (chapters 1-3)

Lettered by
AUBREY AIESE

Cover by
CARA McGEE

Series Designer
MARIE KRUPINA

Collection Designer
JILLIAN CRAB

Assistant Editor
SOPHIE PHILIPS-ROBERTS

Editor
SHANNON WATTERS

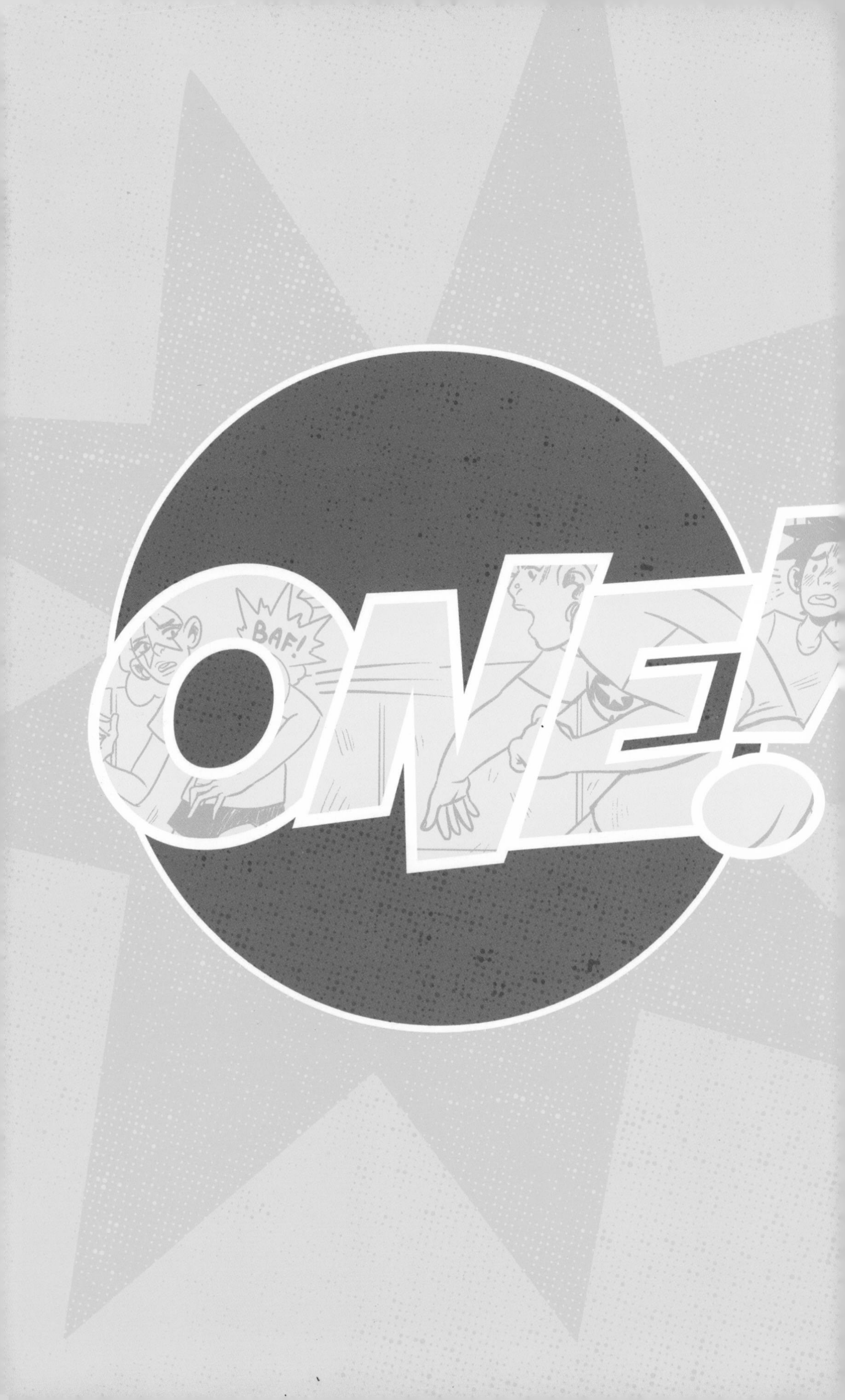
ONE!
BAF!

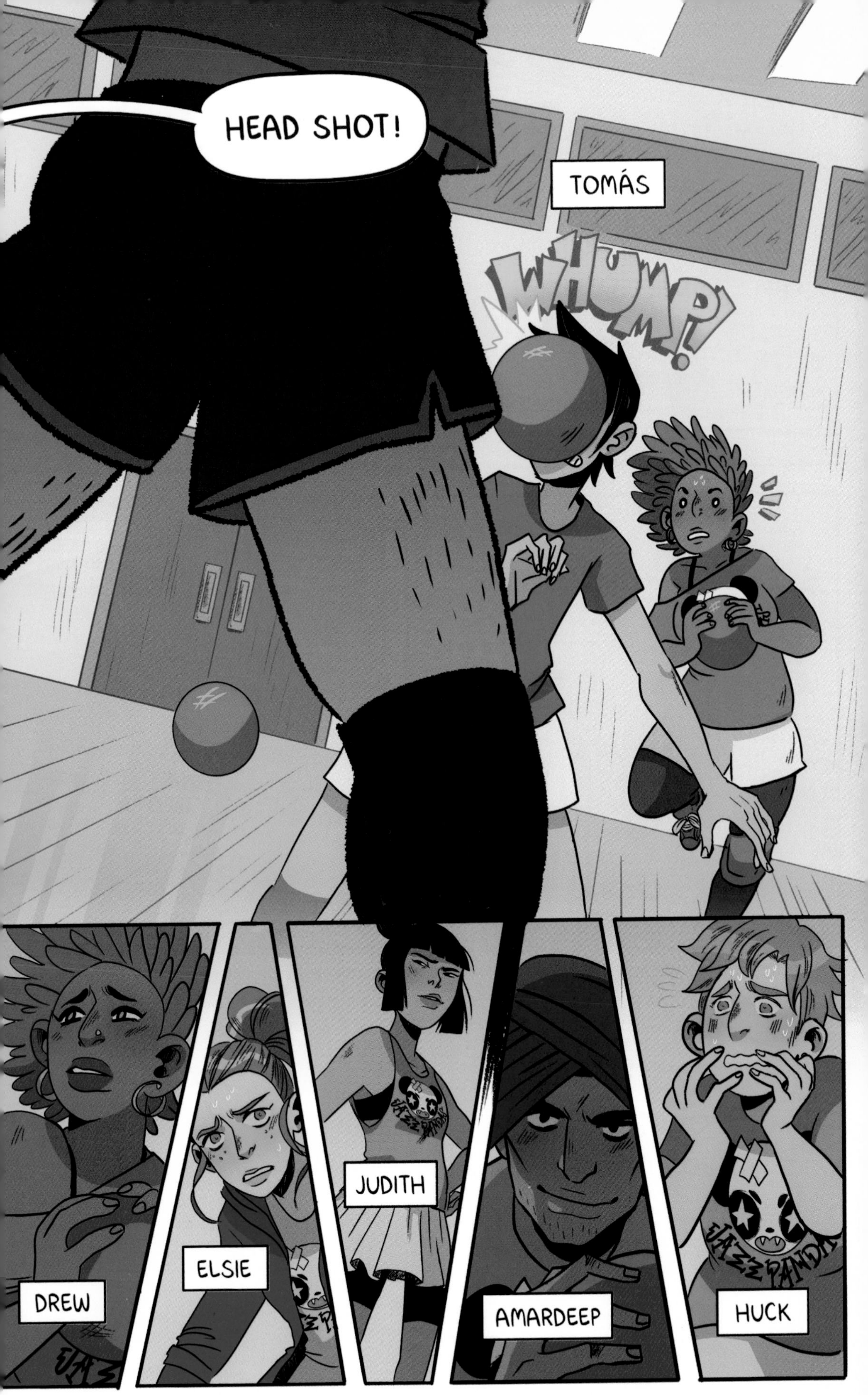
HEAD SHOT!
TOMÁS
WHUMP!
DREW
ELSIE
JUDITH
AMARDEEP
HUCK

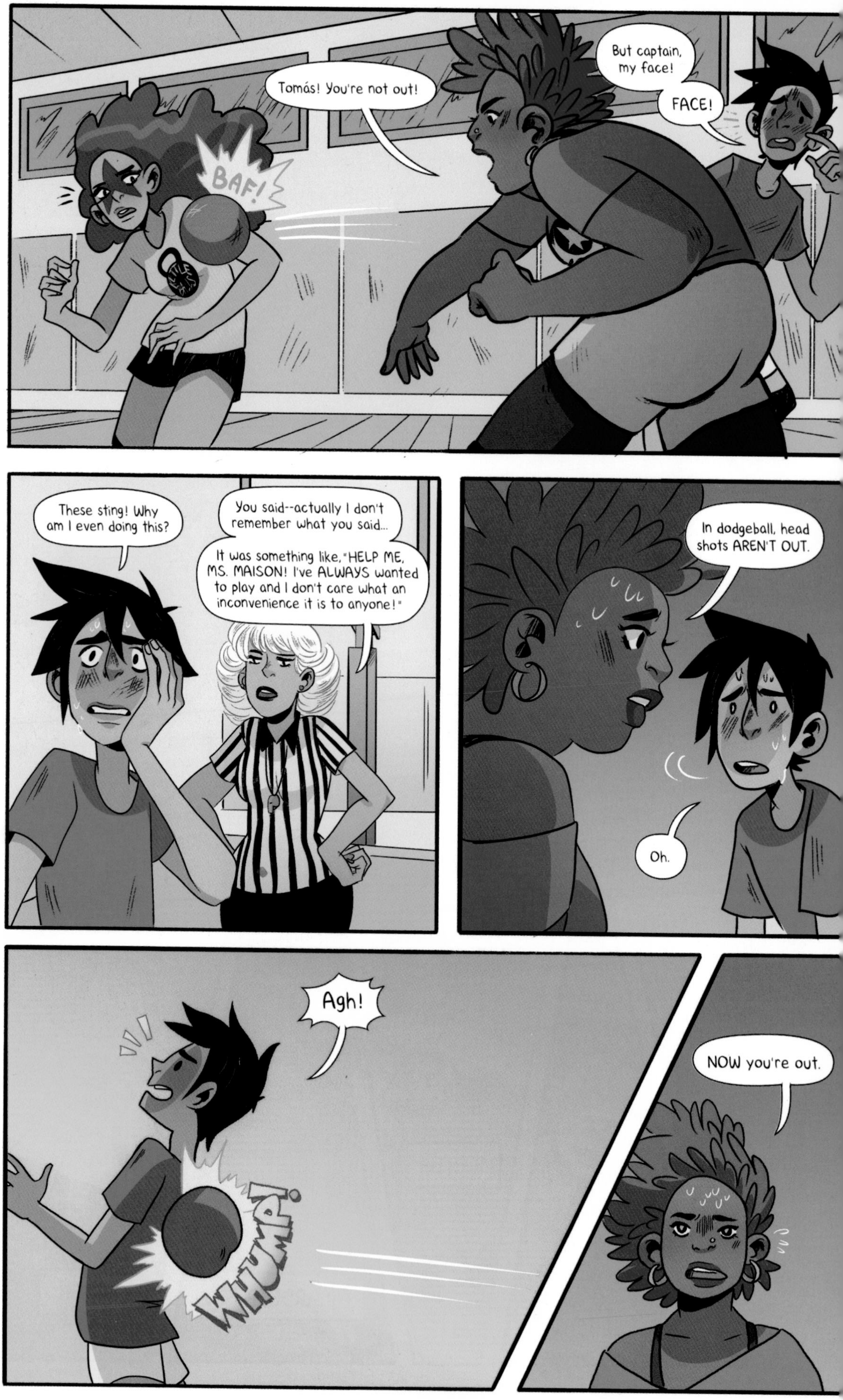

BAF!
Tomás! You're not out!
But captain, my face!
FACE!
These sting! Why am I even doing this?
You said--actually I don't remember what you said...
It was something like, "HELP ME, MS. MAISON! I've ALWAYS wanted to play and I don't care what an inconvenience it is to anyone!"
In dodgeball, head shots AREN'T OUT.
Oh.
Agh!
WHUMP!
NOW you're out.

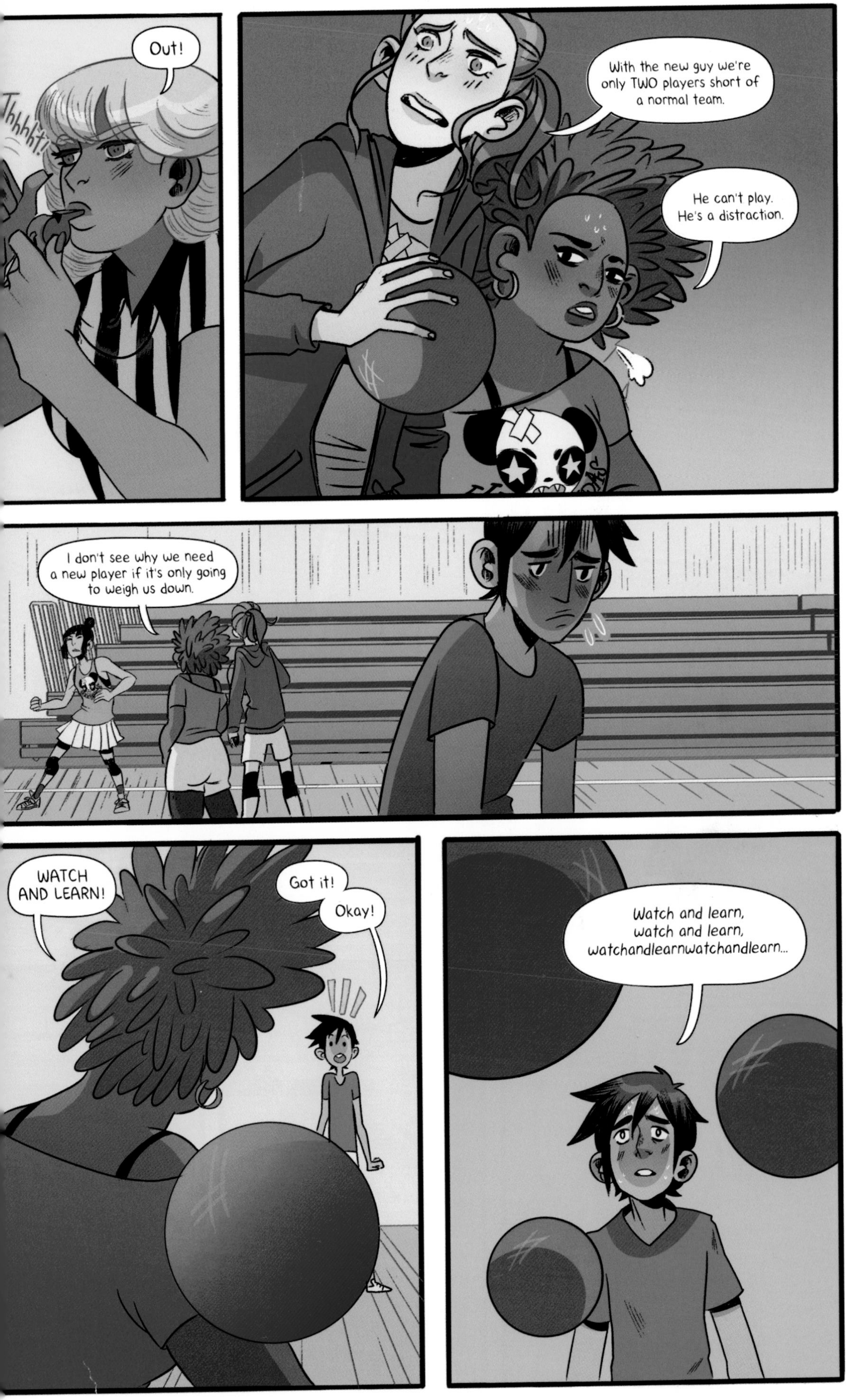
Out!
Thhhht!
With the new guy we're only TWO players short of a normal team.
He can't play. He's a distraction.
I don't see why we need a new player if it's only going to weigh us down.
WATCH AND LEARN!
Got it!
Okay!
Watch and learn, watch and learn, watchandlearnwatchandlearn...

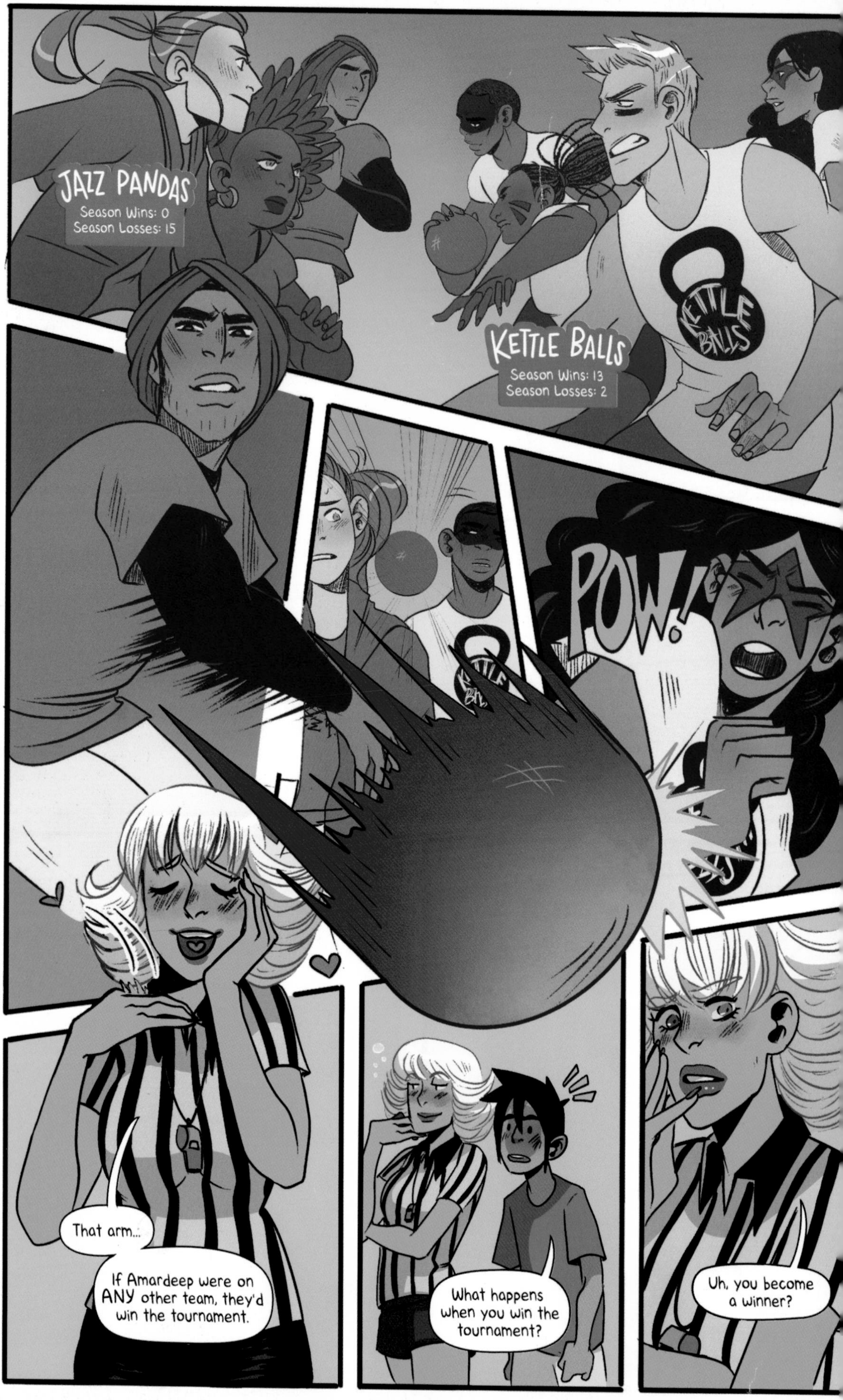
JAZZ PANDAS
Season Wins: 0
Season Losses: 15
KETTLE BALLS
Season Wins: 13
Season Losses: 2
POW!
That arm...
If Amardeep were on ANY other team, they'd win the tournament.
What happens when you win the tournament?
Uh, you become a winner?

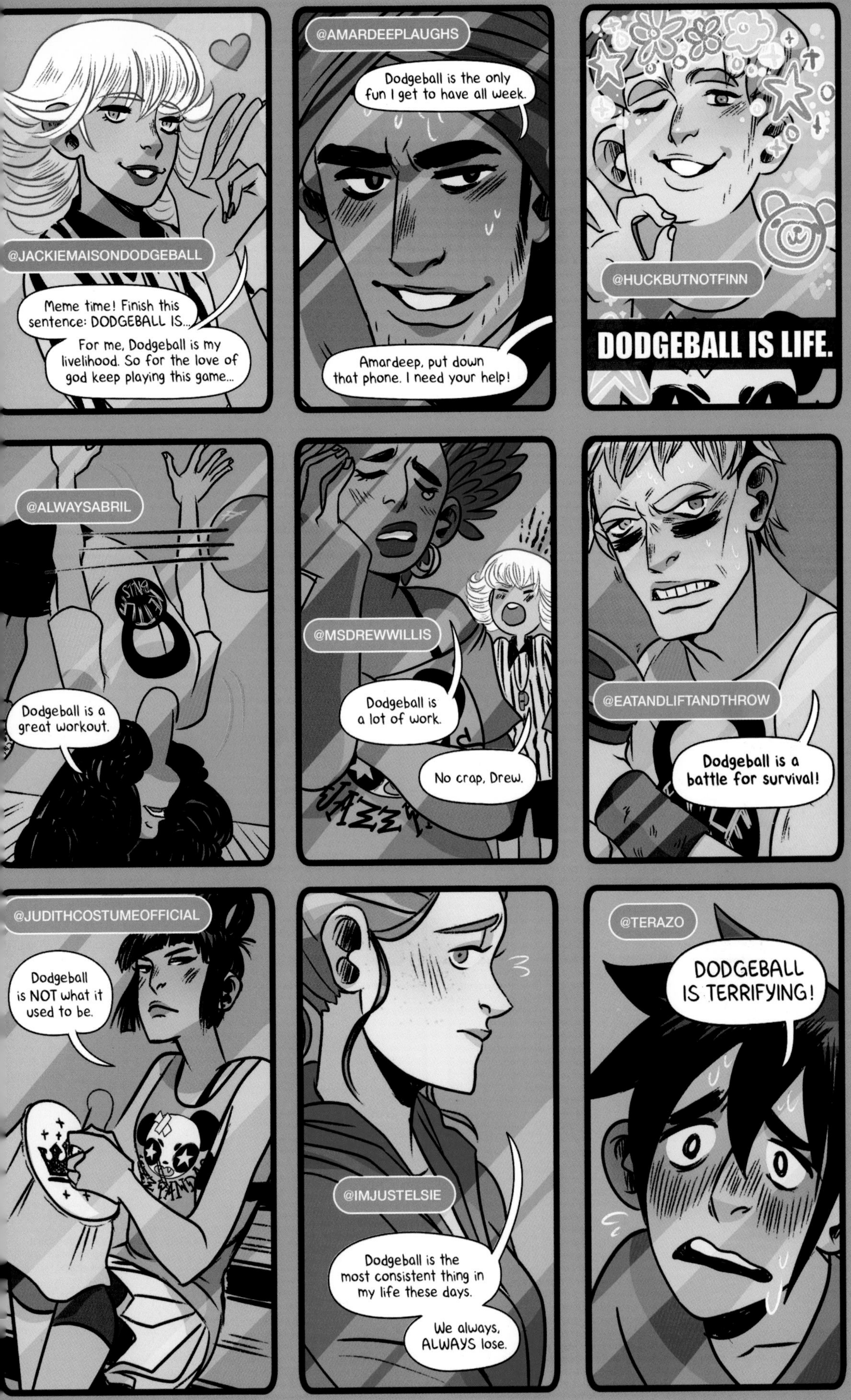
@JACKIEMAISONDODGEBALL
Meme time! Finish this sentence: DODGEBALL IS...
For me, Dodgeball is my livelihood. So for the love of god keep playing this game...
@AMARDEEPLAUGHS
Dodgeball is the only fun I get to have all week.
Amardeep, put down that phone. I need your help!
@HUCKBUTNOTFINN
DODGEBALL IS LIFE.
@ALWAYSABRIL
Dodgeball is a great workout.
@MSDREWWILLIS
Dodgeball is a lot of work.
No crap, Drew.
@EATANDLIFTANDTHROW
Dodgeball is a battle for survival!
@JUDITHCOSTUMEOFFICIAL
Dodgeball is NOT what it used to be.
@IMJUSTELSIE
Dodgeball is the most consistent thing in my life these days.
We always, ALWAYS lose.
@TERAZO
DODGEBALL IS TERRIFYING!

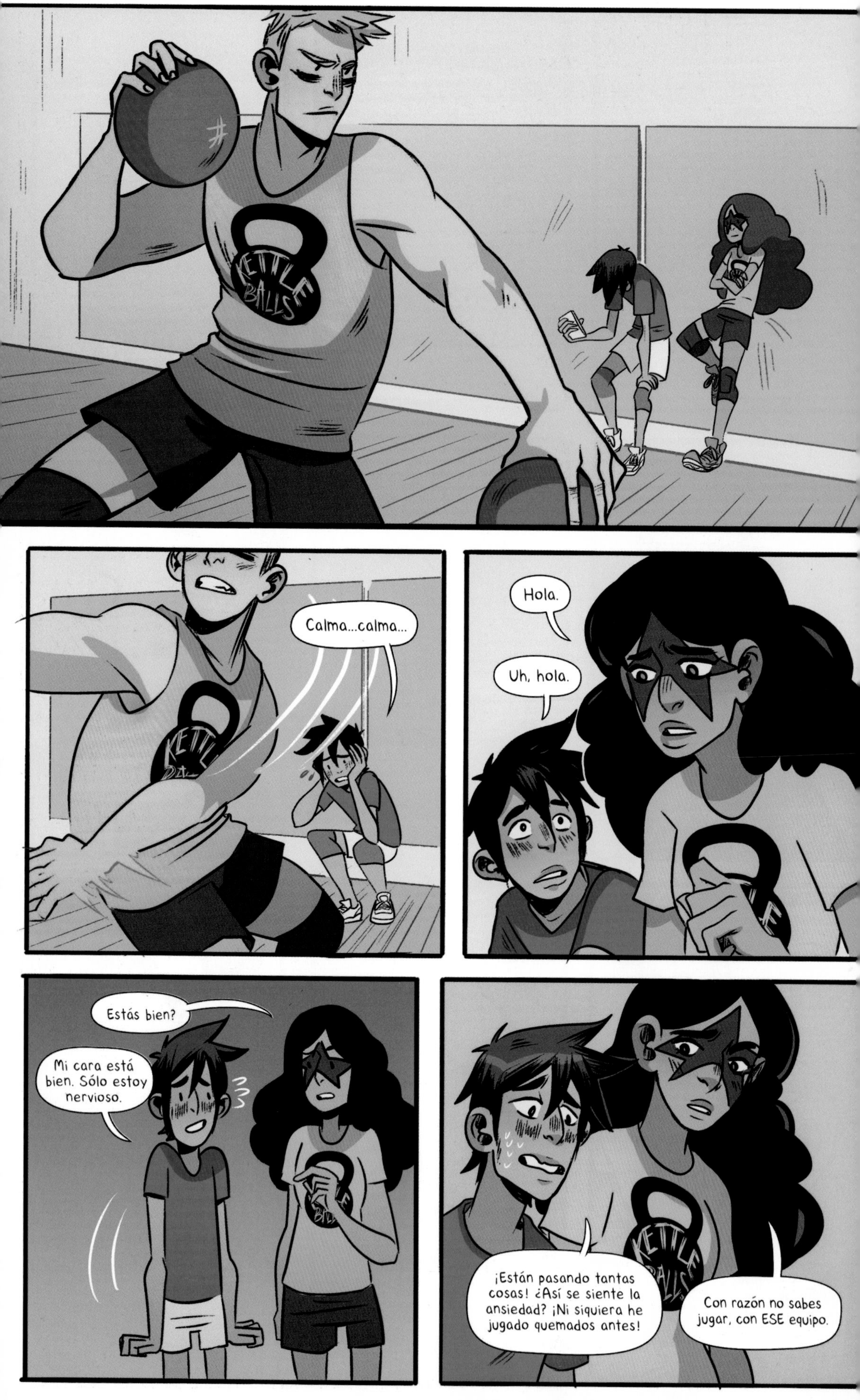
Calma...calma...
Hola.
Uh, hola.
Estás bien?
Mi cara está bien. Sólo estoy nervioso.
¡Están pasando tantas cosas! ¿Así se siente la ansiedad? ¡Ni siquiera he jugado quemados antes!
Con razón no sabes jugar, con ESE equipo.

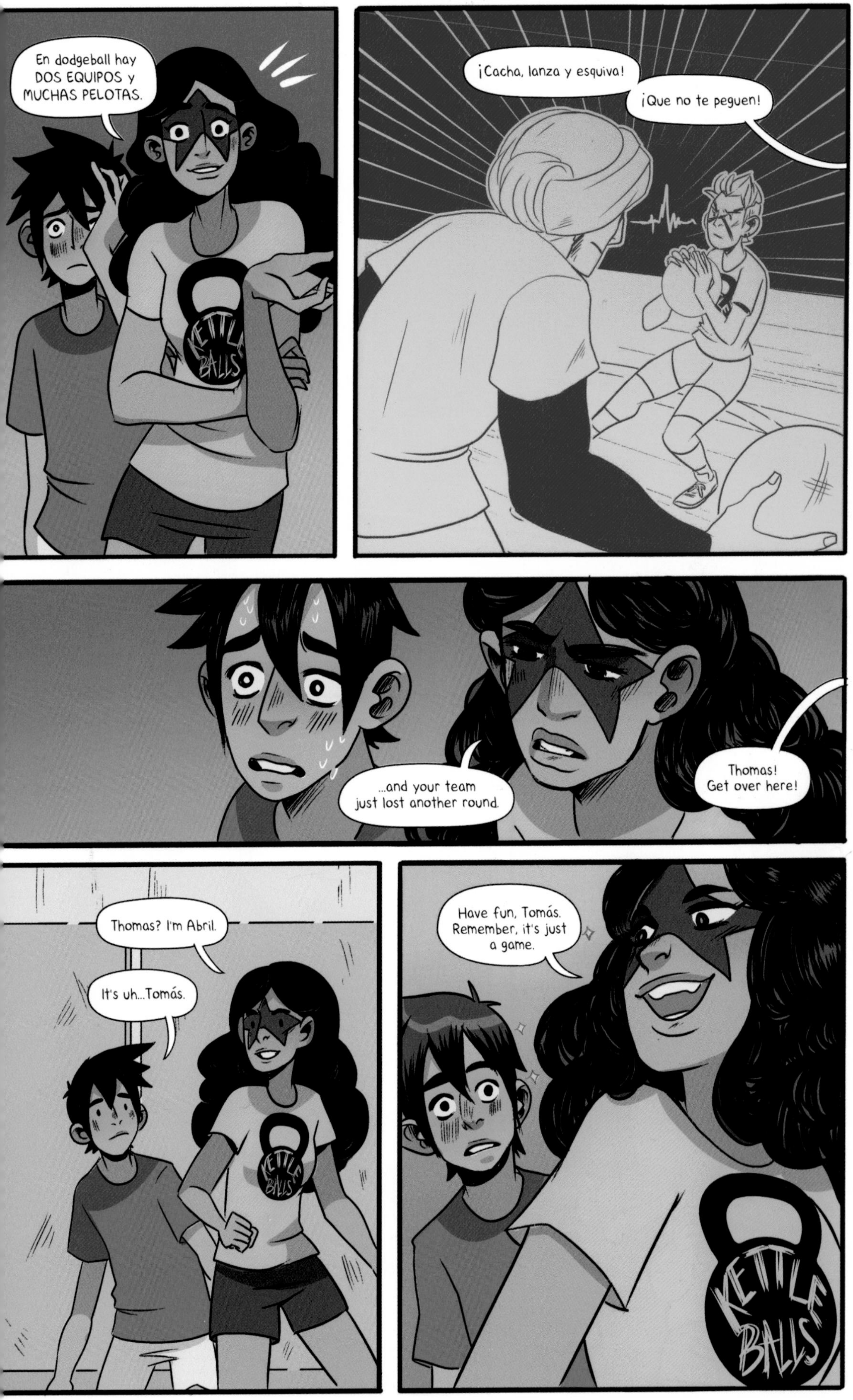

En dodgeball hay DOS EQUIPOS y MUCHAS PELOTAS.
¡Cacha, lanza y esquiva!
¡Que no te peguen!
...and your team just lost another round.
Thomas! Get over here!
Thomas? I'm Abril.
It's uh...Tomás.
Have fun, Tomás. Remember, it's just a game.
KETTLE BALLS

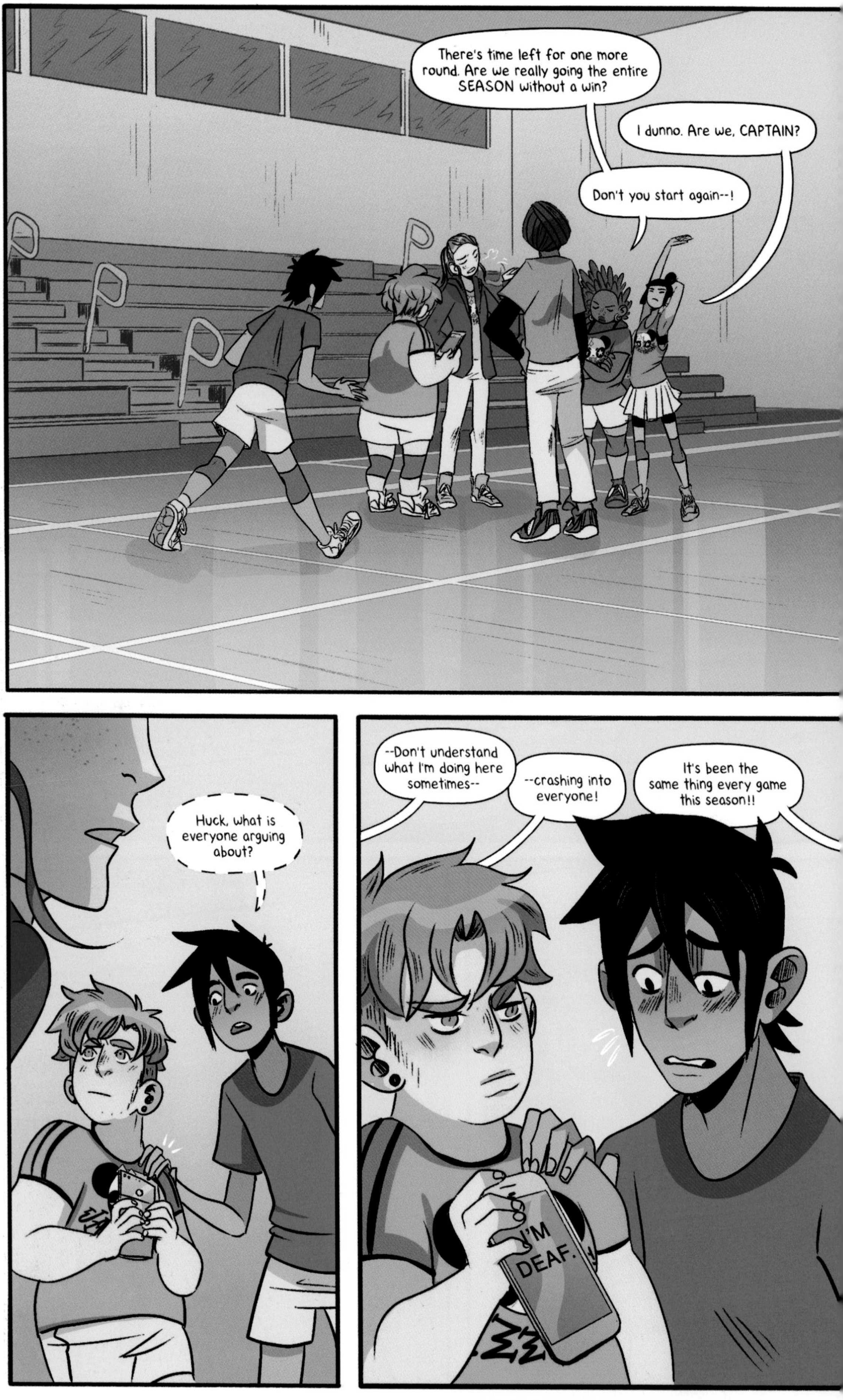
There's time left for one more round. Are we really going the entire SEASON without a win?
I dunno. Are we, CAPTAIN?
Don't you start again--!
Huck, what is everyone arguing about?
--Don't understand what I'm doing here sometimes--
--crashing into everyone!
It's been the same thing every game this season!!
I'M DEAF.

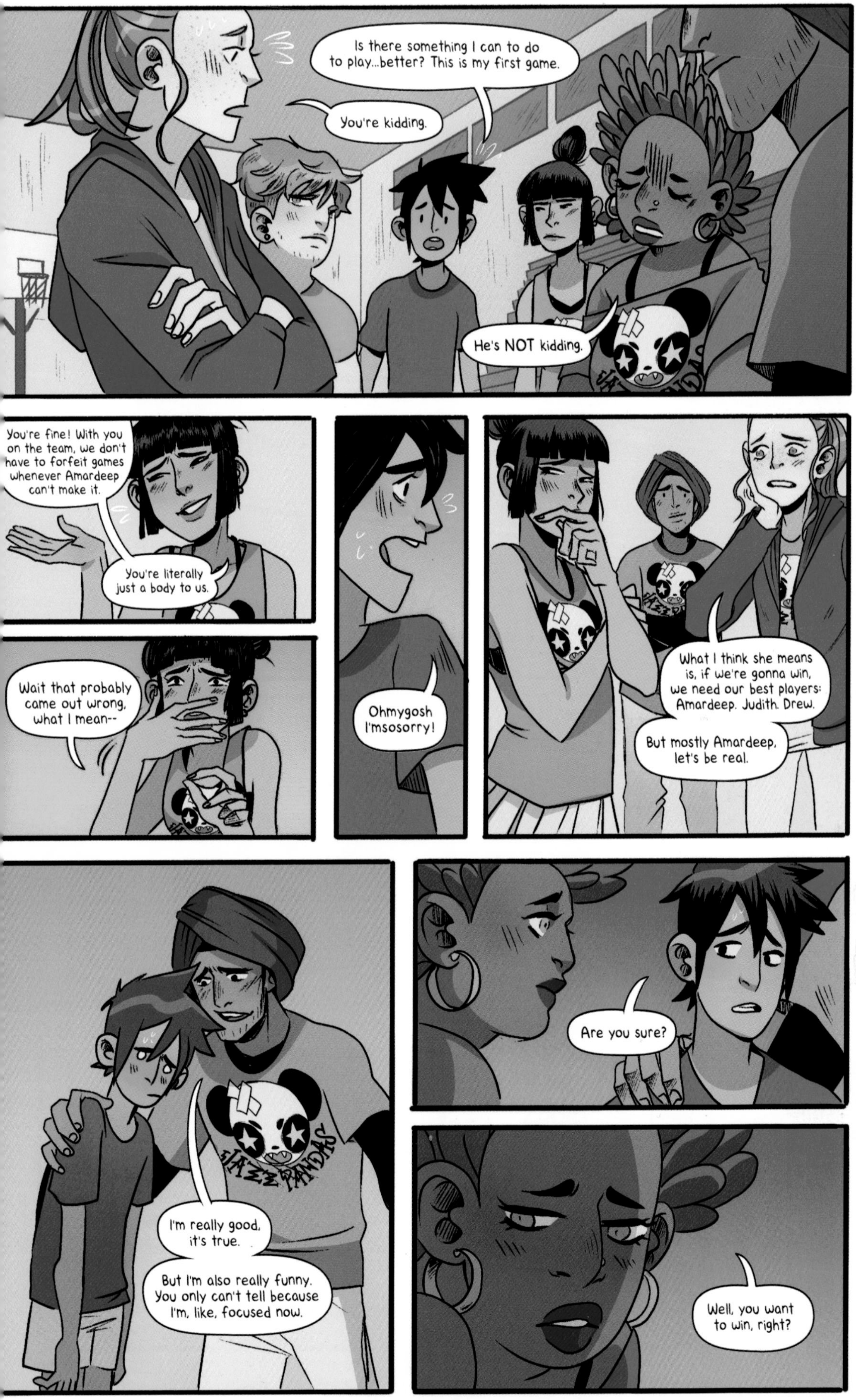
Is there something I can to do to play...better? This is my first game.
You're kidding.
He's NOT kidding.
You're fine! With you on the team, we don't have to forfeit games whenever Amardeep can't make it.
You're literally just a body to us.
Wait that probably came out wrong, what I mean--
Ohmygosh I'msosorry!
What I think she means is, if we're gonna win, we need our best players: Amardeep. Judith. Drew.
But mostly Amardeep, let's be real.
JAZZ PANDAS
I'm really good, it's true.
But I'm also really funny. You only can't tell because I'm, like, focused now.
Are you sure?
Well, you want to win, right?

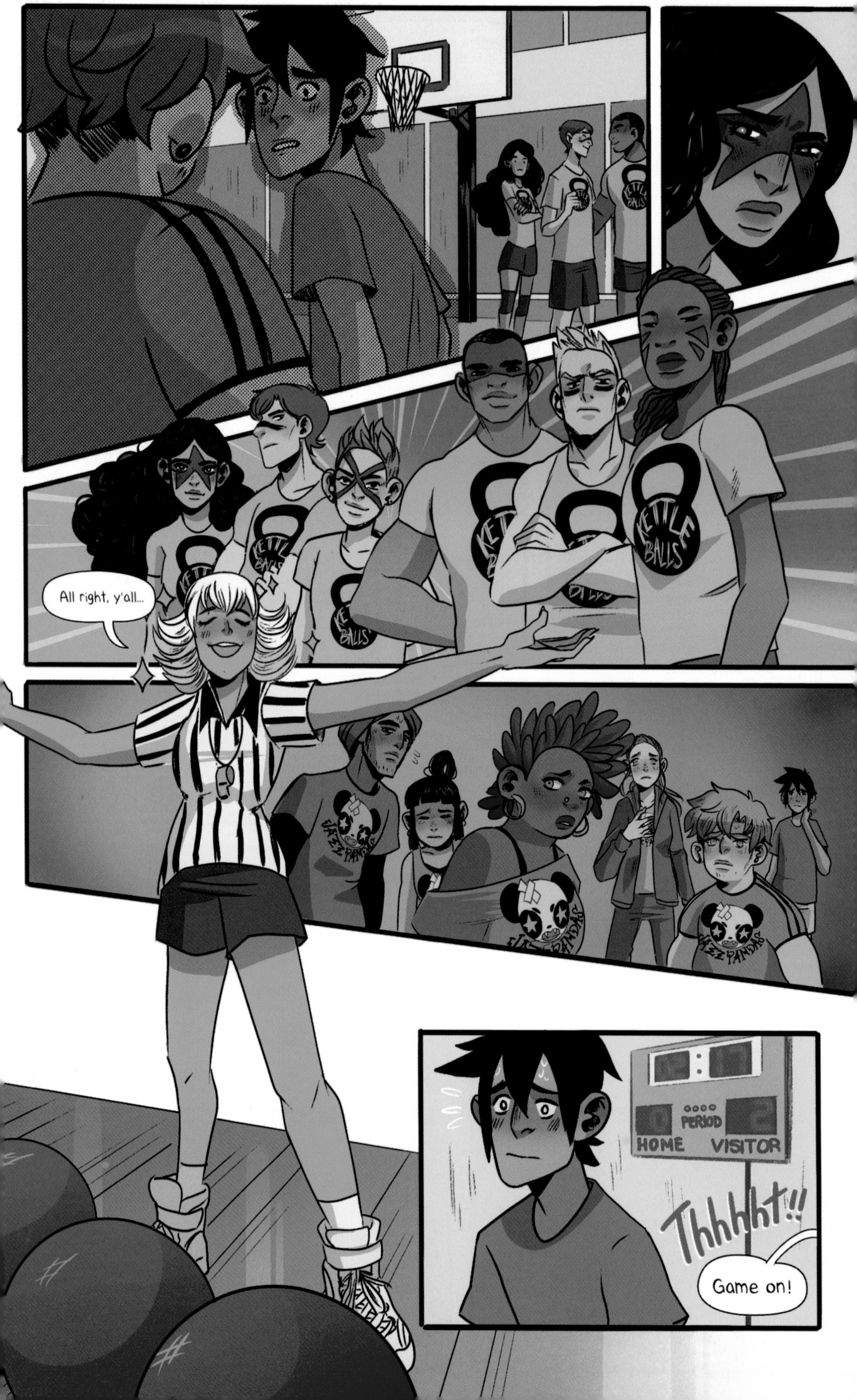
KETTLE BALLS
All right, y'all...
JAZZ PANDAS
PERIOD
HOME
VISITOR
Thhhht!!
Game on!

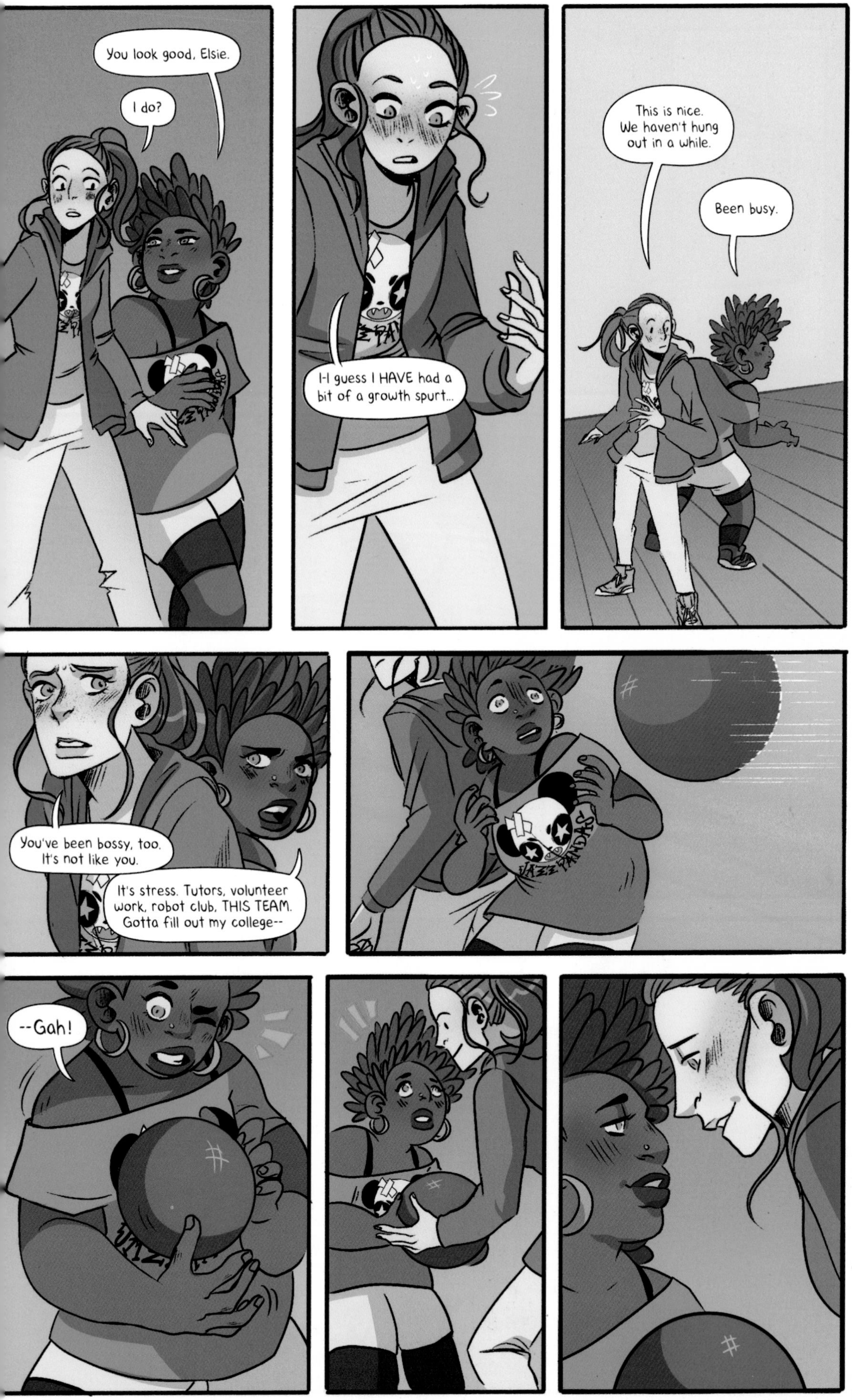
You look good, Elsie.
I do?
I-I guess I HAVE had a bit of a growth spurt...
This is nice. We haven't hung out in a while.
Been busy.
You've been bossy, too. It's not like you.
It's stress. Tutors, volunteer work, robot club, THIS TEAM. Gotta fill out my college--
--Gah!

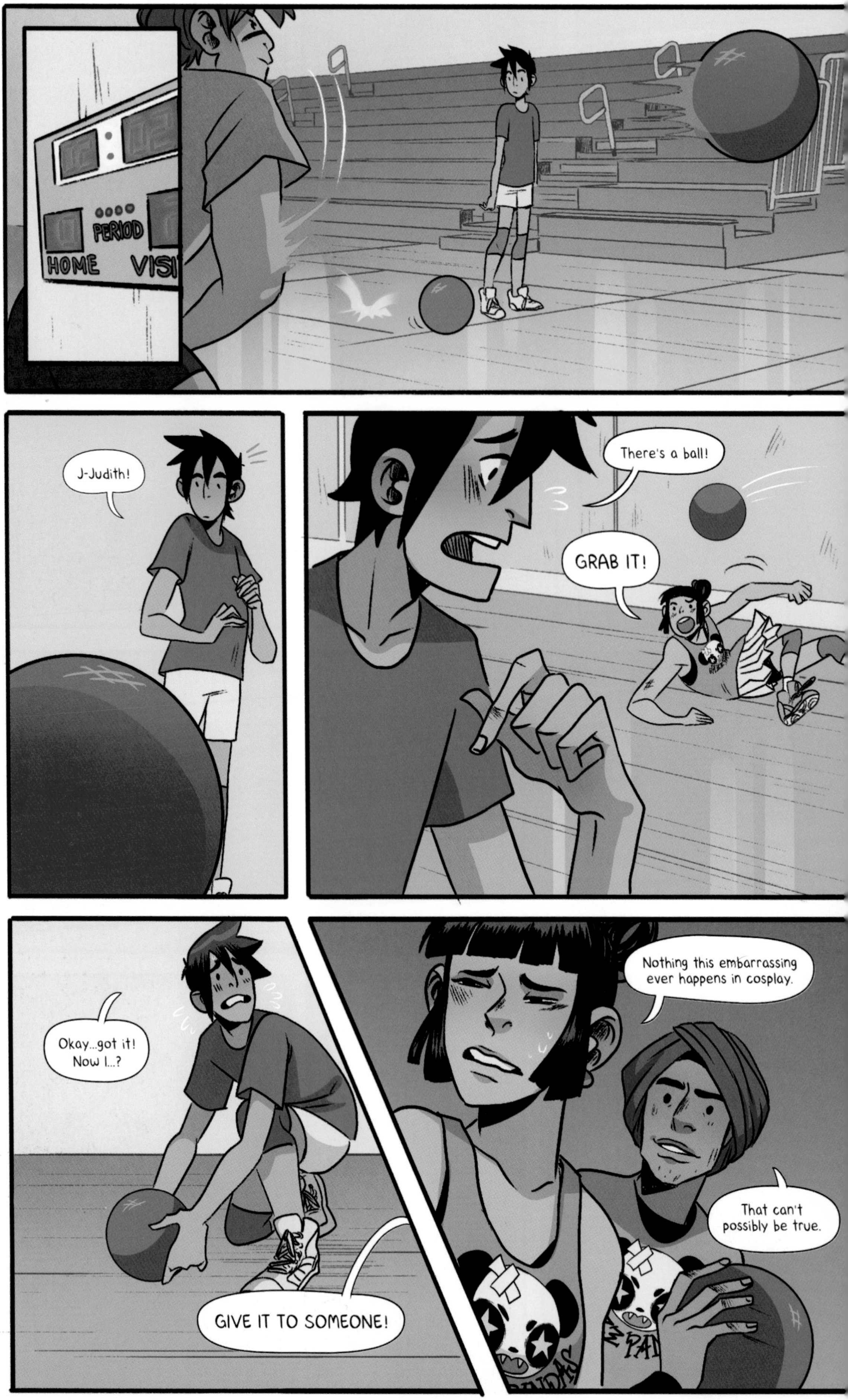
PERIOD
HOME
VISI
J-Judith!
There's a ball!
GRAB IT!
Okay...got it! Now I...?
GIVE IT TO SOMEONE!
Nothing this embarrassing ever happens in cosplay.
That can't possibly be true.

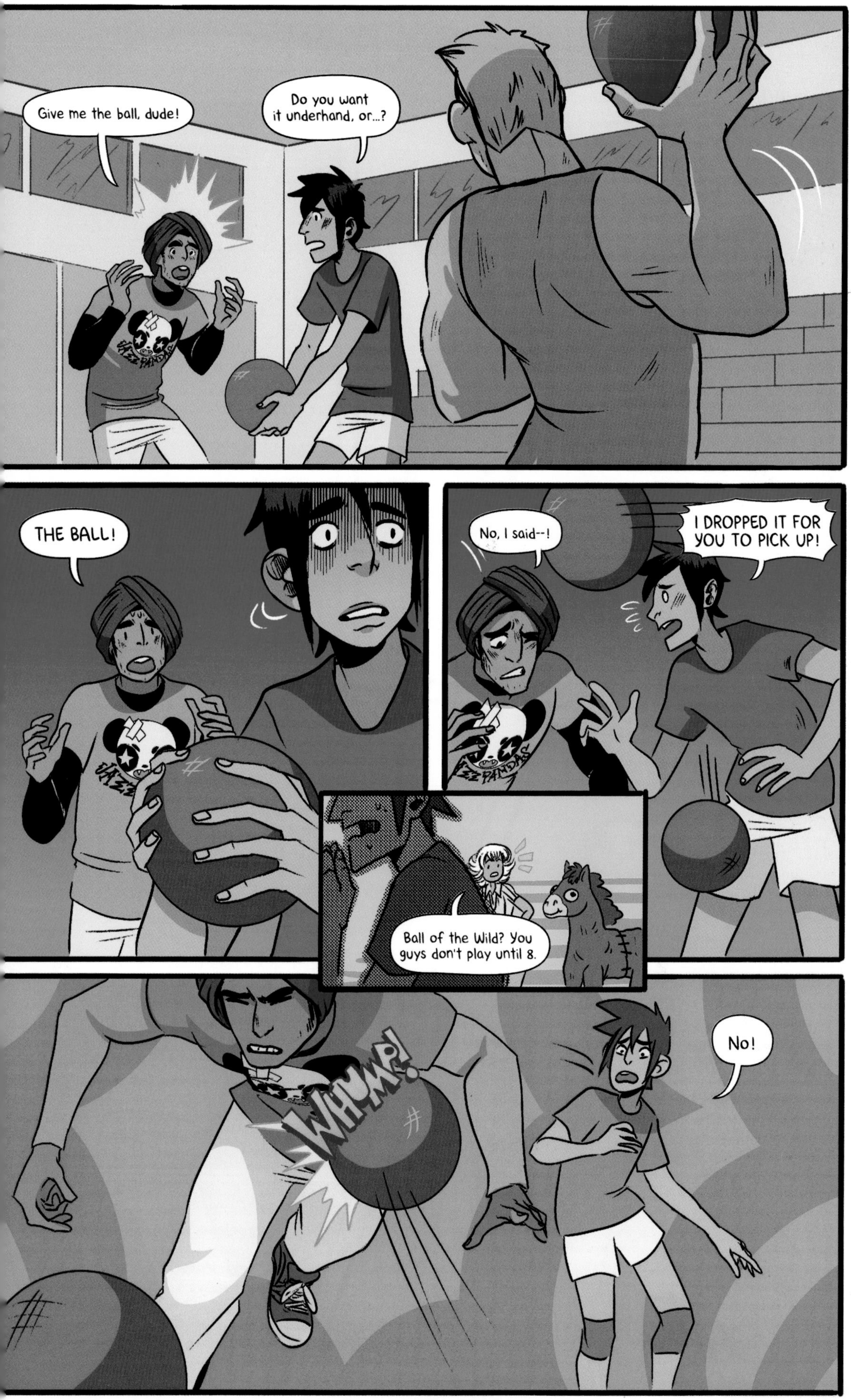
Give me the ball, dude!
Do you want it underhand, or...?
THE BALL!
No, I said--!
I DROPPED IT FOR YOU TO PICK UP!
Ball of the Wild? You guys don't play until 8.
WHUMP!
No!

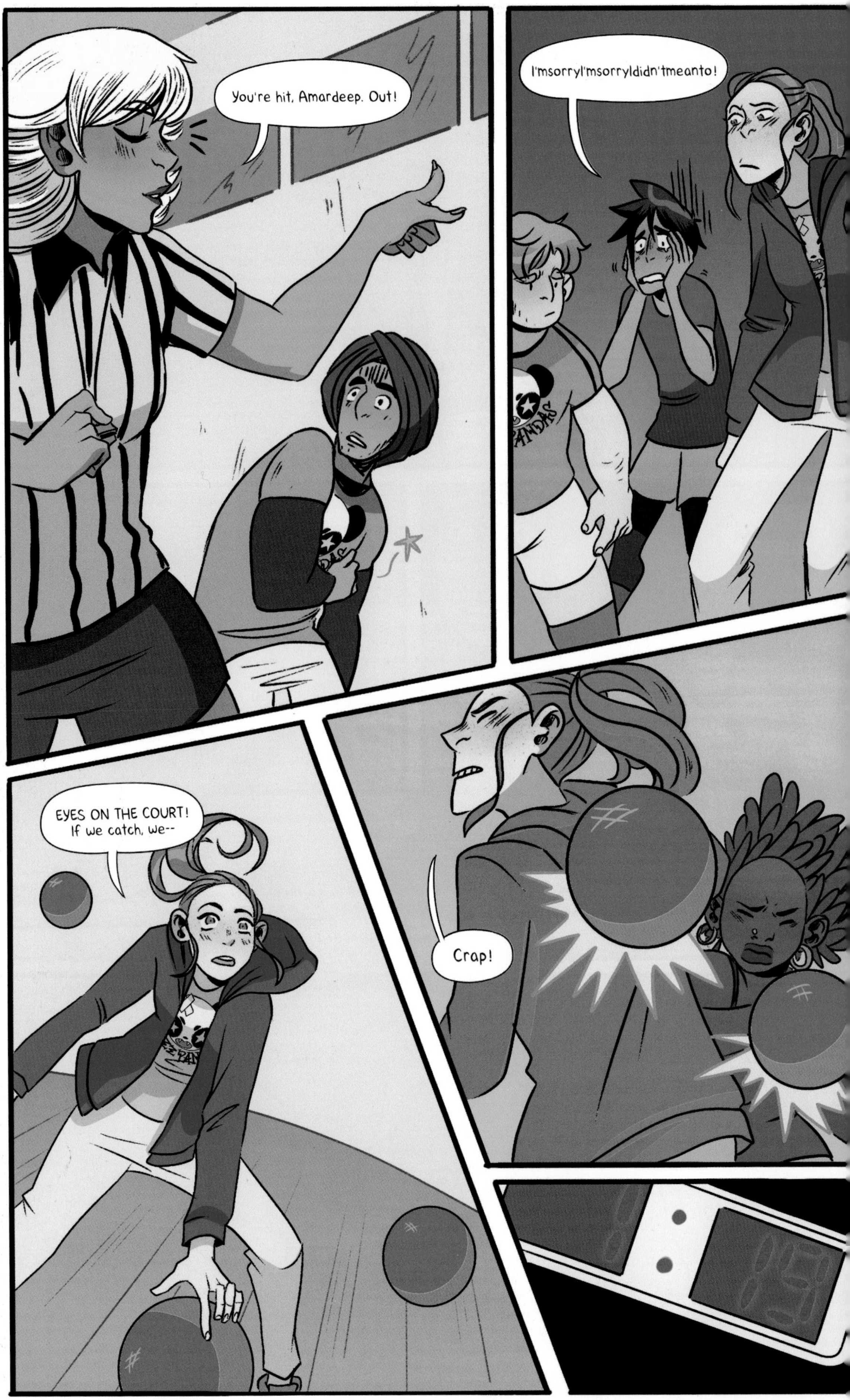
You're hit, Amardeep. Out!
I'msorryI'msorryIdidn'tmeanto!
PANDAS
EYES ON THE COURT! If we catch, we--
Crap!

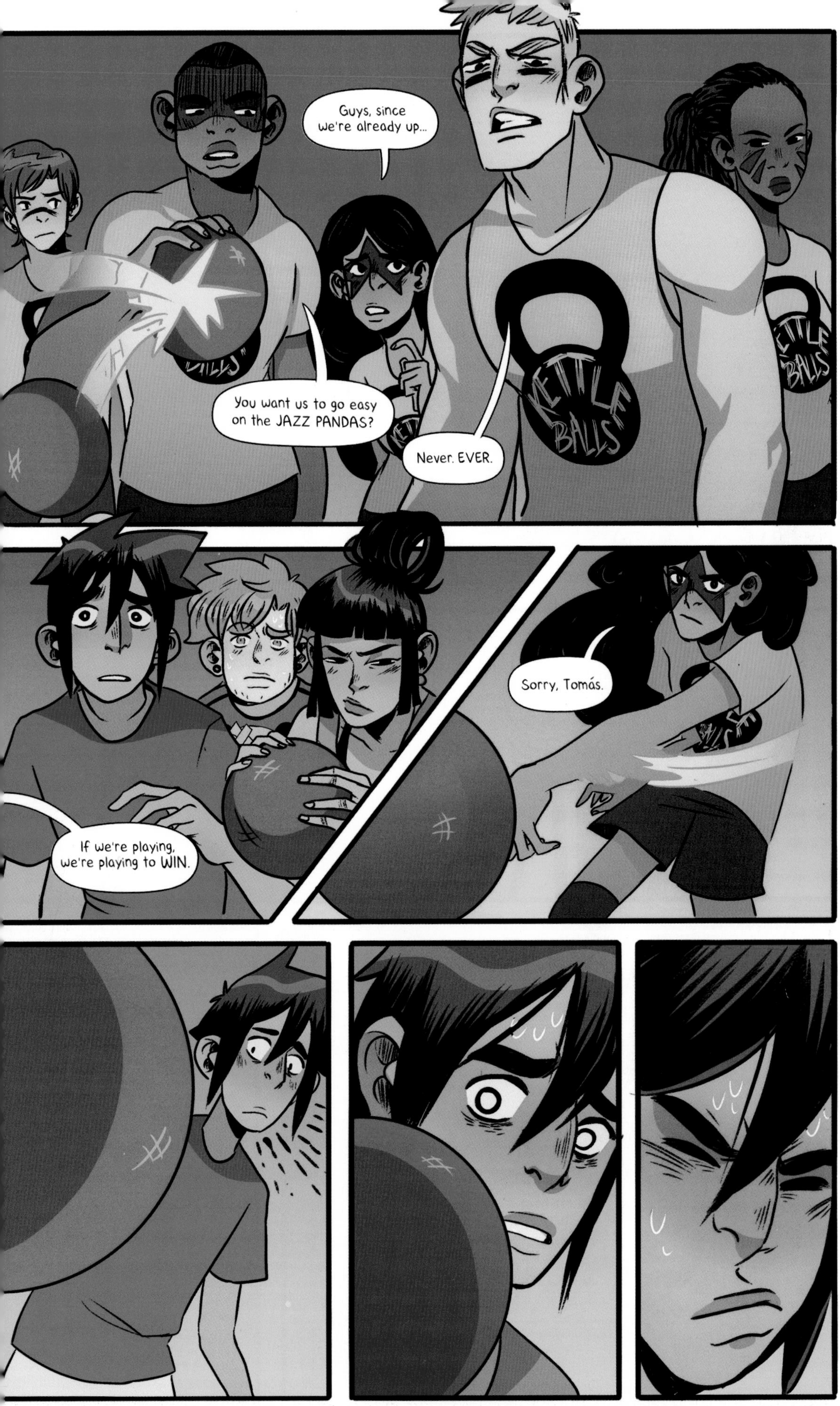
Guys, since we're already up...
You want us to go easy on the JAZZ PANDAS?
Never. EVER.
If we're playing, we're playing to WIN.
Sorry, Tomás.

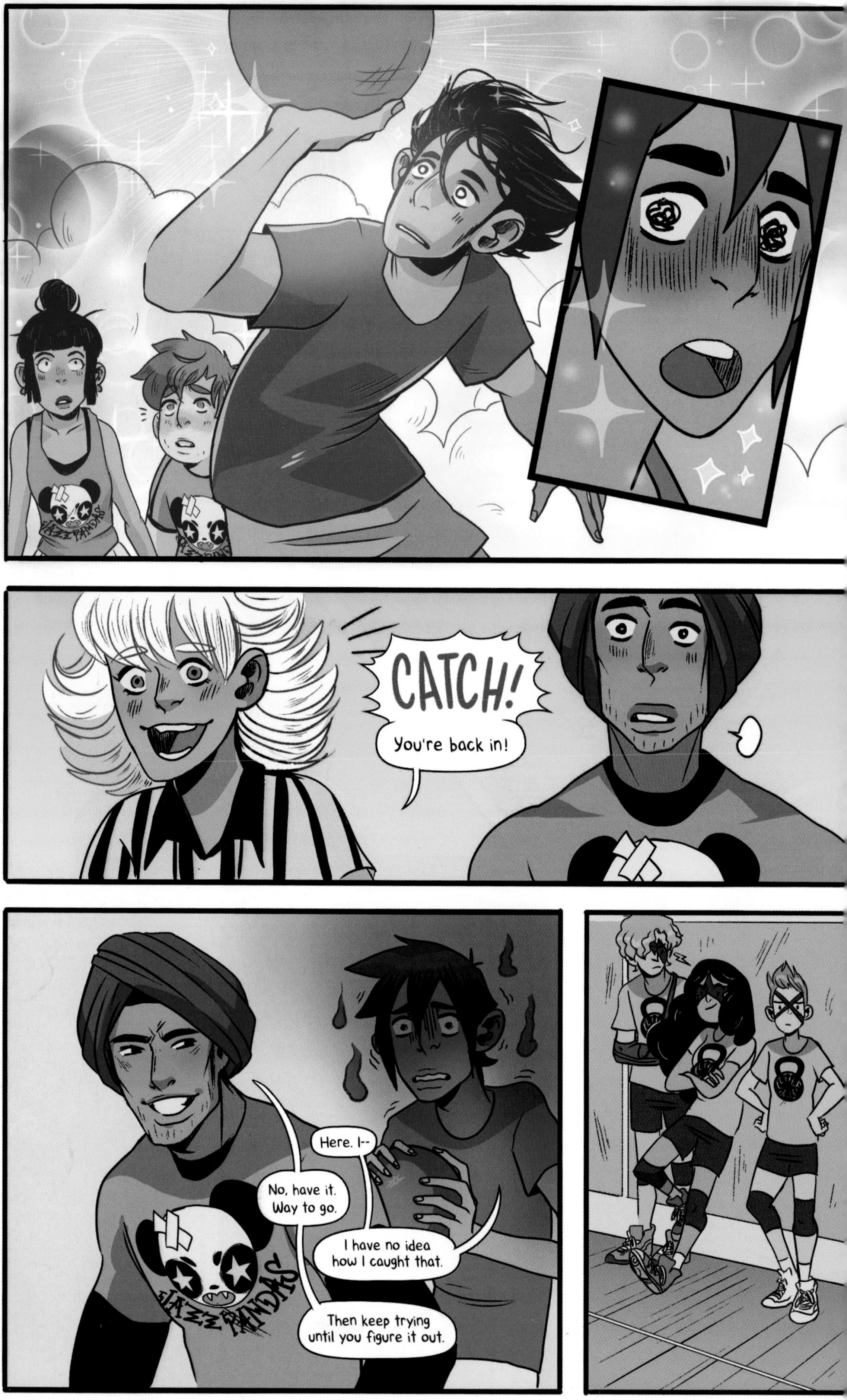
JAZZ PANDAS
CATCH!
You're back in!
Here. I--
No, have it. Way to go.
I have no idea how I caught that.
Then keep trying until you figure it out.
JAZZ PANDAS

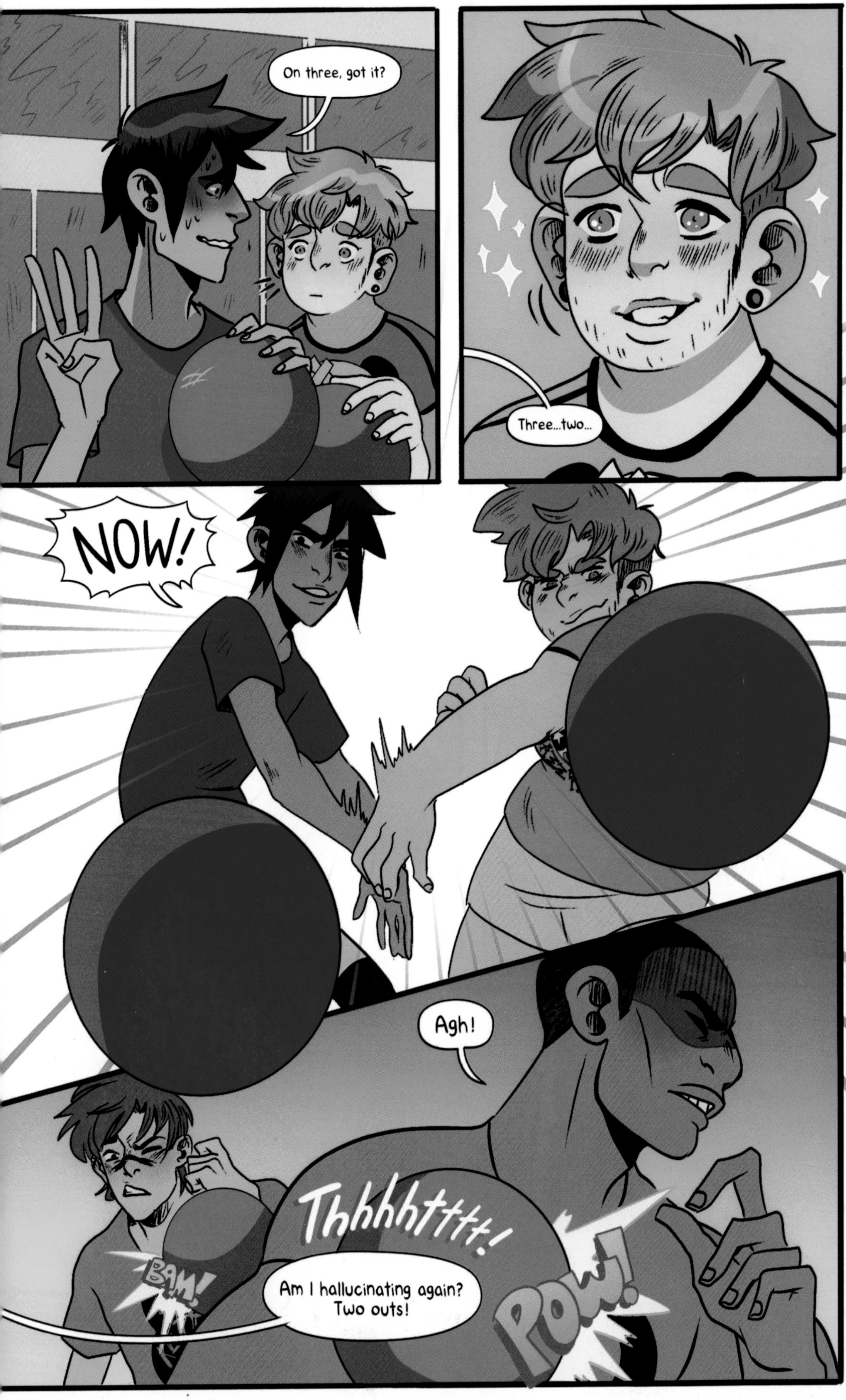
On three, got it?
Three...two...
NOW!
Agh!
Thhhhtttt!
BAM!
POW!
Am I hallucinating again? Two outs!

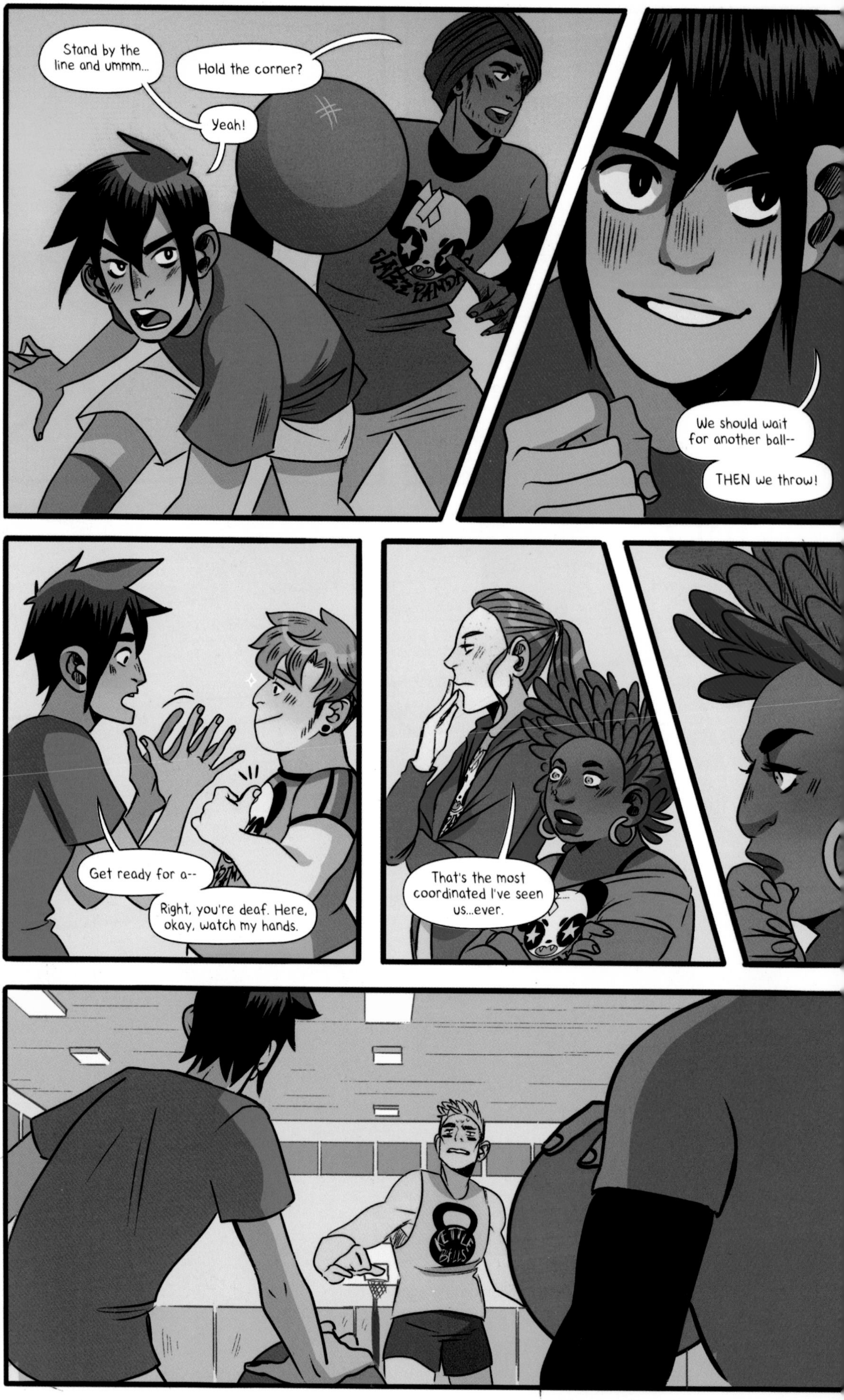
Stand by the line and ummm...
Hold the corner?
Yeah!
We should wait for another ball--
THEN we throw!
Get ready for a--
Right, you're deaf. Here, okay, watch my hands.
That's the most coordinated I've seen us...ever.
KETTLE BELLS

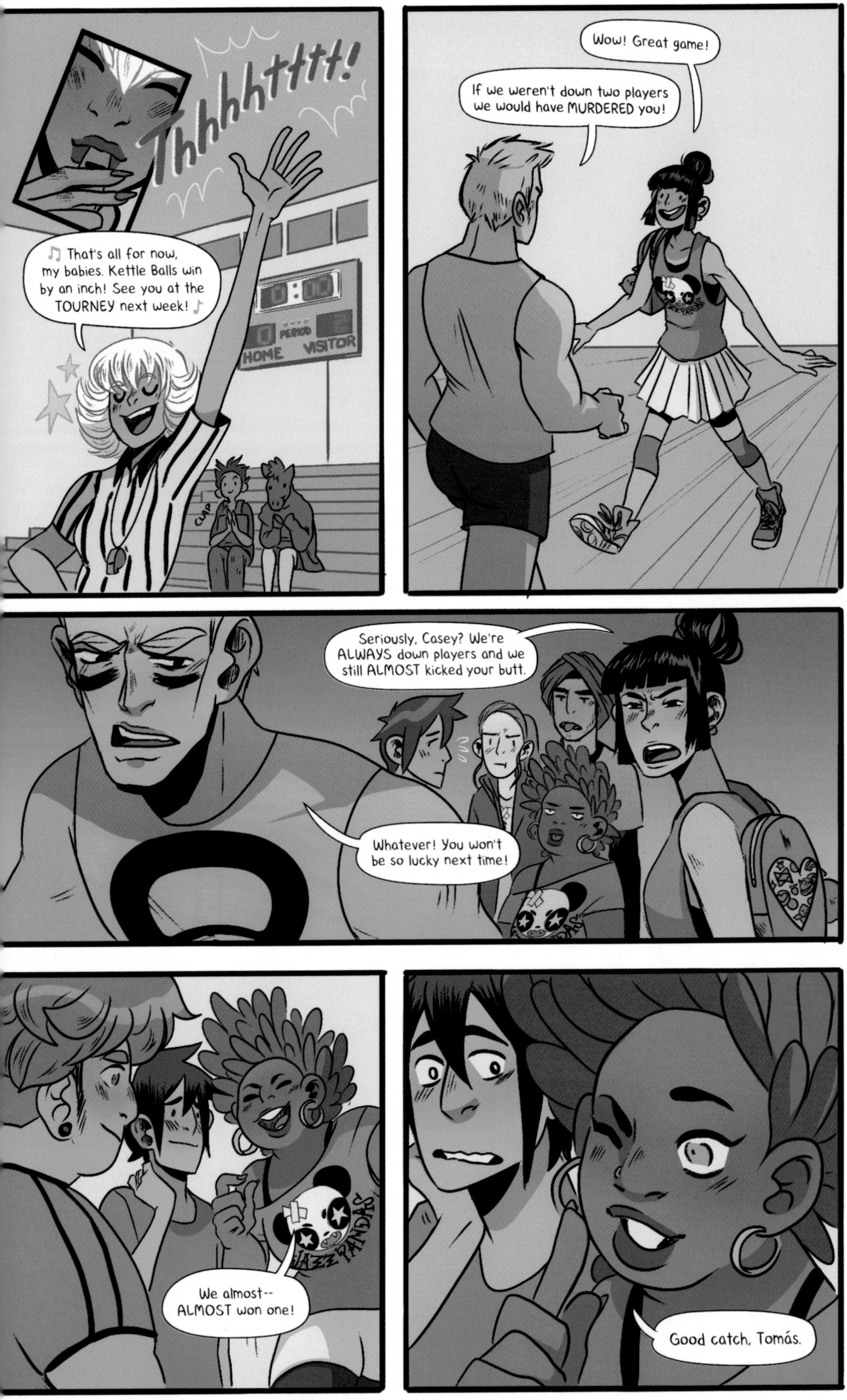
Thhhhttttt!
♫ That's all for now, my babies. Kettle Balls win by an inch! See you at the TOURNEY next week! ♪
PERIOD
HOME VISITOR
CLAP
Wow! Great game!
If we weren't down two players we would have MURDERED you!
Seriously, Casey? We're ALWAYS down players and we still ALMOST kicked your butt.
Whatever! You won't be so lucky next time!
JAZZ PANDAS
We almost-- ALMOST won one!
Good catch, Tomás.

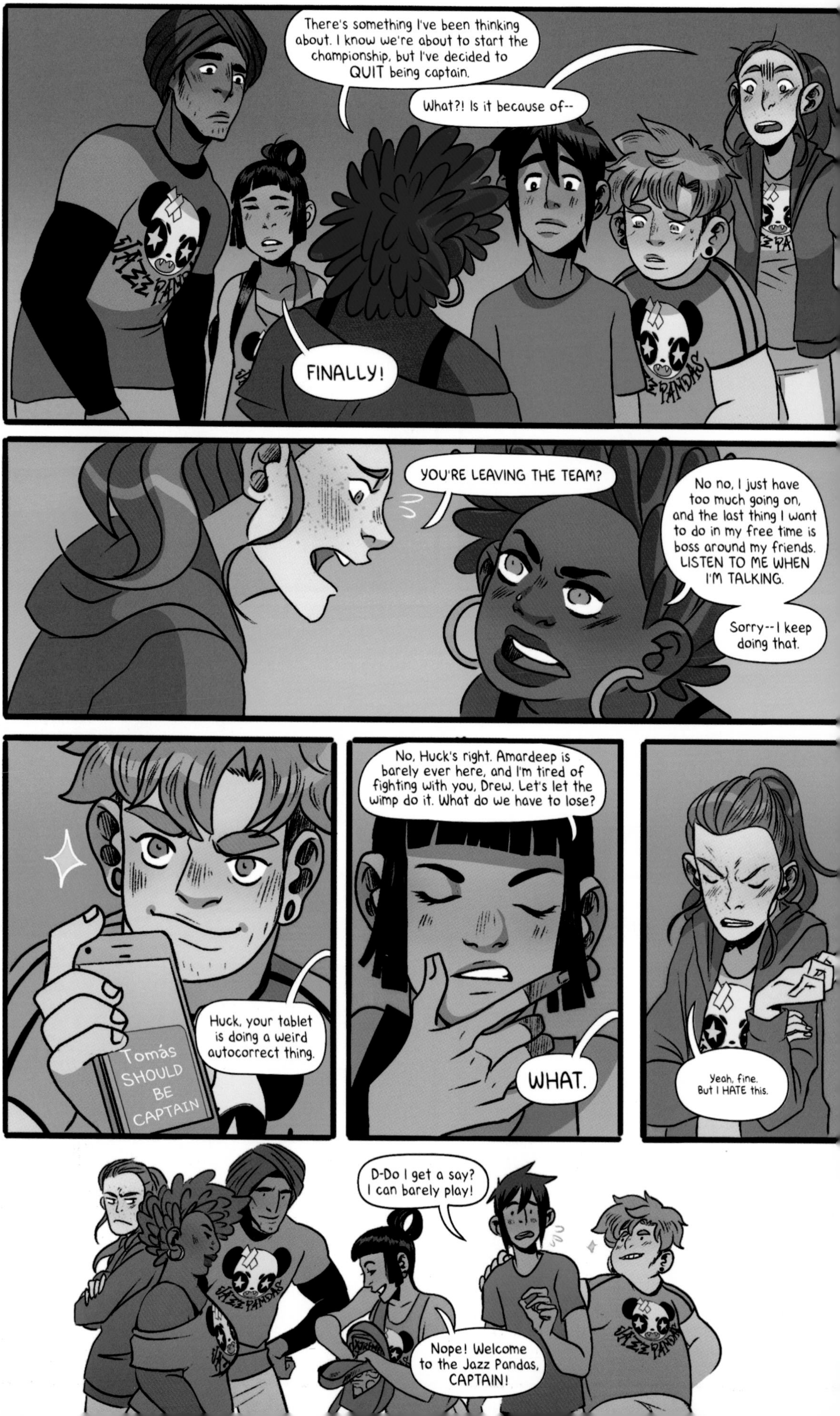
There's something I've been thinking about. I know we're about to start the championship, but I've decided to QUIT being captain.
What?! Is it because of--
FINALLY!
YOU'RE LEAVING THE TEAM?
No no, I just have too much going on, and the last thing I want to do in my free time is boss around my friends. LISTEN TO ME WHEN I'M TALKING.
Sorry--I keep doing that.
Tomás SHOULD BE CAPTAIN
Huck, your tablet is doing a weird autocorrect thing.
No, Huck's right. Amardeep is barely ever here, and I'm tired of fighting with you, Drew. Let's let the wimp do it. What do we have to lose?
WHAT.
Yeah, fine. But I HATE this.
D-Do I get a say? I can barely play!
Nope! Welcome to the Jazz Pandas, CAPTAIN!

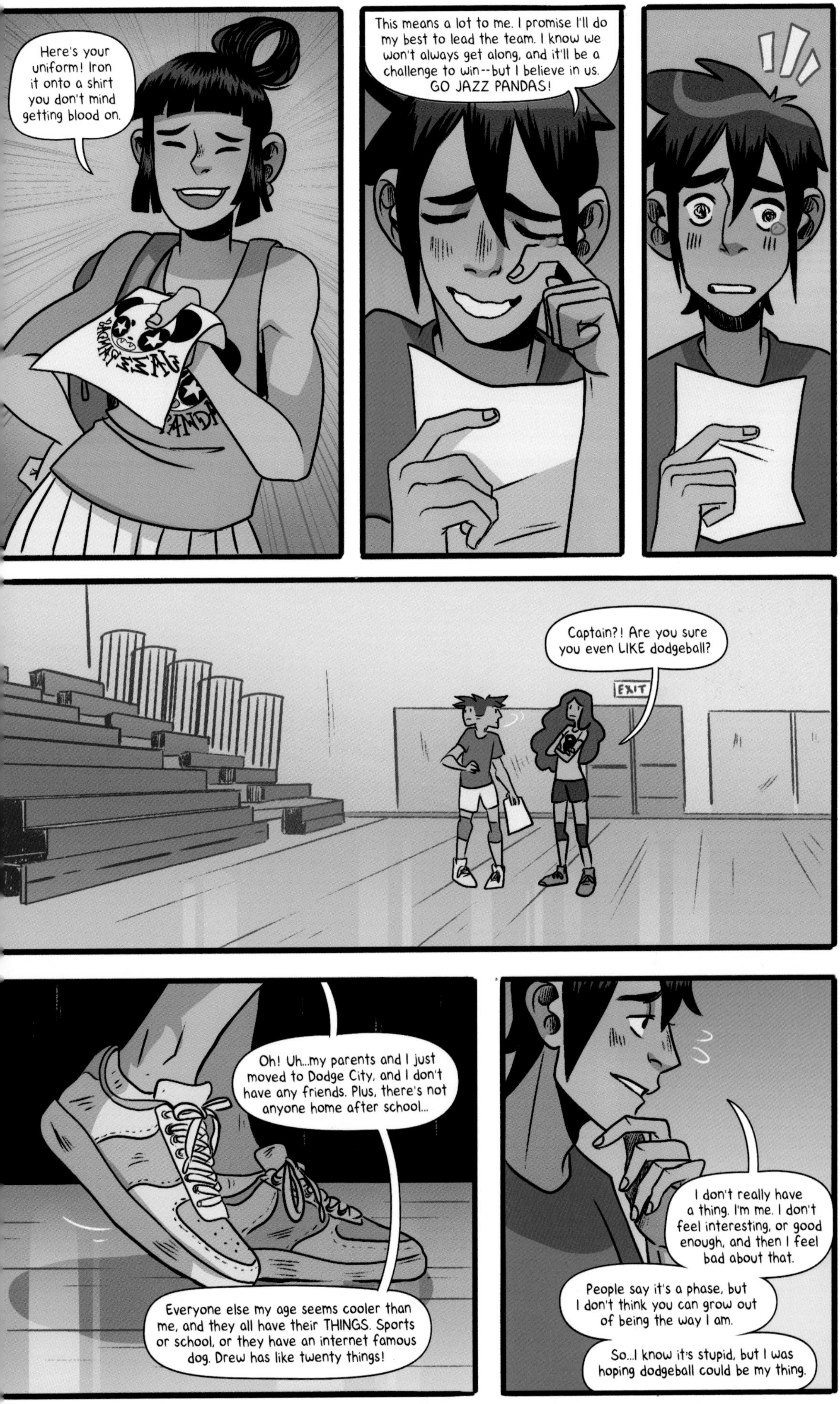
Here's your uniform! Iron it onto a shirt you don't mind getting blood on.
This means a lot to me. I promise I'll do my best to lead the team. I know we won't always get along, and it'll be a challenge to win--but I believe in us. GO JAZZ PANDAS!
Captain?! Are you sure you even LIKE dodgeball?
EXIT
Oh! Uh...my parents and I just moved to Dodge City, and I don't have any friends. Plus, there's not anyone home after school...
Everyone else my age seems cooler than me, and they all have their THINGS. Sports or school, or they have an internet famous dog. Drew has like twenty things!
I don't really have a thing. I'm me. I don't feel interesting, or good enough, and then I feel bad about that.
People say it's a phase, but I don't think you can grow out of being the way I am.
So...I know it's stupid, but I was hoping dodgeball could be my thing.

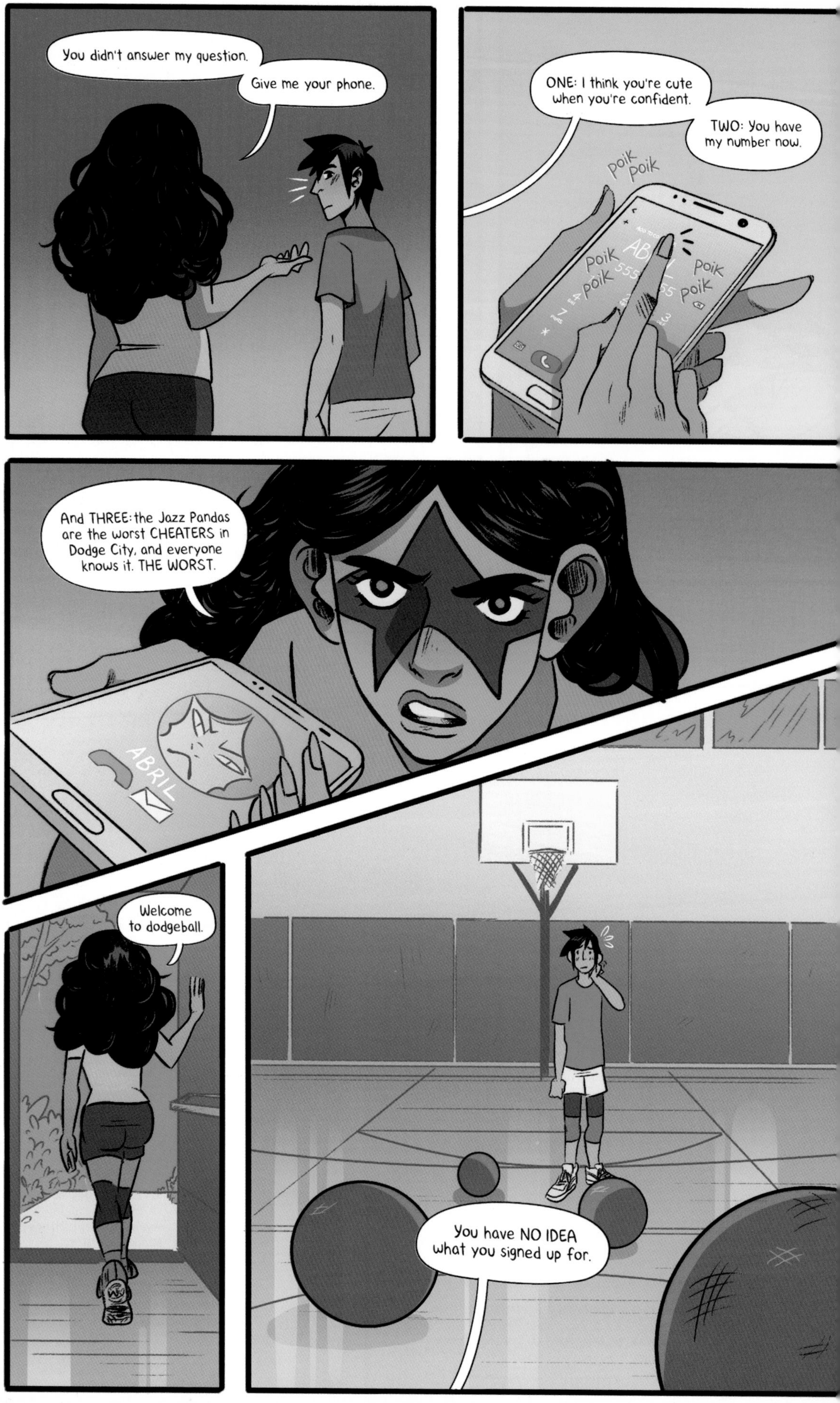
You didn't answer my question.
Give me your phone.
ONE: I think you're cute when you're confident.
TWO: You have my number now.
poik poik
poik poik
poik poik
And THREE: the Jazz Pandas are the worst CHEATERS in Dodge City, and everyone knows it. THE WORST.
ABRIL
Welcome to dodgeball.
You have NO IDEA what you signed up for.

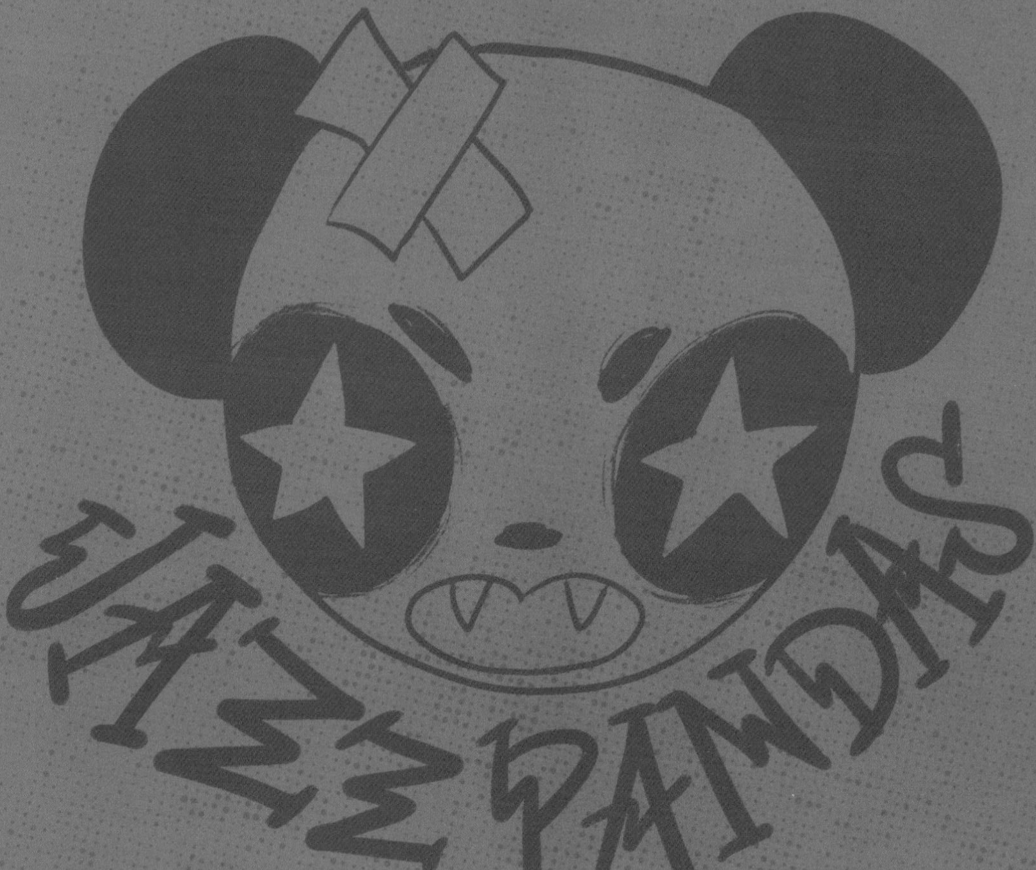
JAZZ PANDAS

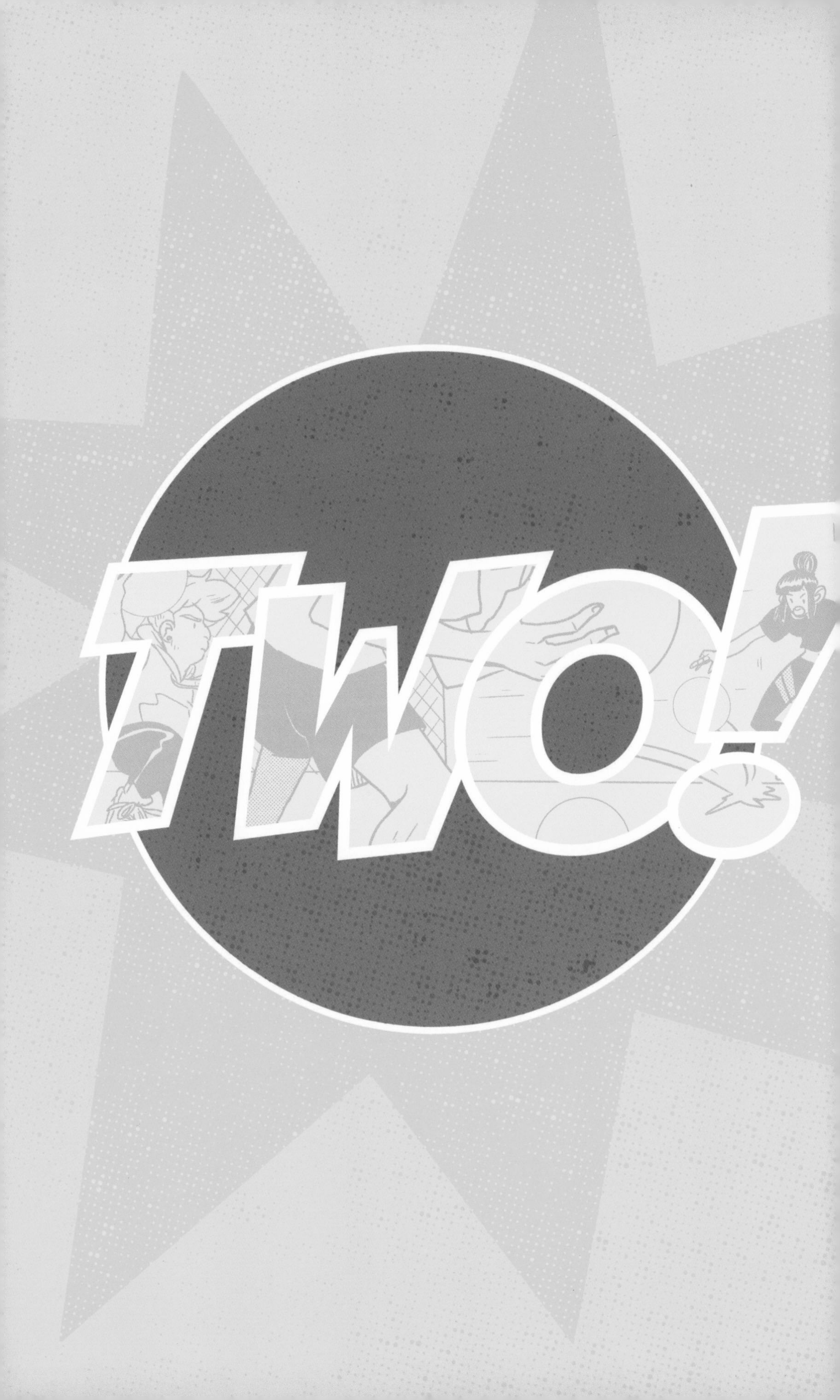
TWO!

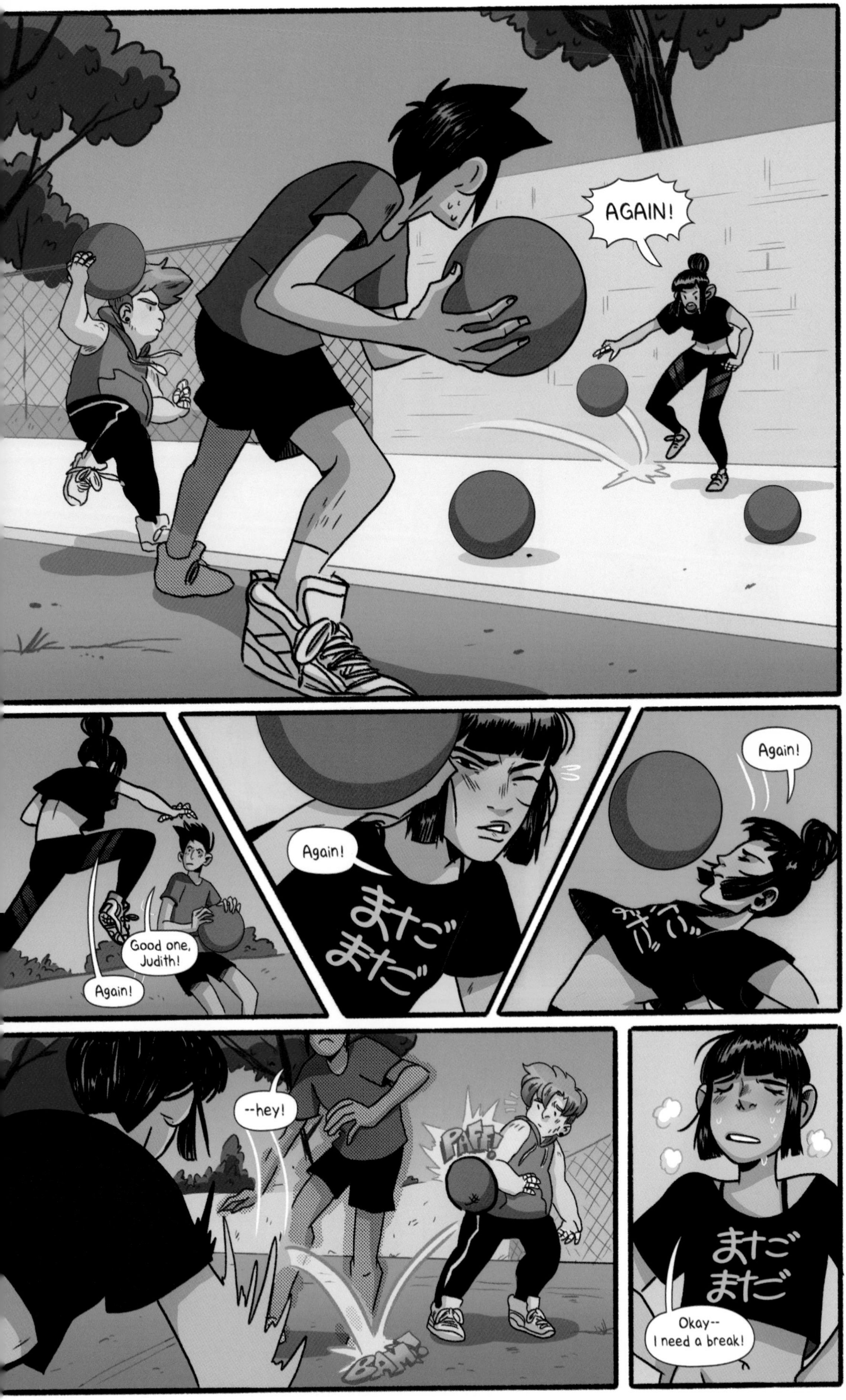
AGAIN!
Good one, Judith!
Again!
Again!
まだ
まだ
Again!
--hey!
PAFF!
BAM!
まだ
まだ
Okay-- I need a break!

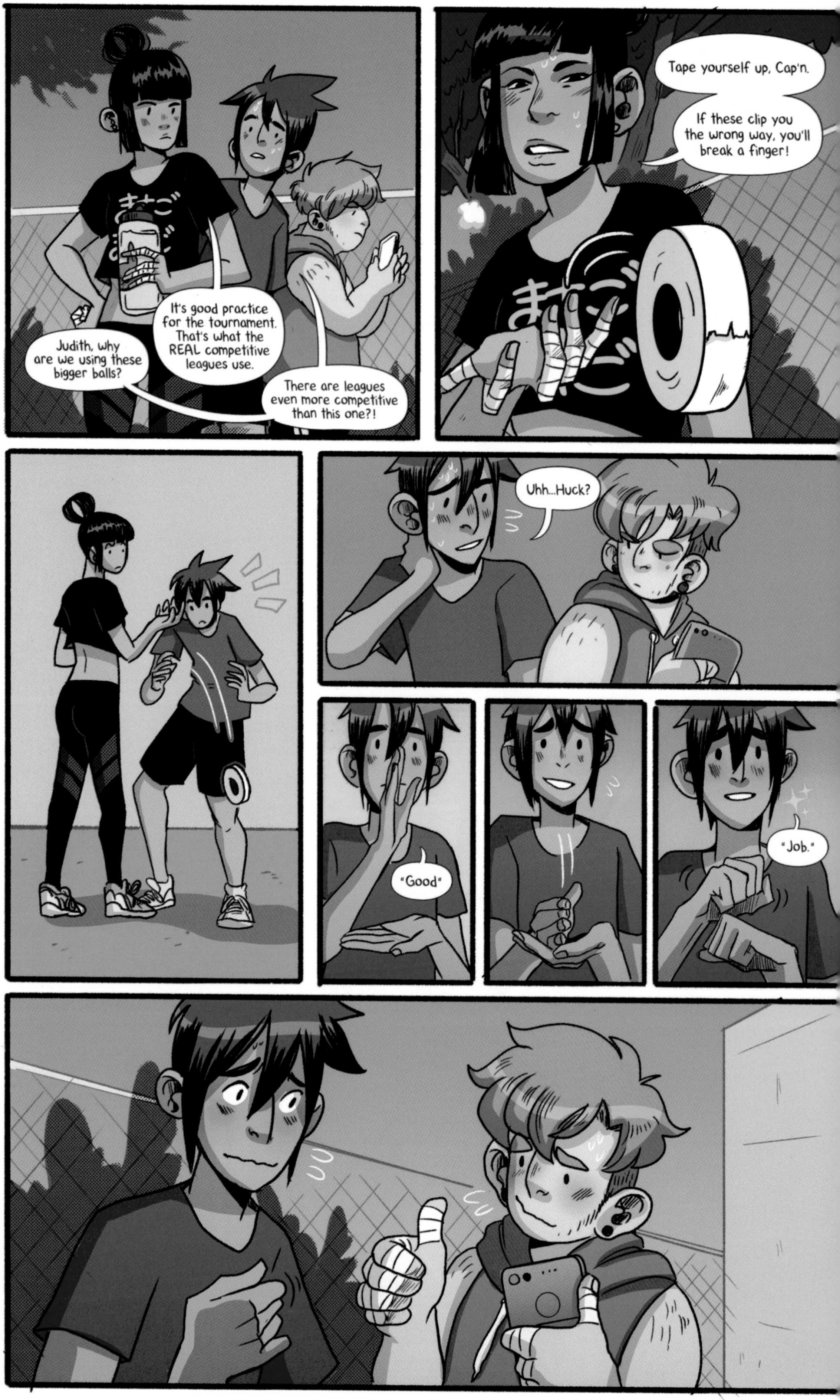
Judith, why are we using these bigger balls?
It's good practice for the tournament. That's what the REAL competitive leagues use.
There are leagues even more competitive than this one?!
Tape yourself up, Cap'n.
If these clip you the wrong way, you'll break a finger!
Uhh...Huck?
"Good"
"Job."

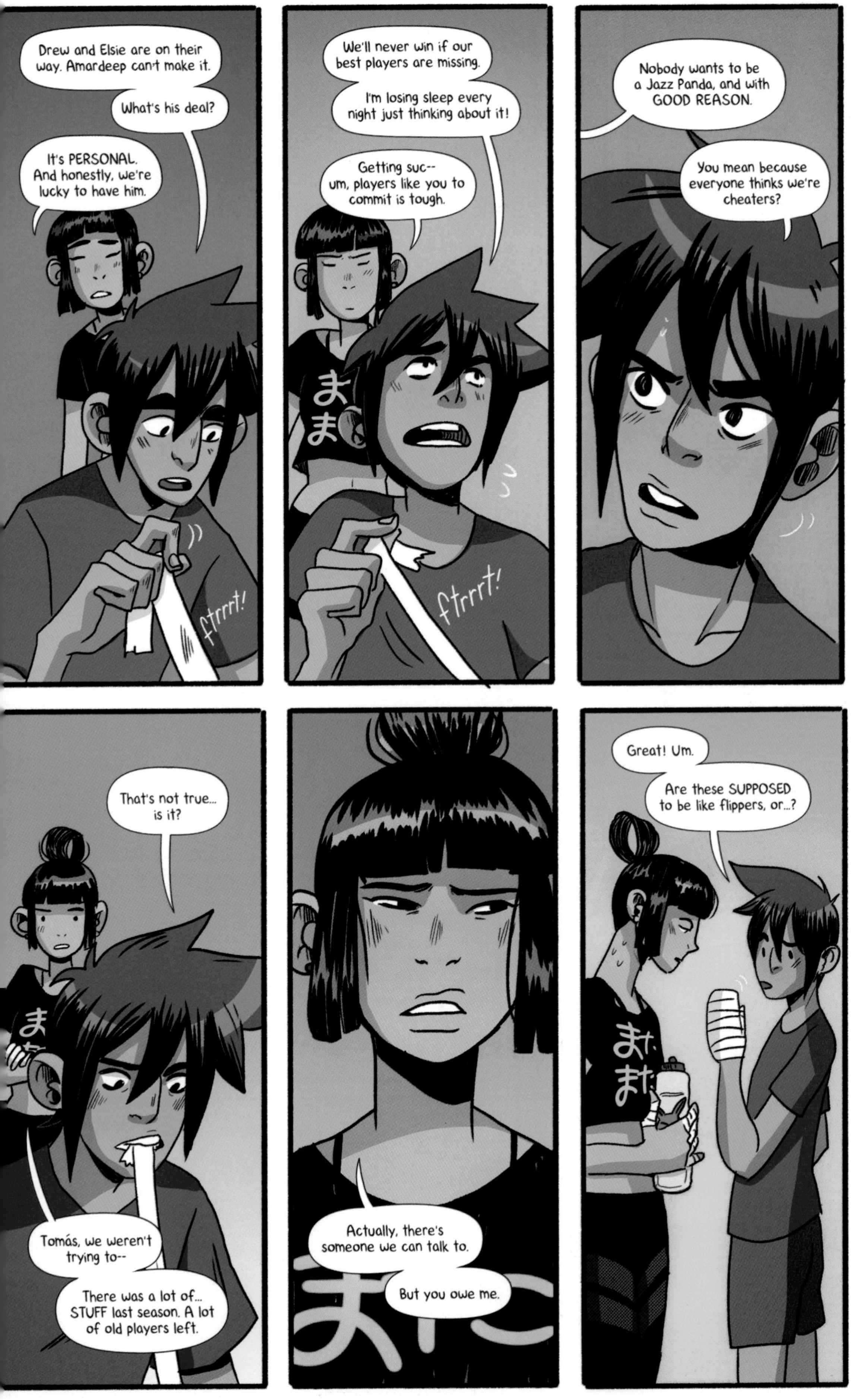
Drew and Elsie are on their way. Amardeep can't make it.
What's his deal?
It's PERSONAL. And honestly, we're lucky to have him.
ftrrrt!
We'll never win if our best players are missing.
I'm losing sleep every night just thinking about it!
Getting suc-- um, players like you to commit is tough.
まま
ftrrrt!
Nobody wants to be a Jazz Panda, and with GOOD REASON.
You mean because everyone thinks we're cheaters?
That's not true... is it?
Tomás, we weren't trying to--
There was a lot of... STUFF last season. A lot of old players left.
Actually, there's someone we can talk to.
But you owe me.
Great! Um.
Are these SUPPOSED to be like flippers, or...?

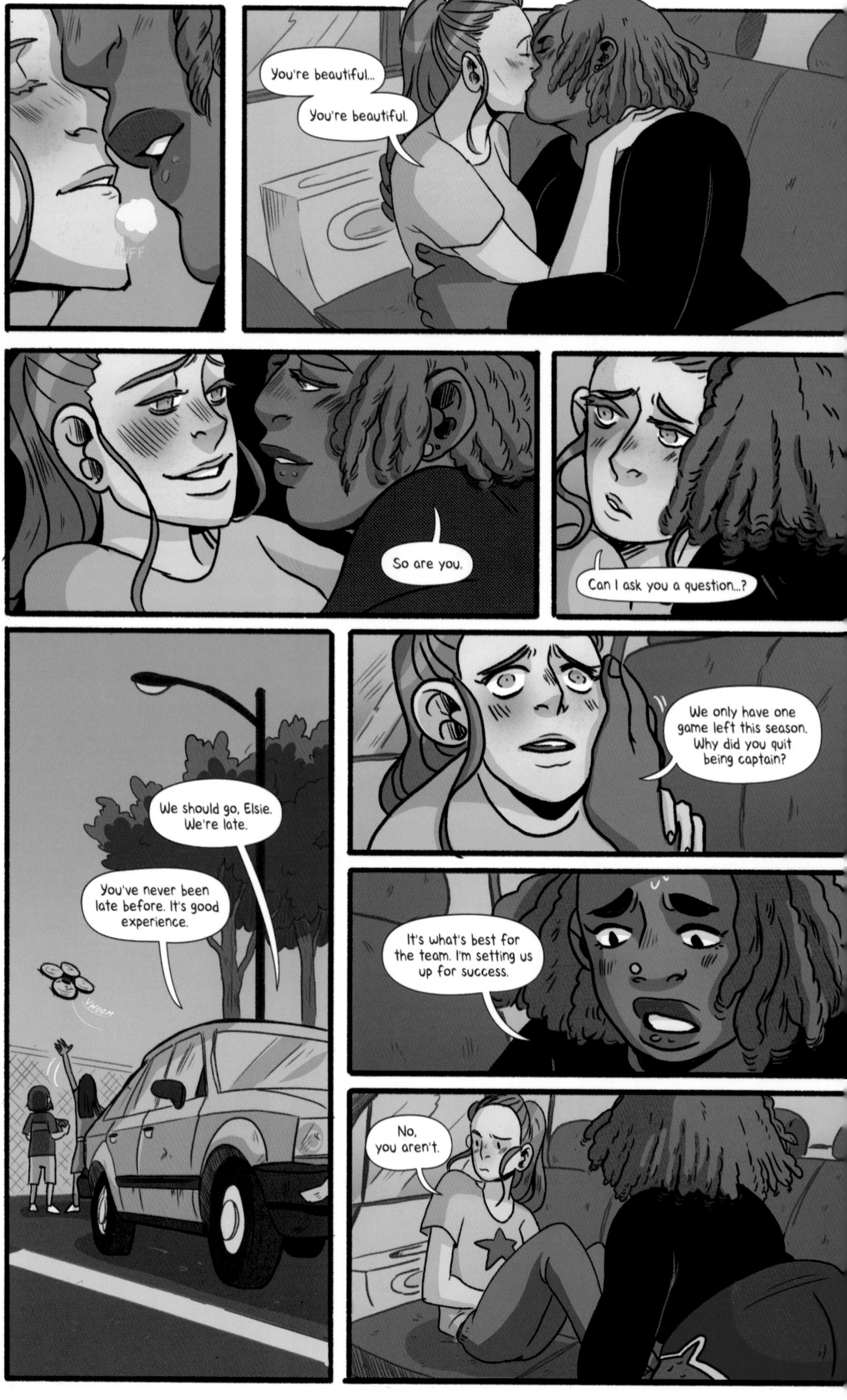
You're beautiful...
You're beautiful.
So are you.
Can I ask you a question...?
We should go, Elsie. We're late.
You've never been late before. It's good experience.
VWOOM
We only have one game left this season. Why did you quit being captain?
It's what's best for the team. I'm setting us up for success.
No, you aren't.

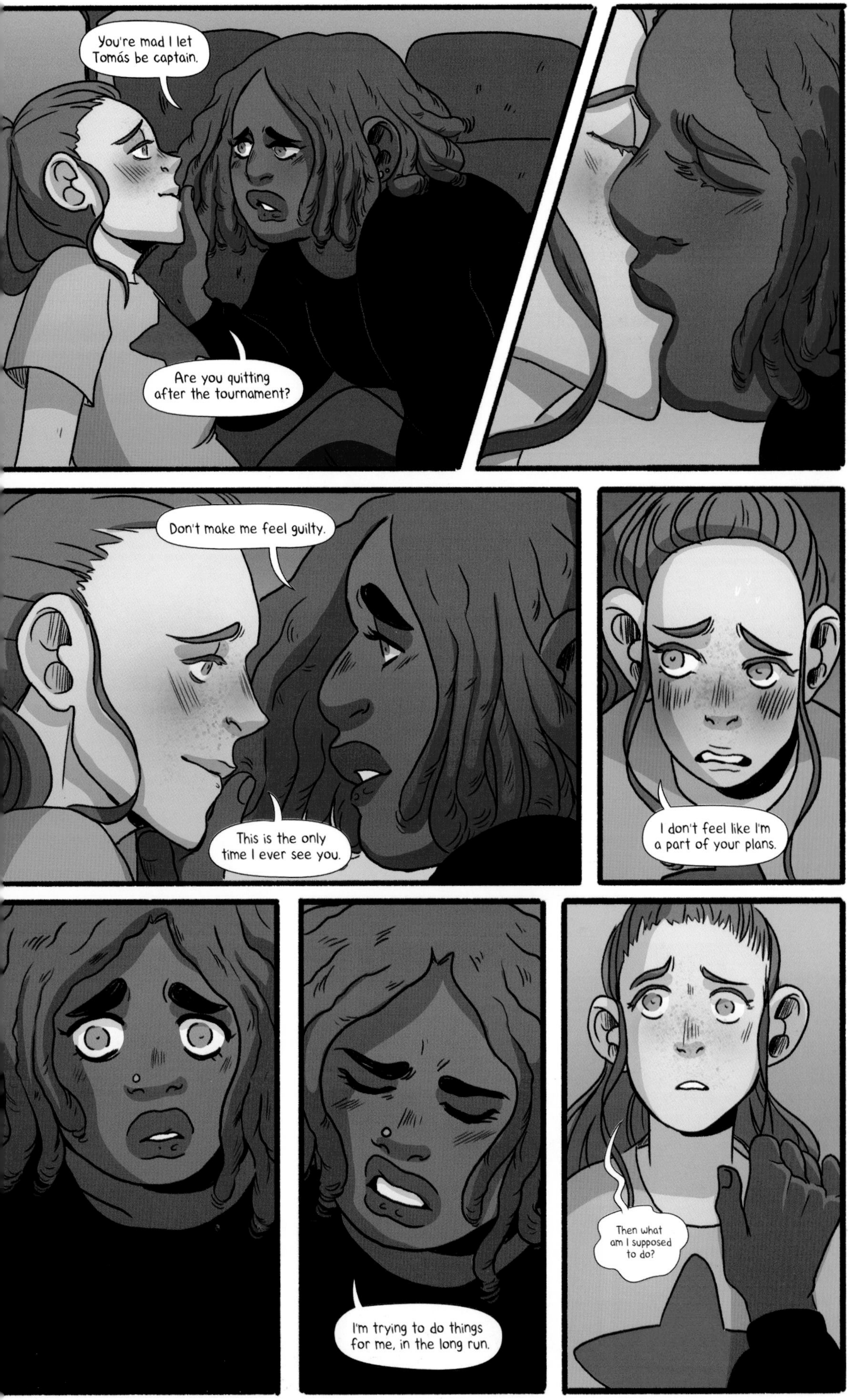
You're mad I let Tomás be captain.
Are you quitting after the tournament?
Don't make me feel guilty.
This is the only time I ever see you.
I don't feel like I'm a part of your plans.
I'm trying to do things for me, in the long run.
Then what am I supposed to do?

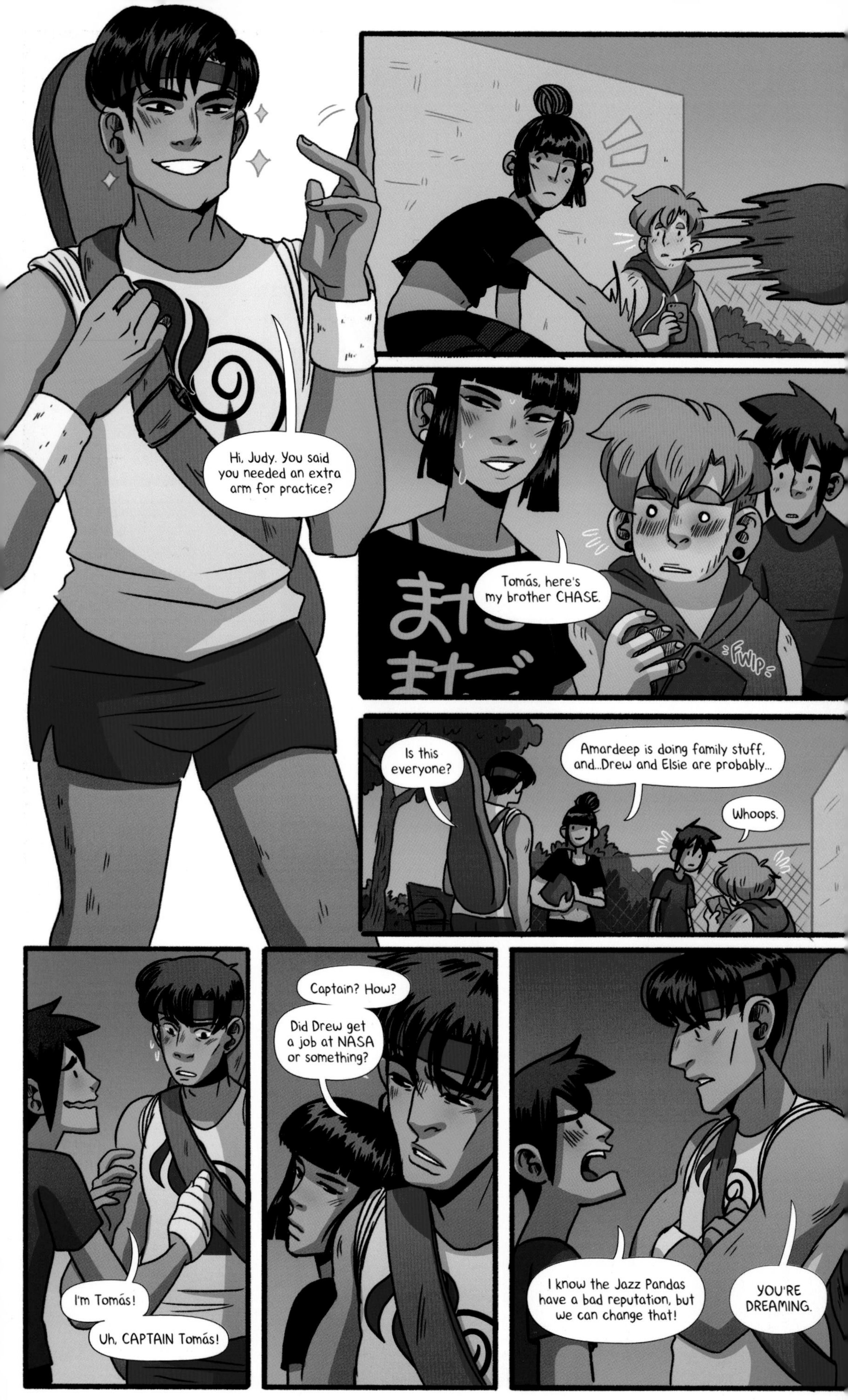

Hi, Judy. You said you needed an extra arm for practice?
Tomás, here's my brother CHASE.
FWIP
Is this everyone?
Amardeep is doing family stuff, and...Drew and Elsie are probably...
Whoops.
I'm Tomás!
Uh, CAPTAIN Tomás!
Captain? How?
Did Drew get a job at NASA or something?
I know the Jazz Pandas have a bad reputation, but we can change that!
YOU'RE DREAMING.

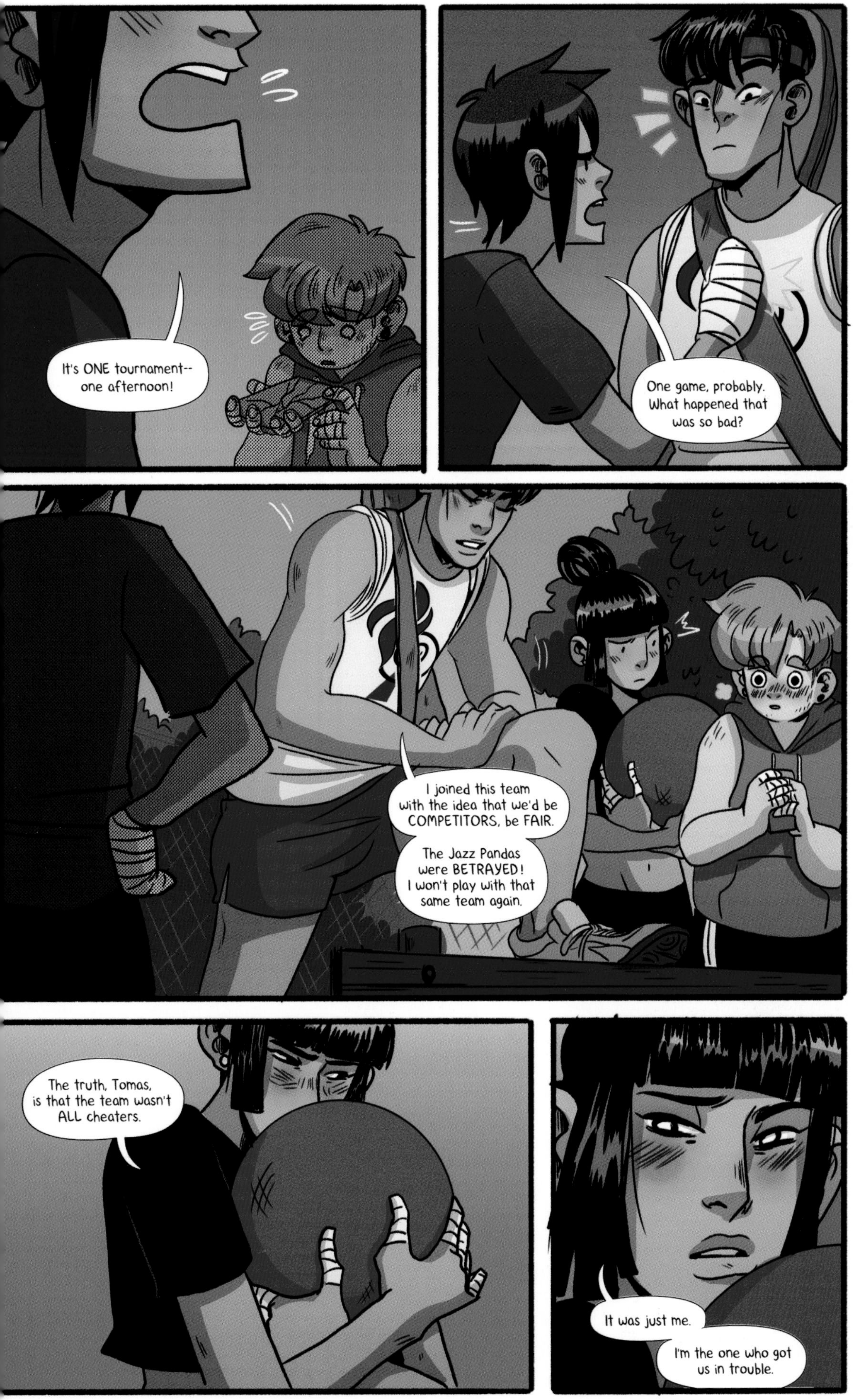
It's ONE tournament--
one afternoon!
One game, probably.
What happened that
was so bad?
I joined this team
with the idea that we'd be
COMPETITORS, be FAIR.
The Jazz Pandas
were BETRAYED!
I won't play with that
same team again.
The truth, Tomas,
is that the team wasn't
ALL cheaters.
It was just me.
I'm the one who got
us in trouble.

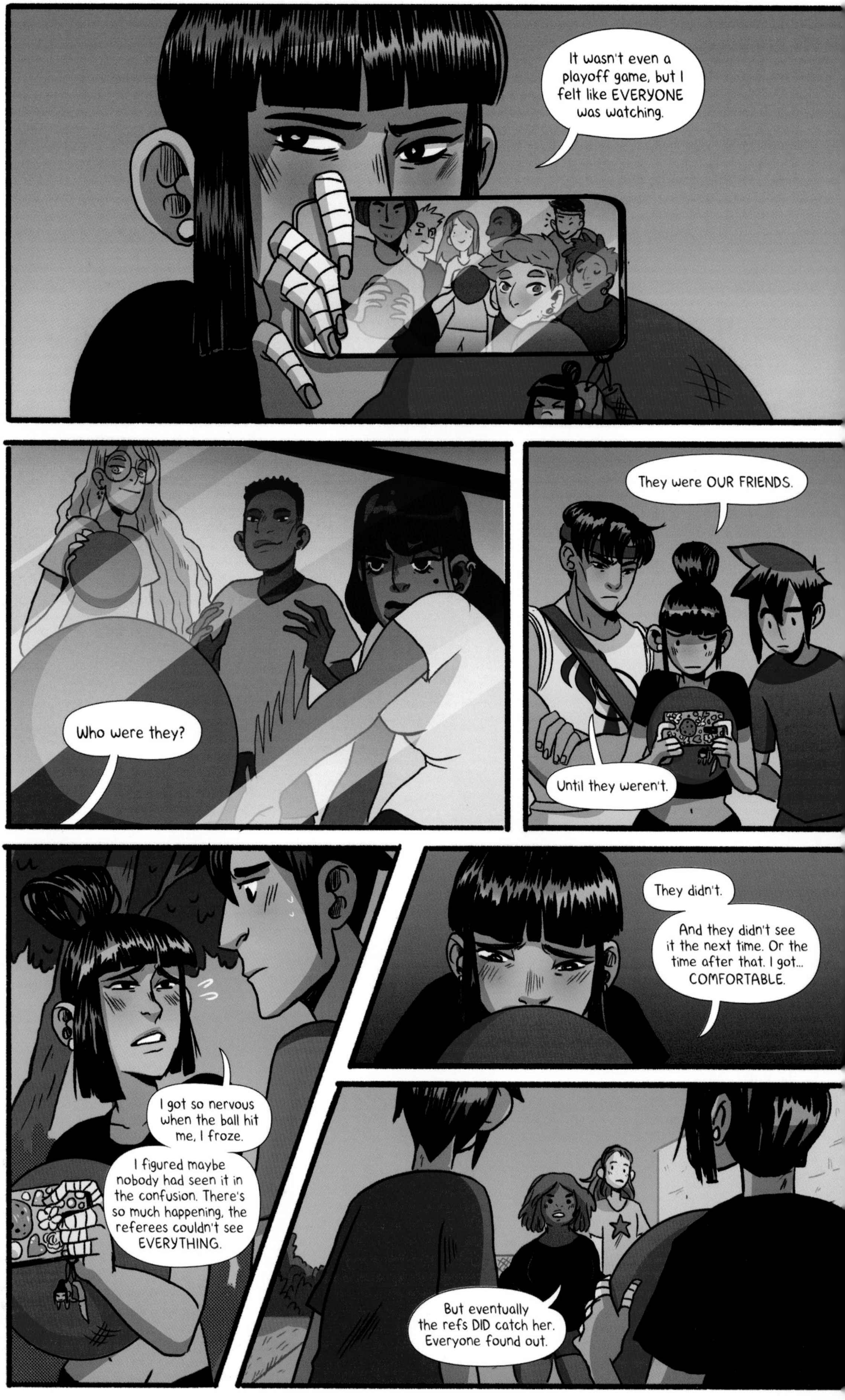
It wasn't even a playoff game, but I felt like EVERYONE was watching.
Who were they?
They were OUR FRIENDS.
Until they weren't.
I got so nervous when the ball hit me, I froze.
I figured maybe nobody had seen it in the confusion. There's so much happening, the referees couldn't see EVERYTHING.
They didn't.
And they didn't see it the next time. Or the time after that. I got... COMFORTABLE.
But eventually the refs DID catch her. Everyone found out.

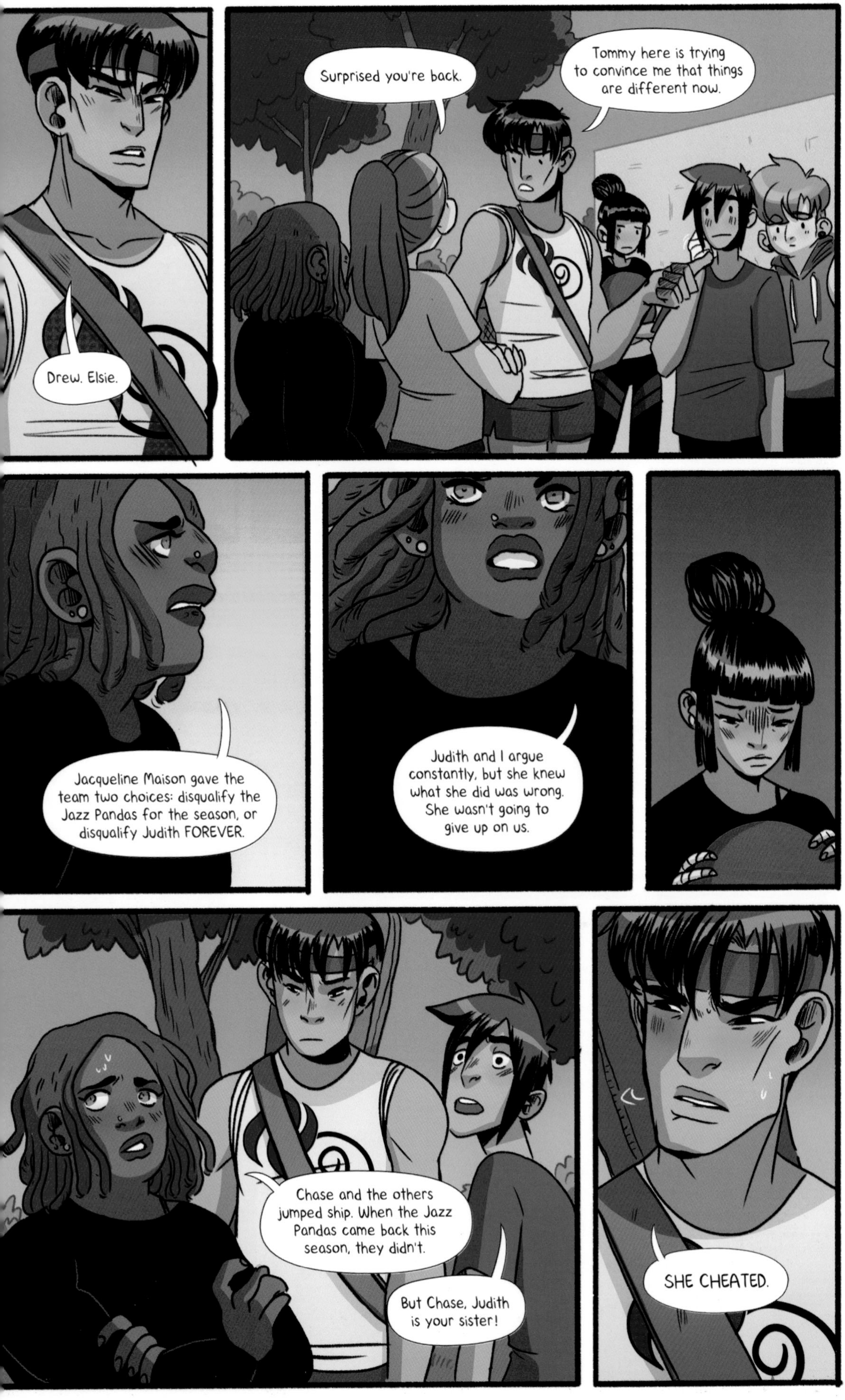
Drew. Elsie.
Surprised you're back.
Tommy here is trying to convince me that things are different now.
Jacqueline Maison gave the team two choices: disqualify the Jazz Pandas for the season, or disqualify Judith FOREVER.
Judith and I argue constantly, but she knew what she did was wrong. She wasn't going to give up on us.
Chase and the others jumped ship. When the Jazz Pandas came back this season, they didn't.
But Chase, Judith is your sister!
SHE CHEATED.

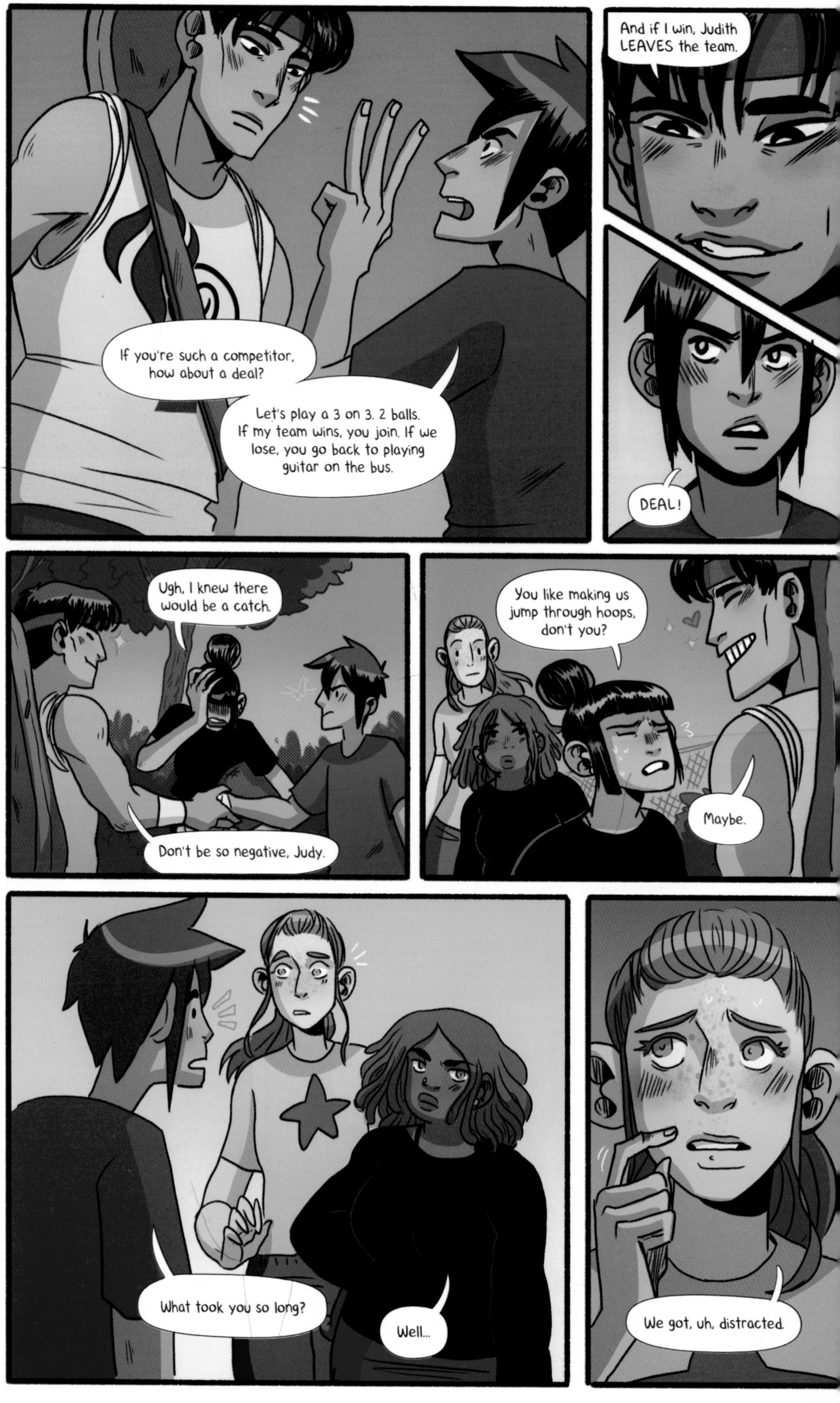
If you're such a competitor, how about a deal?
Let's play a 3 on 3. 2 balls. If my team wins, you join. If we lose, you go back to playing guitar on the bus.
And if I win, Judith LEAVES the team.
DEAL!
Ugh, I knew there would be a catch.
Don't be so negative, Judy.
You like making us jump through hoops, don't you?
Maybe.
What took you so long?
Well...
We got, uh, distracted.

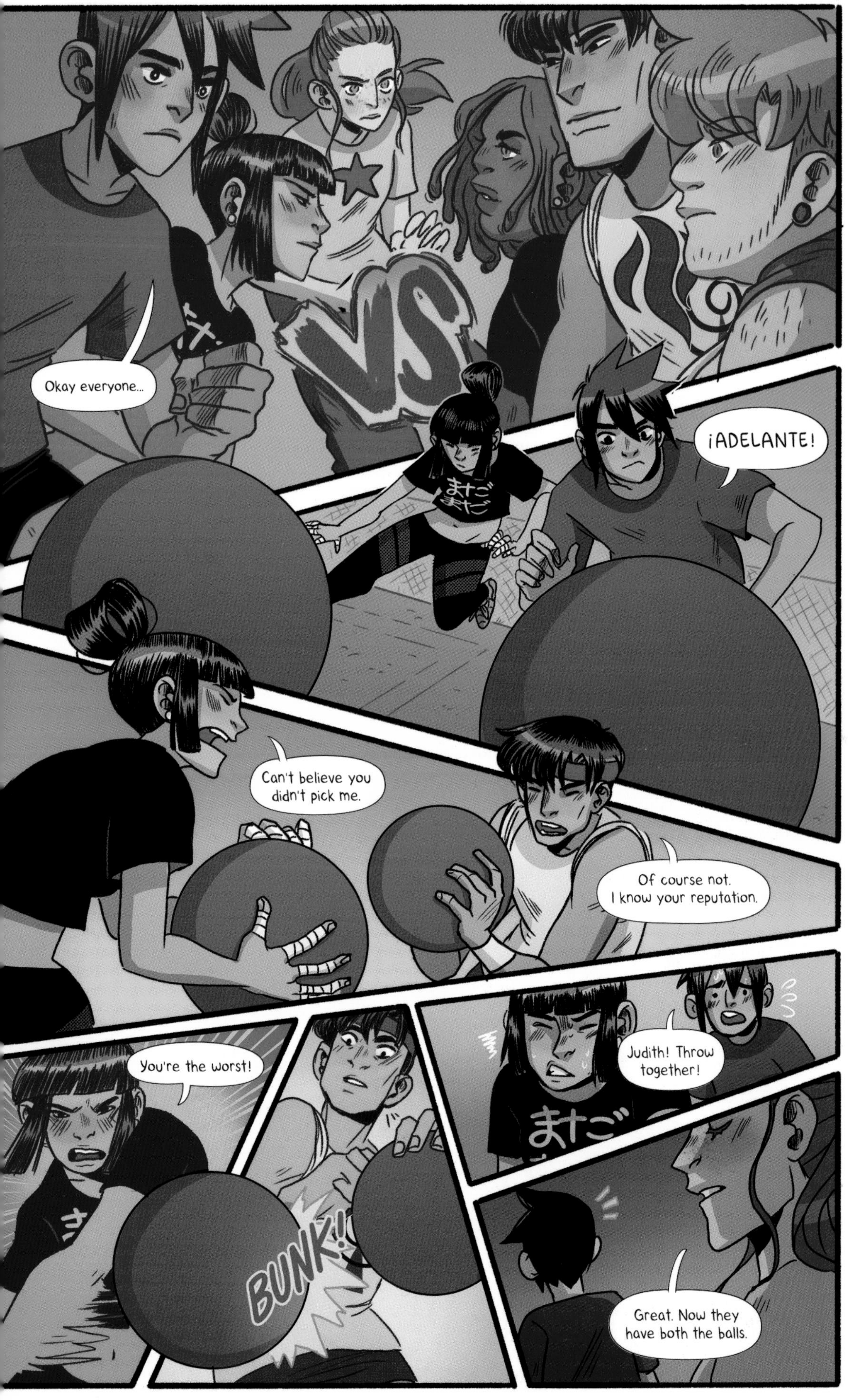
VS
Okay everyone...
¡ADELANTE!
Can't believe you didn't pick me.
Of course not. I know your reputation.
You're the worst!
BUNK!
Judith! Throw together!
Great. Now they have both the balls.

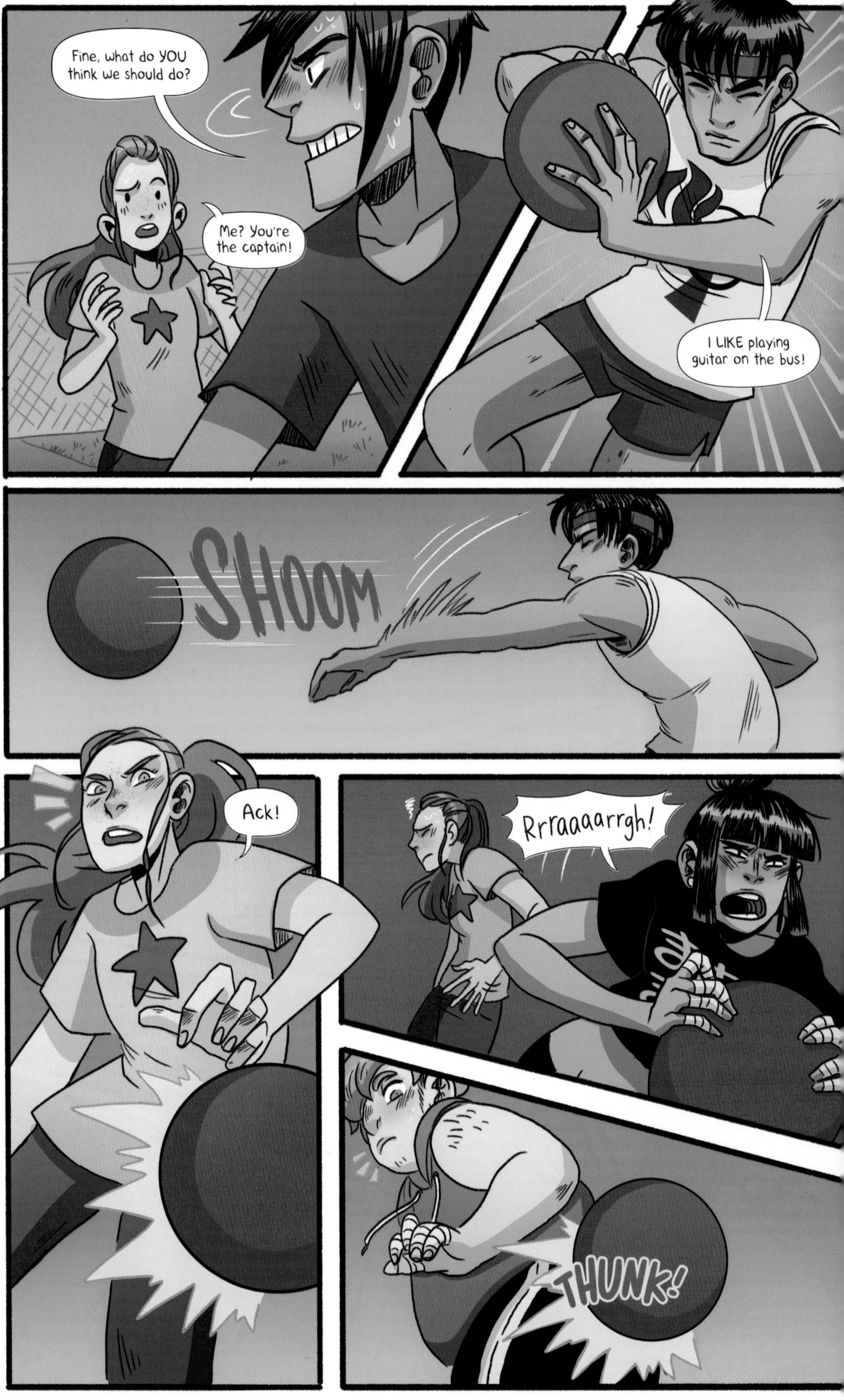
Fine, what do YOU think we should do?
Me? You're the captain!
I LIKE playing guitar on the bus!
SHOOM
Ack!
Rrraaaarrgh!
THUNK!

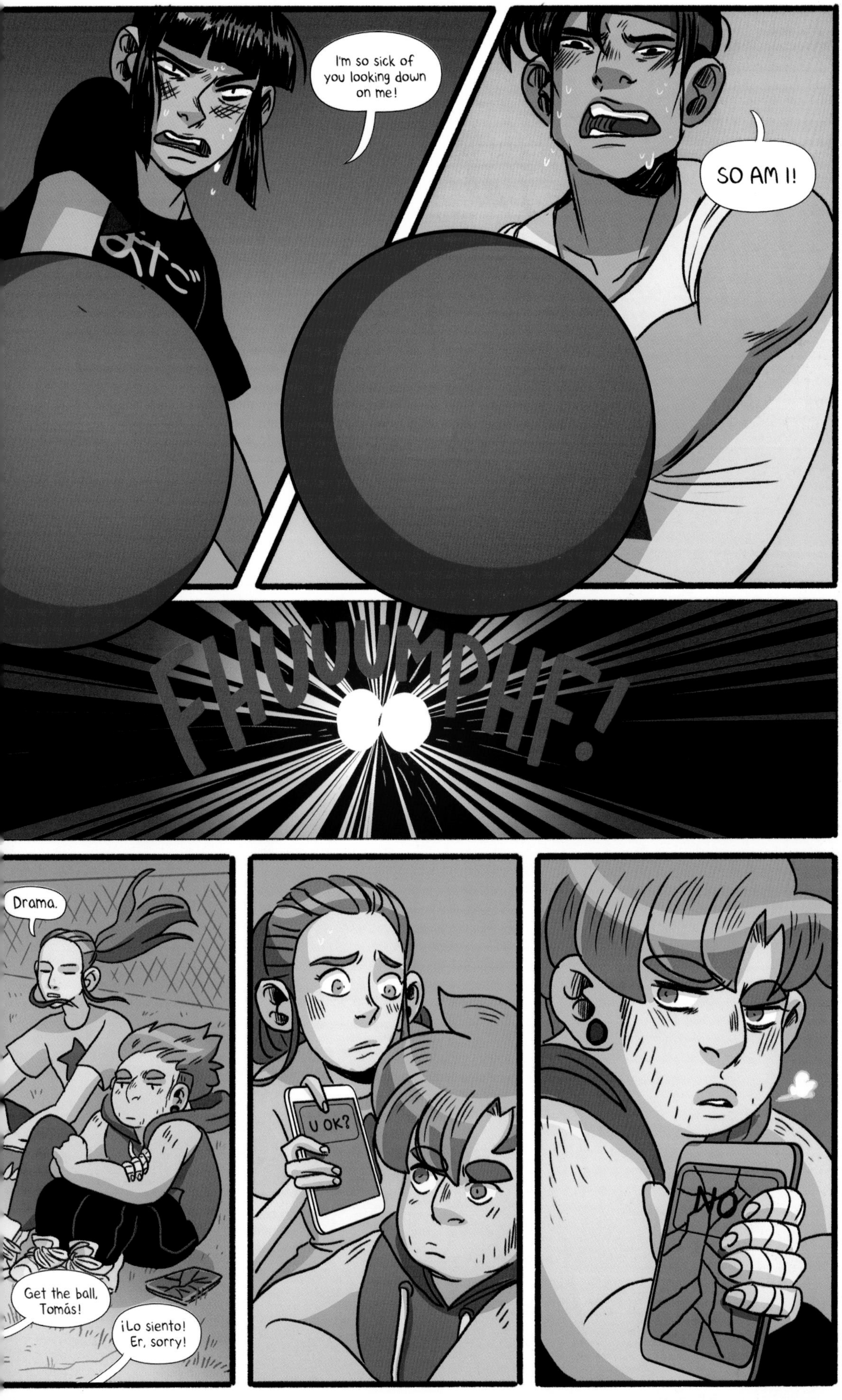
I'm so sick of you looking down on me!
SO AM I!
FHUUUMPHF!
Drama.
Get the ball, Tomás!
¡Lo siento! Er, sorry!
U OK?
NO

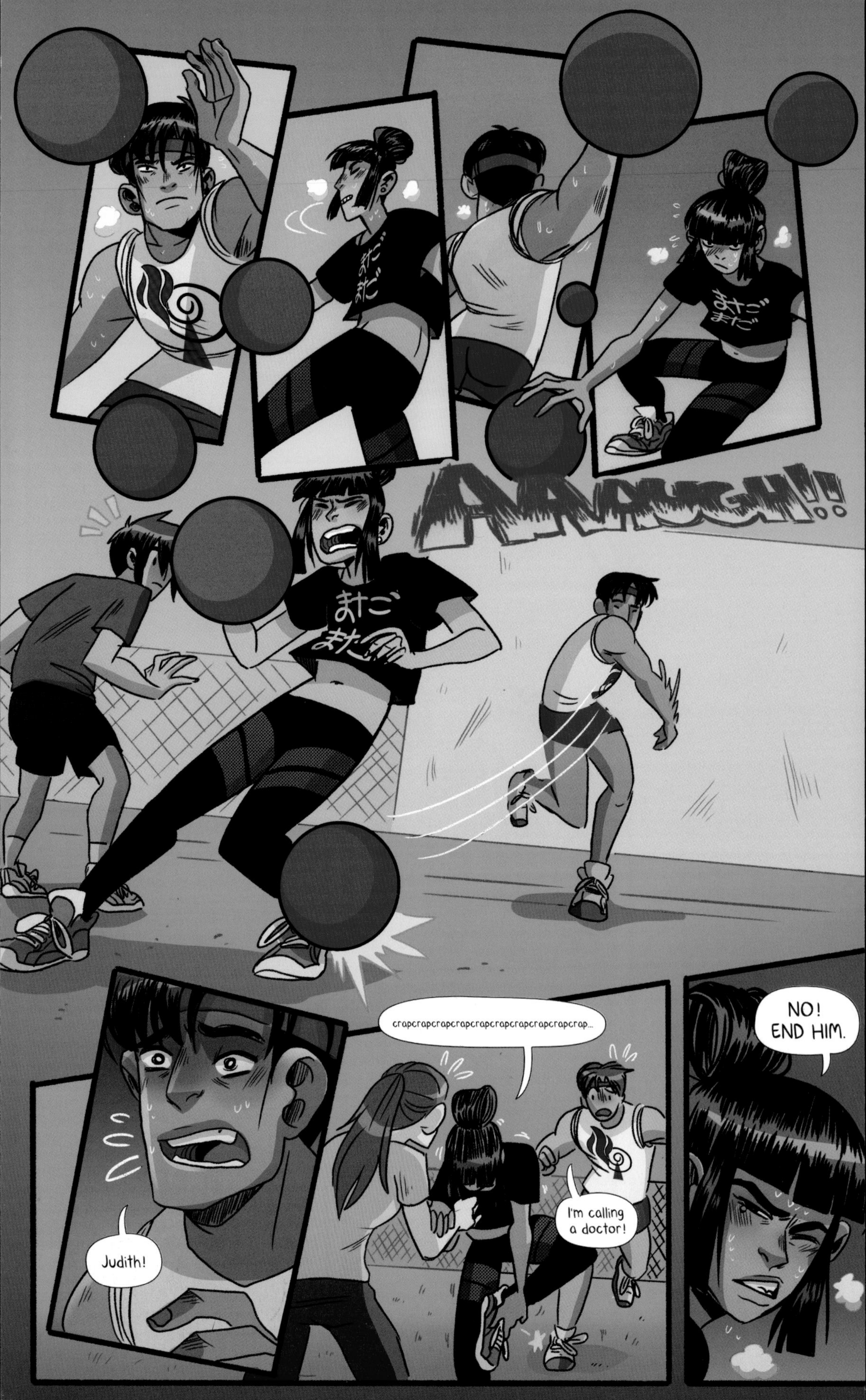
AAAUGH!!
Judith!
crapcrapcrapcrapcrapcrapcrapcrapcrapcrap...
I'm calling a doctor!
NO! END HIM.

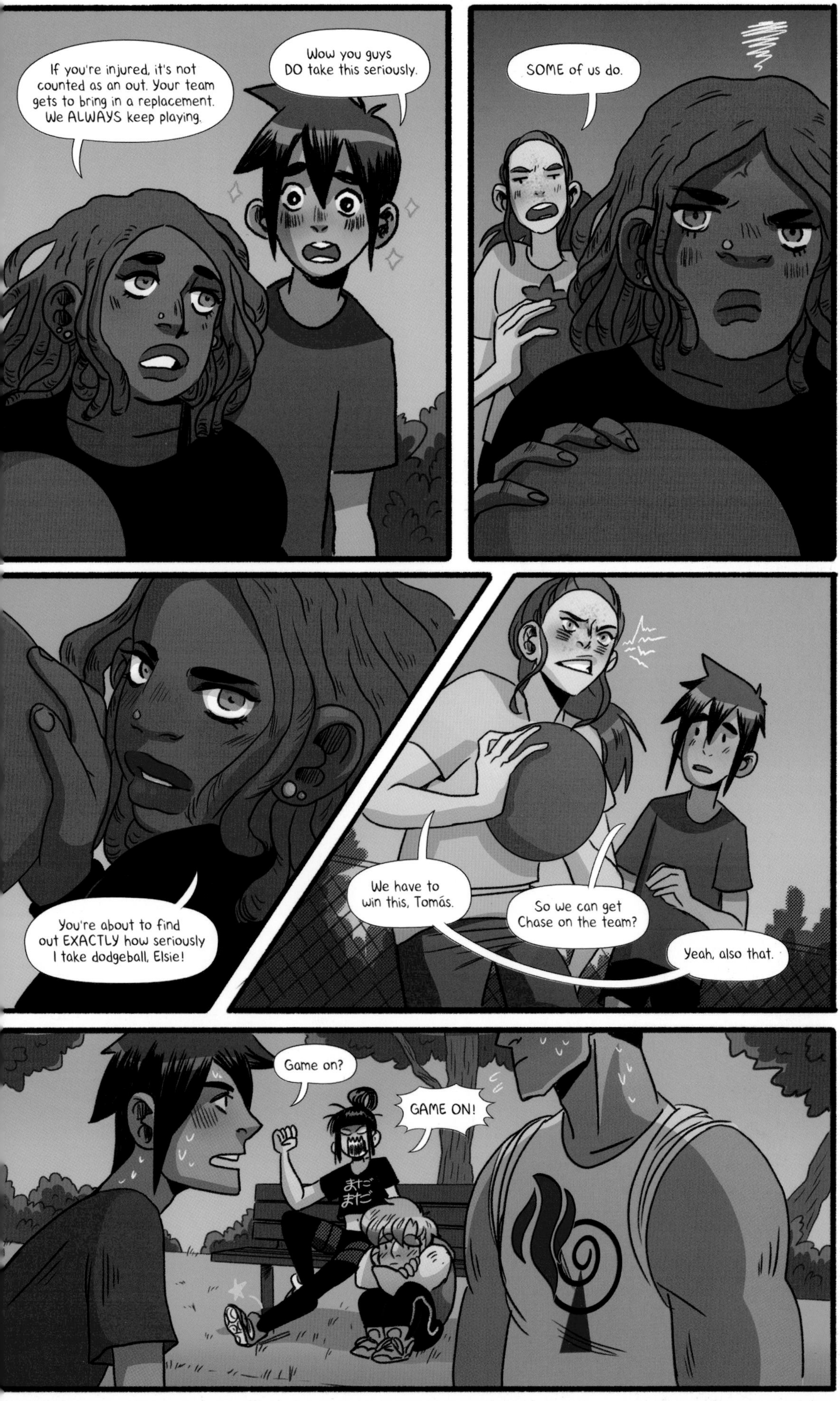
If you're injured, it's not counted as an out. Your team gets to bring in a replacement. We ALWAYS keep playing.
Wow you guys DO take this seriously.
SOME of us do.
You're about to find out EXACTLY how seriously I take dodgeball, Elsie!
We have to win this, Tomás.
So we can get Chase on the team?
Yeah, also that.
Game on?
GAME ON!
まだ まだ

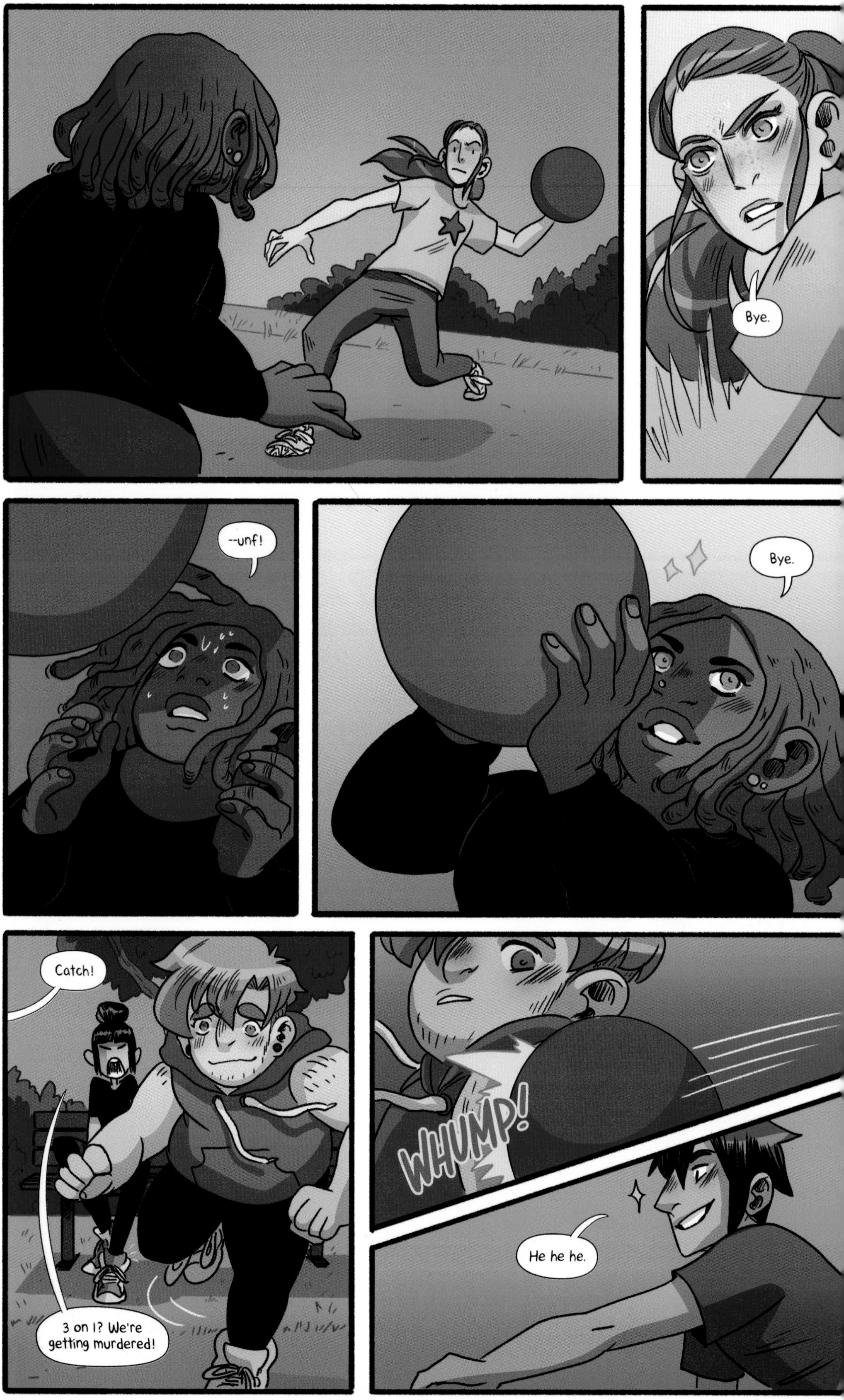
Bye.
--unf!
Bye.
Catch!
3 on 1? We're getting murdered!
WHUMP!
He he he.

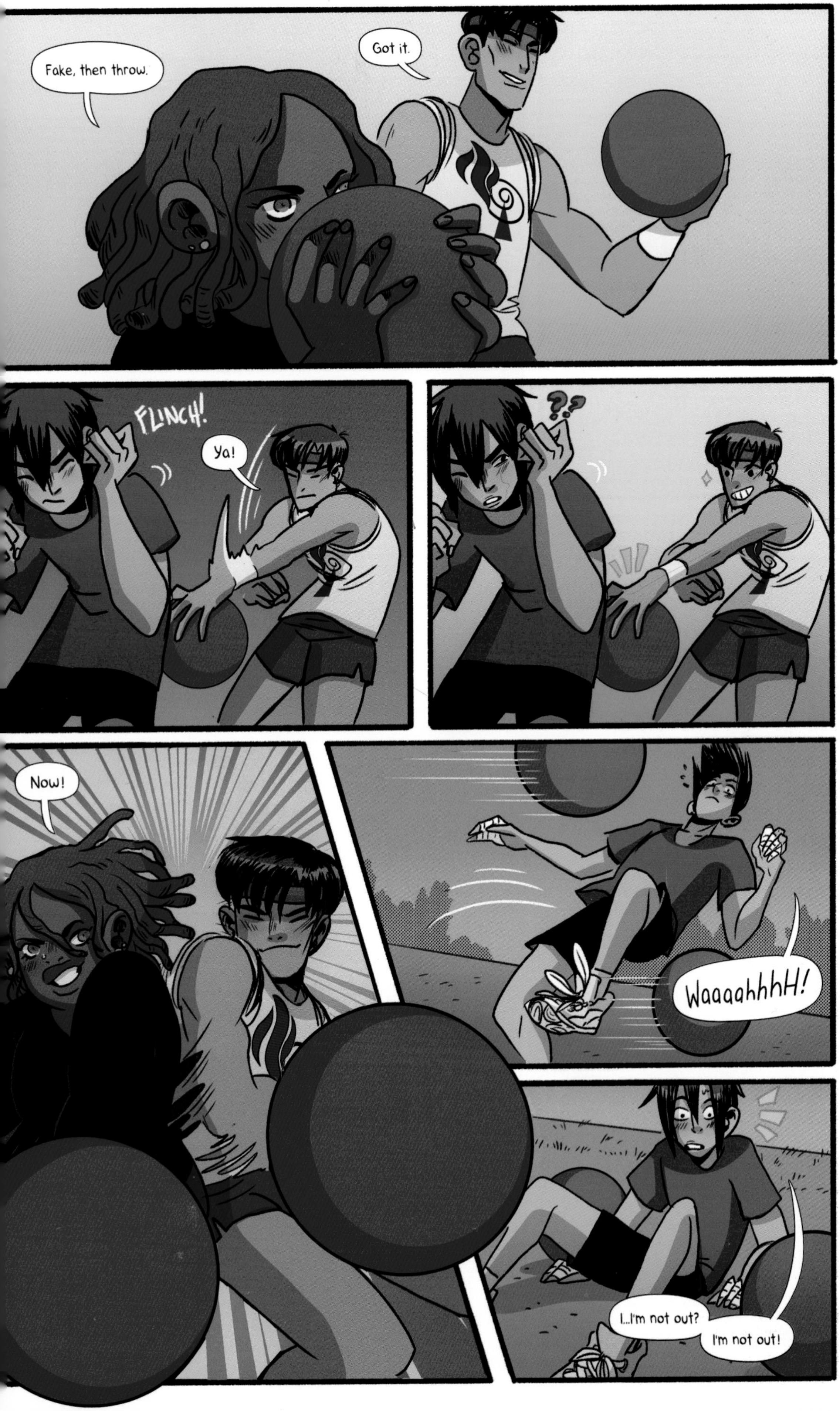
Fake, then throw.
Got it.
FLINCH!
Ya!
??
Now!
WaaaahhhH!
I...I'm not out?
I'm not out!

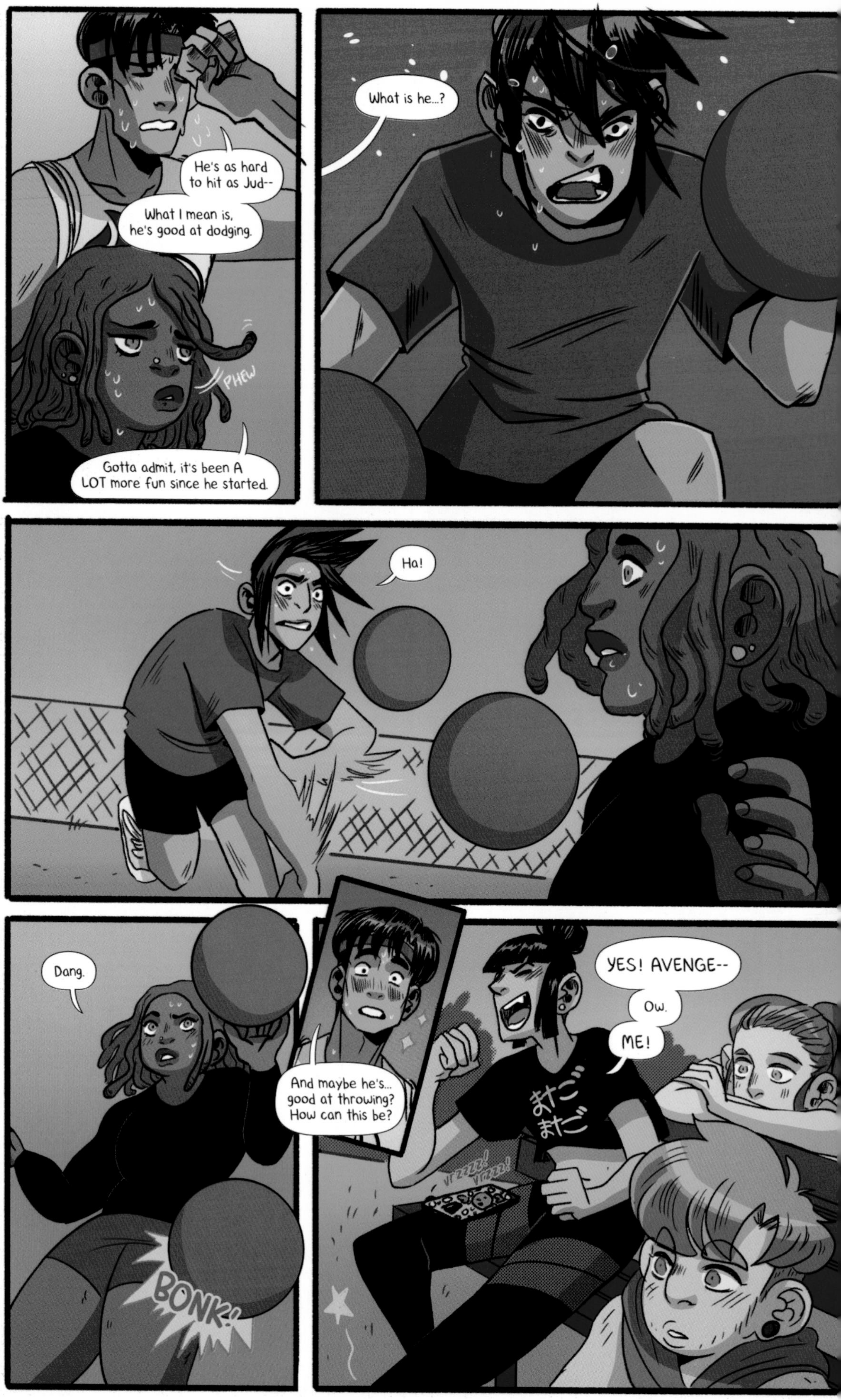

He's as hard to hit as Jud--
What I mean is, he's good at dodging.
PHEW
Gotta admit, it's been A LOT more fun since he started.
What is he...?
Ha!
Dang.
BONK!
And maybe he's... good at throwing? How can this be?
YES! AVENGE--
Ow.
ME!
まご
まご

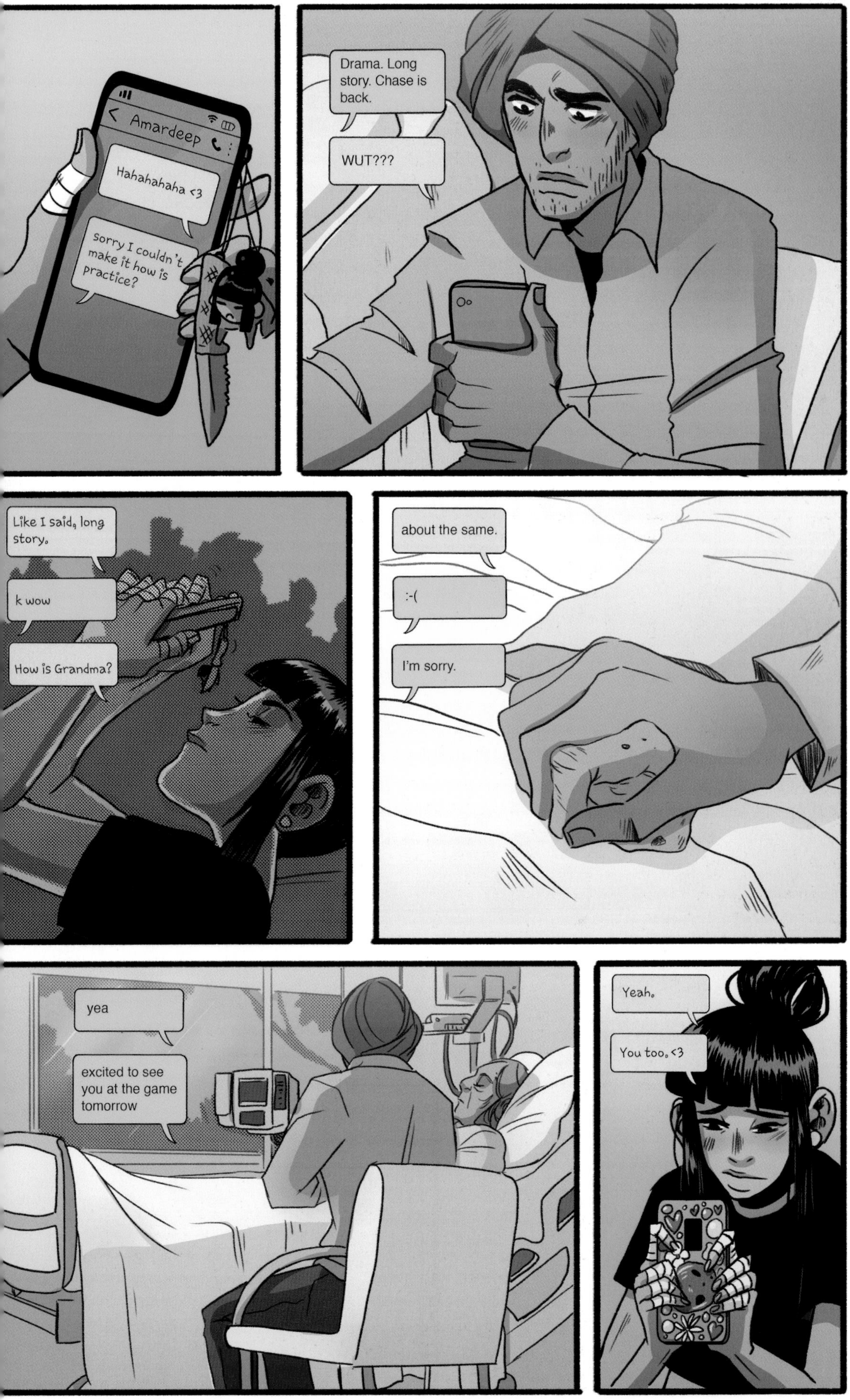
Amardeep
Hahahahaha <3
Sorry I couldn't make it how is practice?
Drama. Long story. Chase is back.
WUT???
Like I said, long story.
k wow
How is Grandma?
about the same.
:-(
I'm sorry.
yea
excited to see you at the game tomorrow
Yeah.
You too. <3

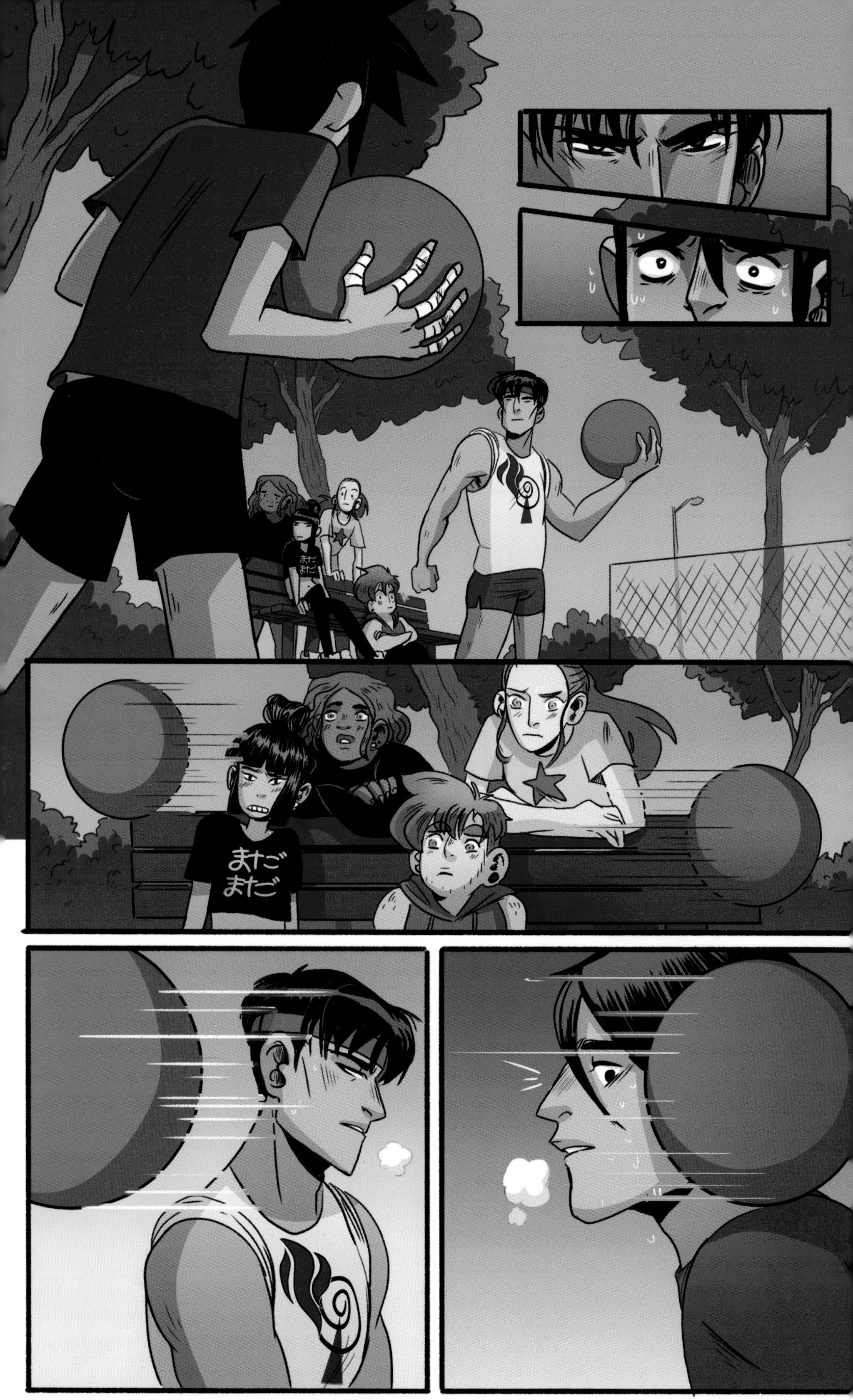
まだ
まだ

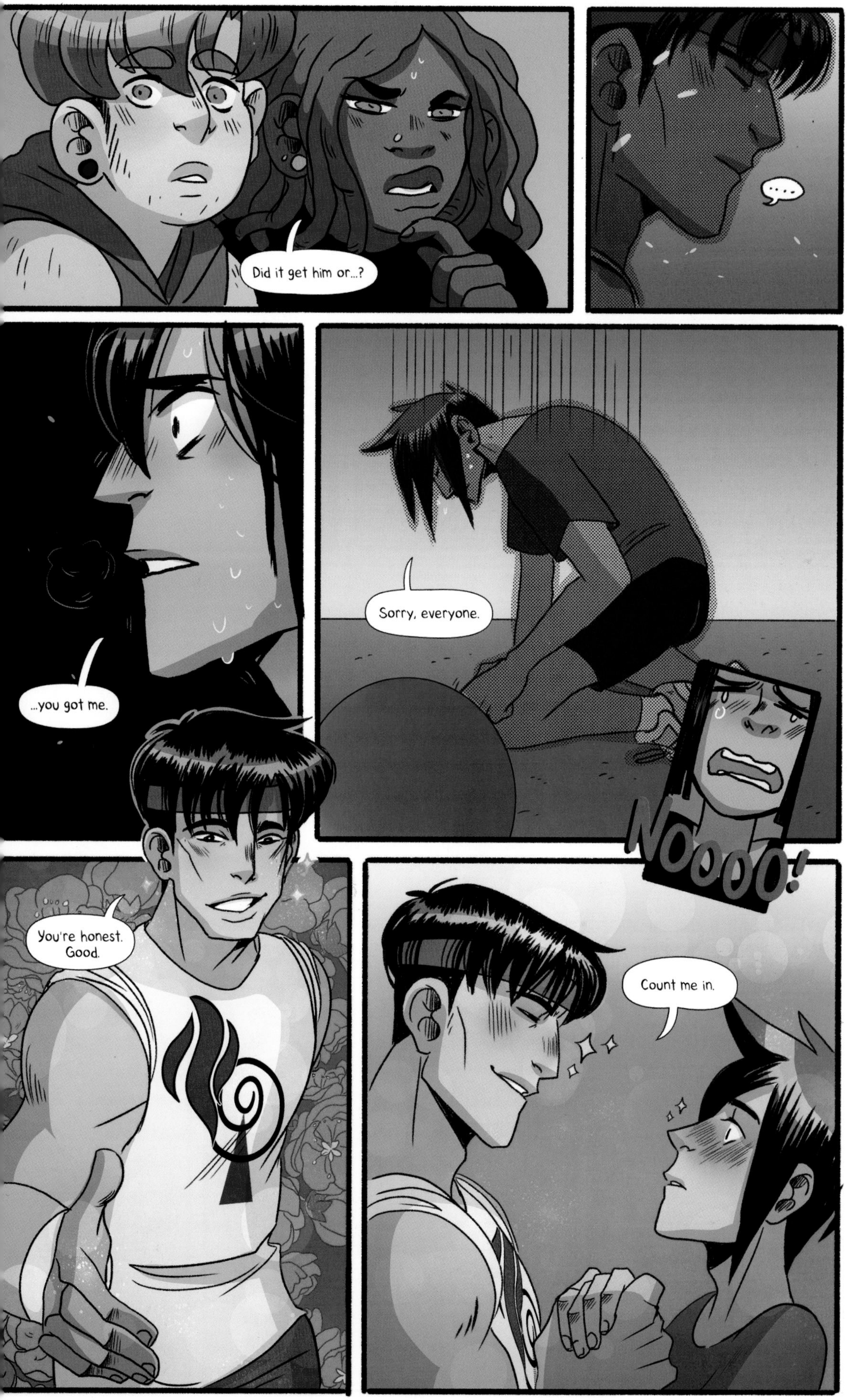
Did it get him or...?
...
...you got me.
Sorry, everyone.
NOOOO!
You're honest. Good.
Count me in.

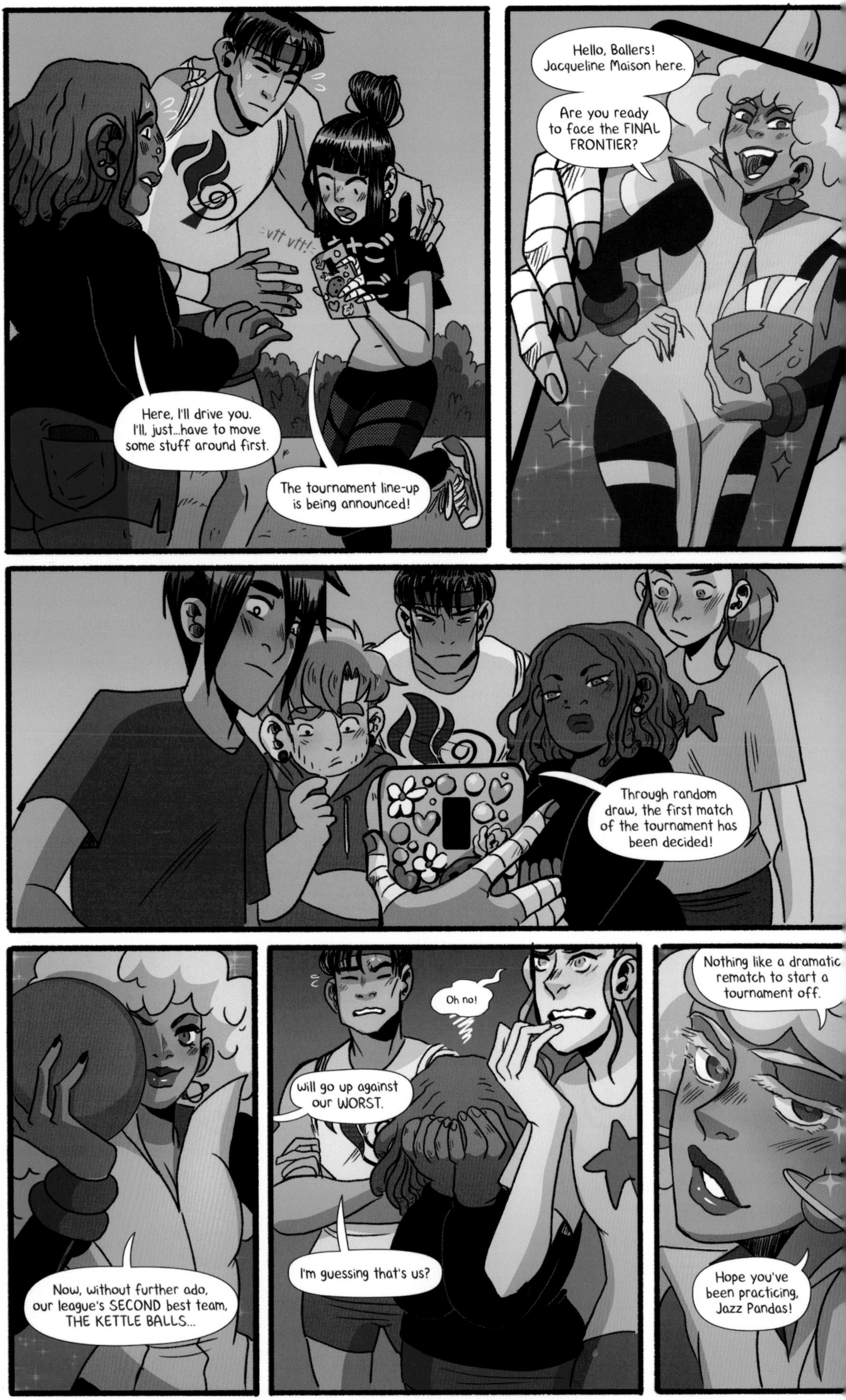
vtt vtt!
Here, I'll drive you. I'll, just...have to move some stuff around first.
The tournament line-up is being announced!
Hello, Ballers! Jacqueline Maison here.
Are you ready to face the FINAL FRONTIER?
Through random draw, the first match of the tournament has been decided!
Now, without further ado, our league's SECOND best team, THE KETTLE BALLS...
will go up against our WORST.
Oh no!
I'm guessing that's us?
Nothing like a dramatic rematch to start a tournament off.
Hope you've been practicing, Jazz Pandas!

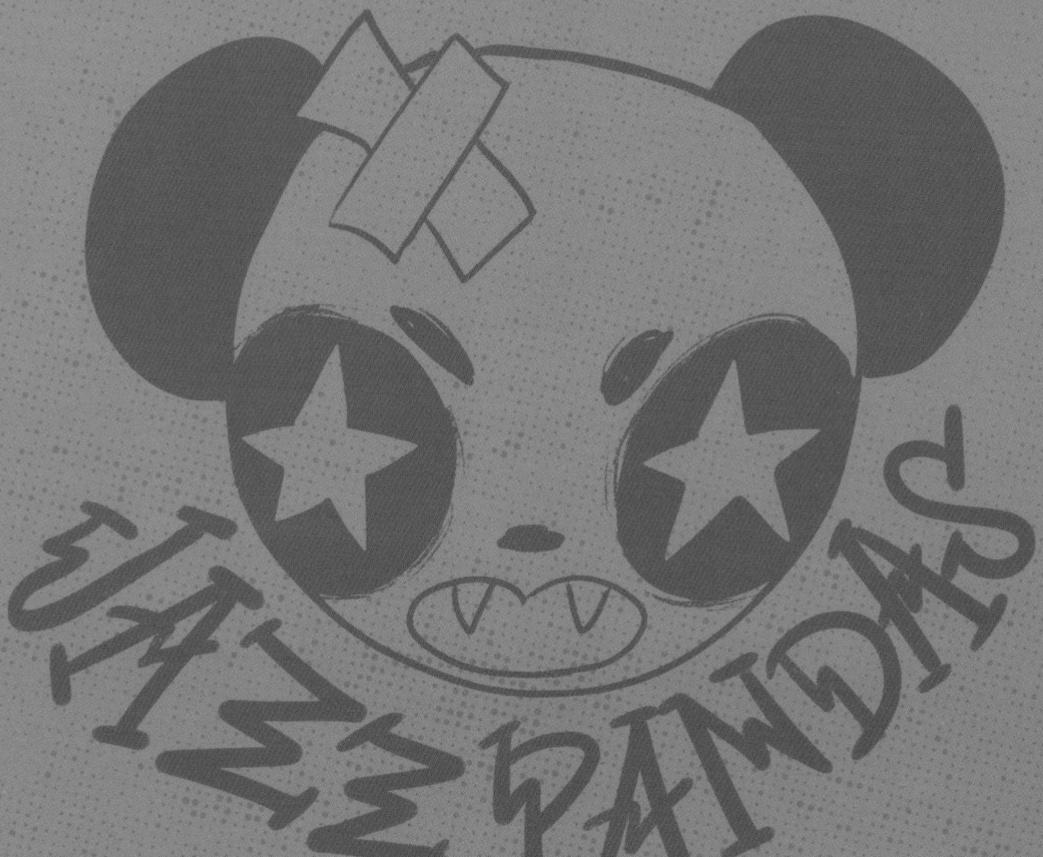
JAZZ PANDAS

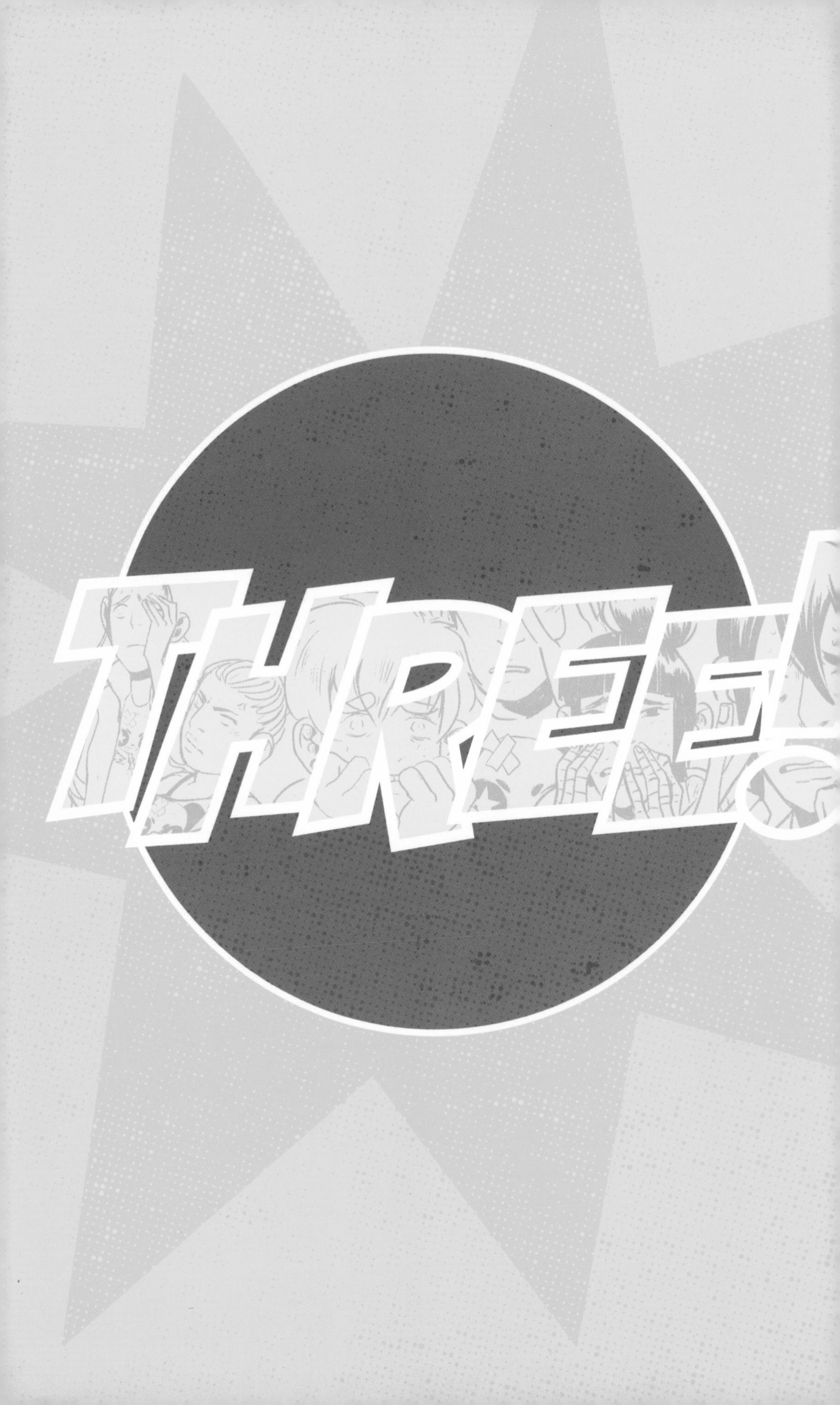
THREE!

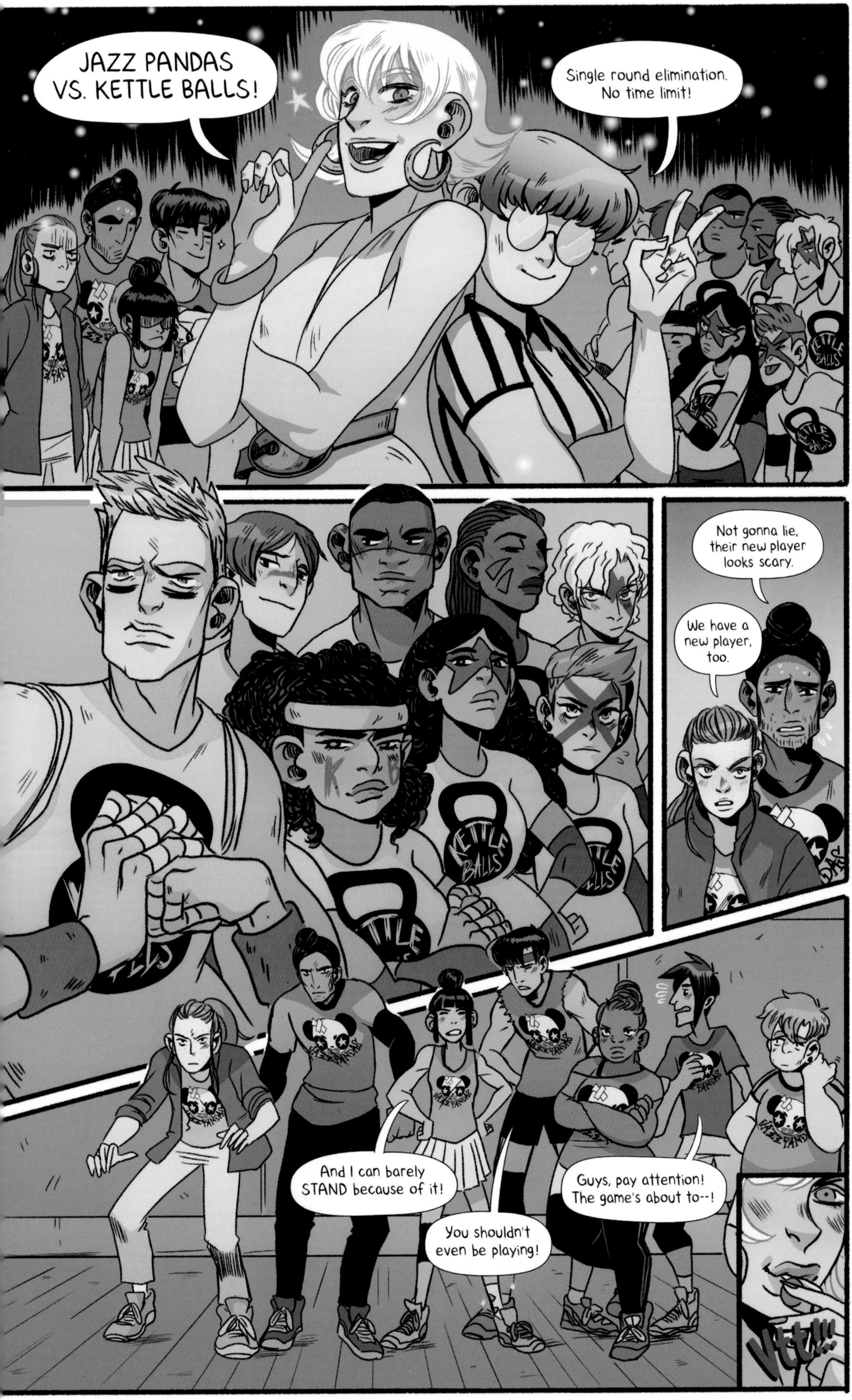
JAZZ PANDAS VS. KETTLE BALLS!
Single round elimination. No time limit!
KETTLE BALLS
Not gonna lie, their new player looks scary.
We have a new player, too.
JAZZ PANDAS
And I can barely STAND because of it!
You shouldn't even be playing!
Guys, pay attention! The game's about to--!
VTT!!!

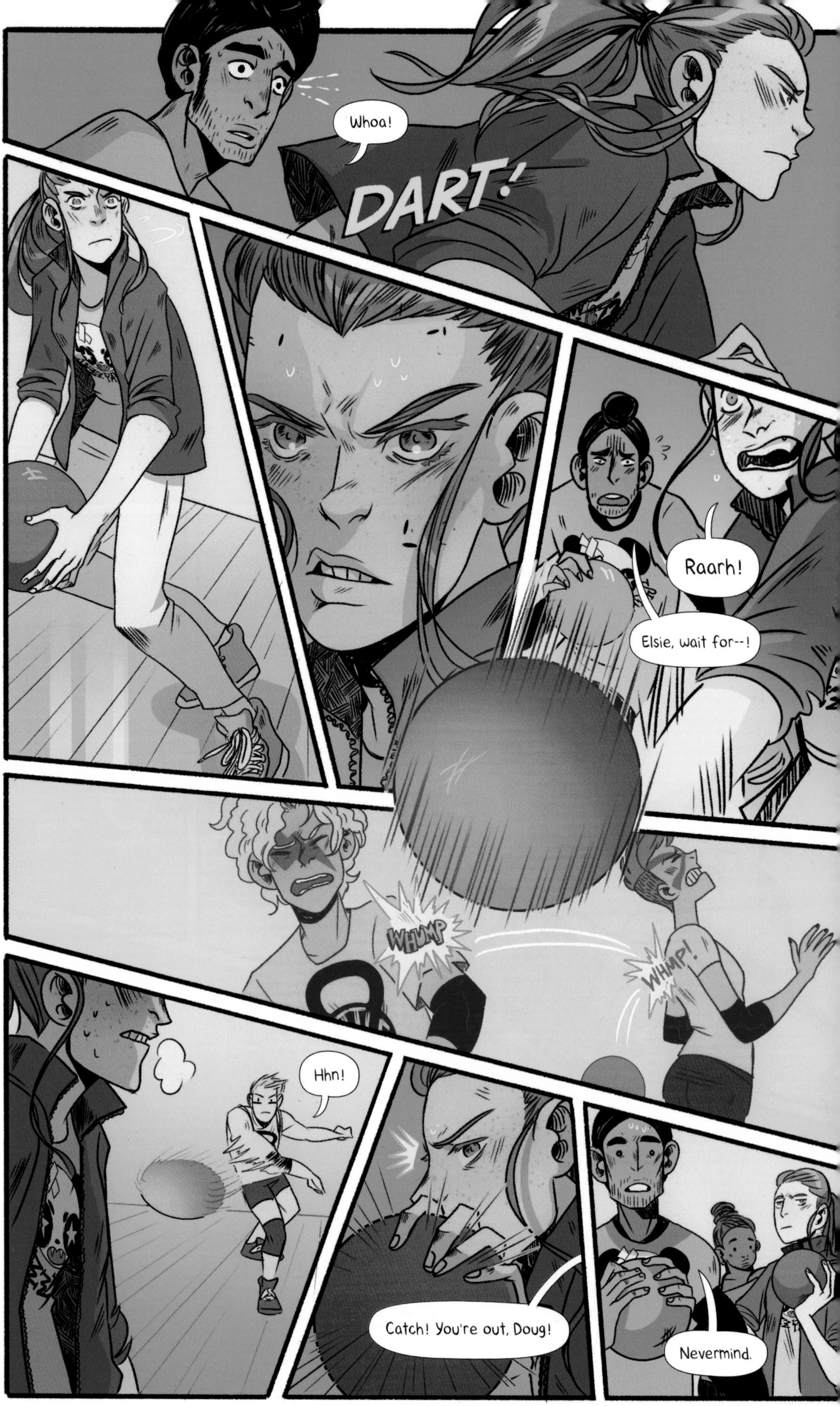
Whoa!
DART!
Raarh!
Elsie, wait for--!
WHUMP
WHMP!
Hhn!
Catch! You're out, Doug!
Nevermind.

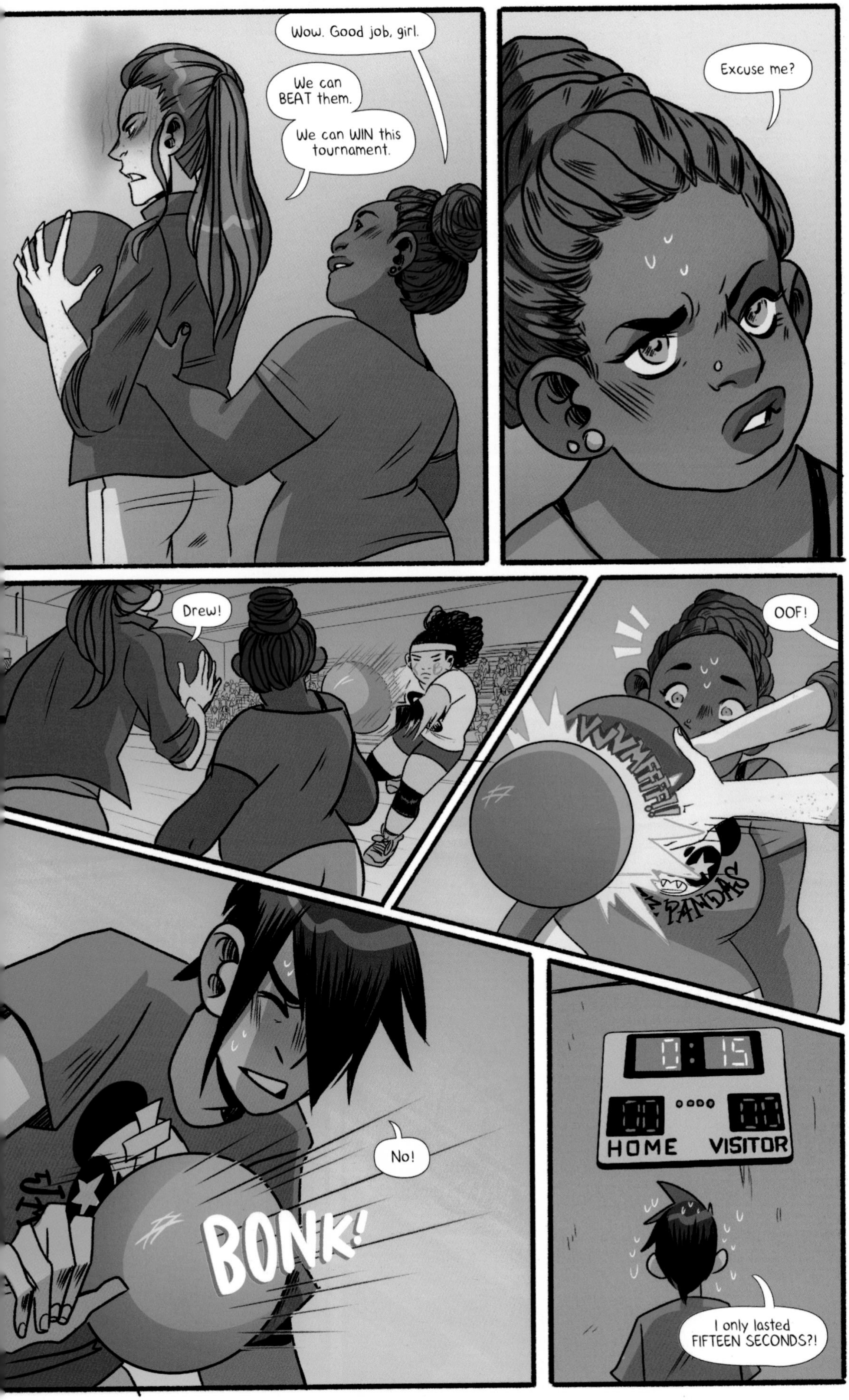
Wow. Good job, girl.
We can BEAT them.
We can WIN this tournament.
Excuse me?
Drew!
OOF!
PANDAS
No!
BONK!
0:15
HOME
VISITOR
I only lasted FIFTEEN SECONDS?!

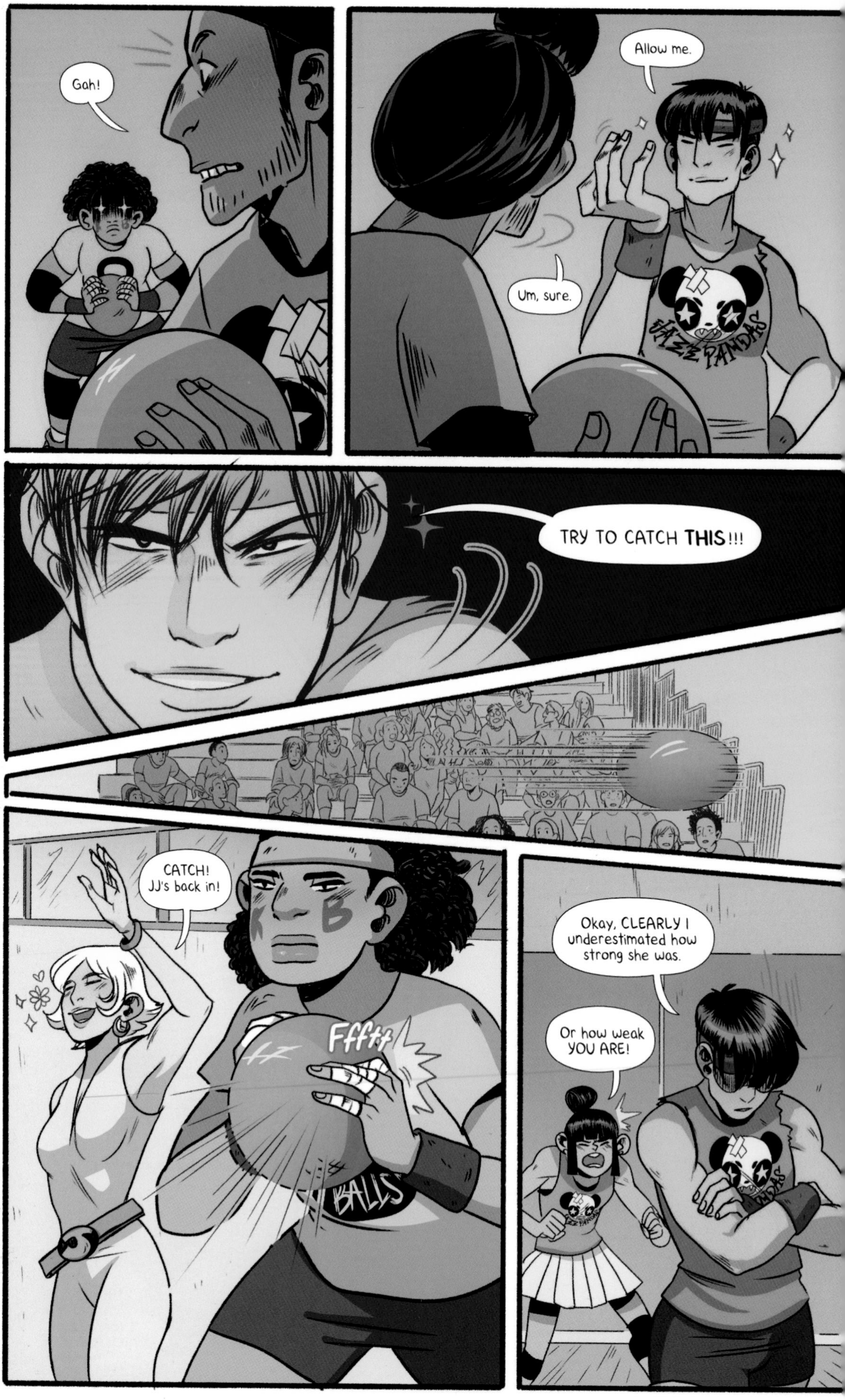
Gah!
Allow me.
Um, sure.
TRY TO CATCH **THIS**!!!
CATCH! JJ's back in!
Fffft
BALLS
Okay, CLEARLY I underestimated how strong she was.
Or how weak YOU ARE!

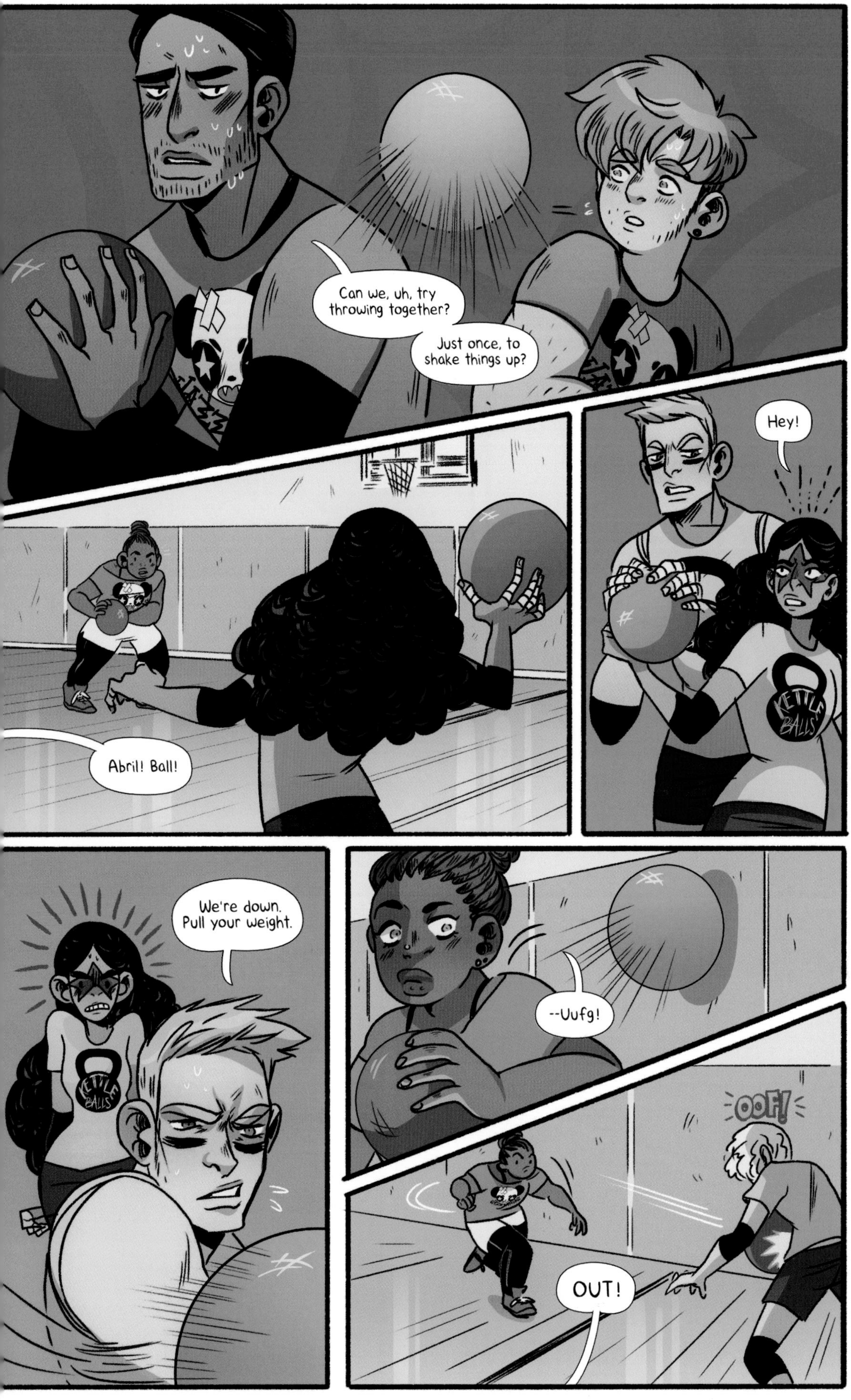
Can we, uh, try throwing together?
Just once, to shake things up?
Hey!
Abril! Ball!
We're down. Pull your weight.
--Uufg!
OOF!
OUT!

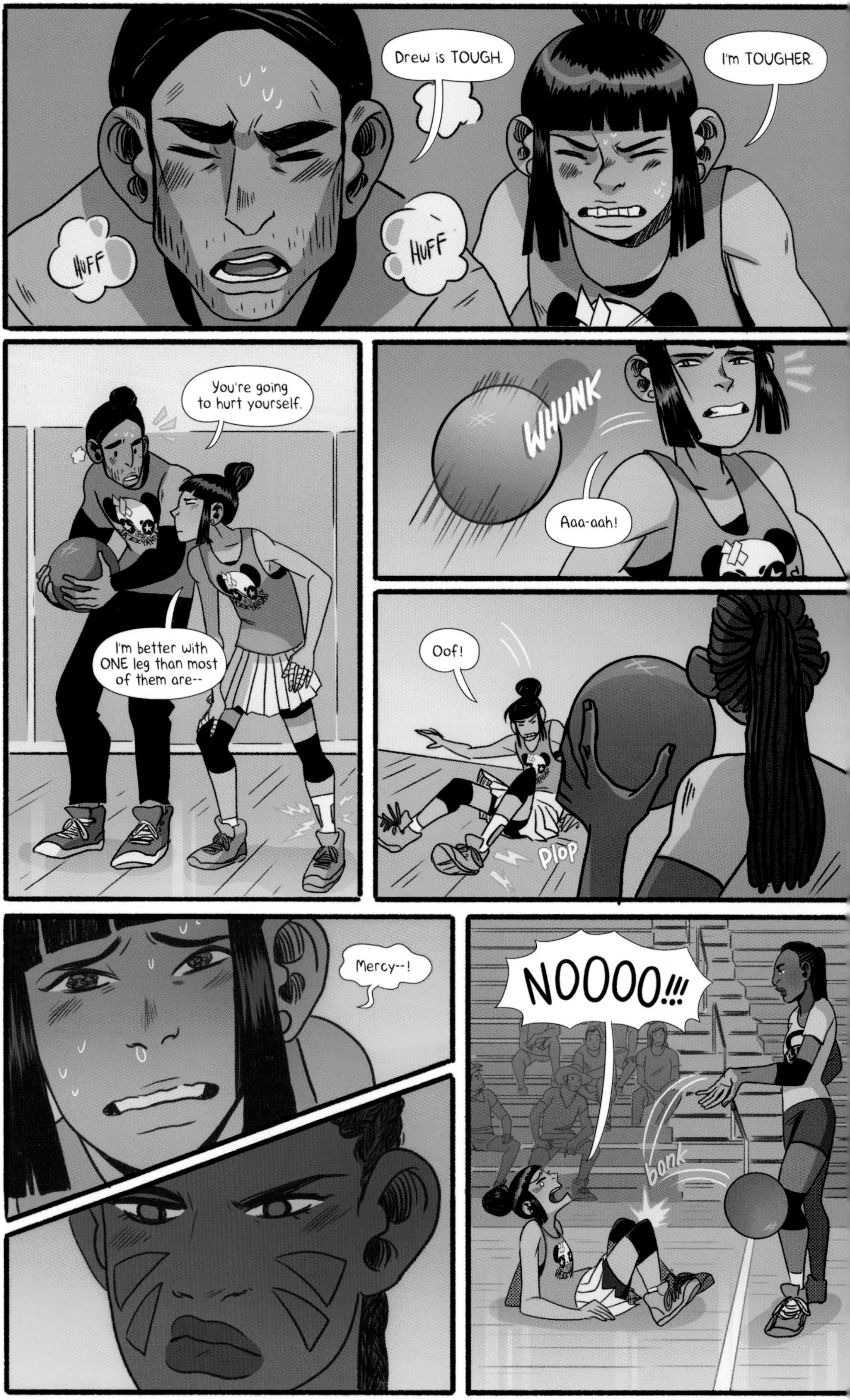
Drew is TOUGH.
I'm TOUGHER.
HUFF
HUFF
You're going to hurt yourself.
I'm better with ONE leg than most of them are--
WHUNK
Aaa-aah!
Oof!
PLOP
Mercy--!
NOOOO!!!
bonk

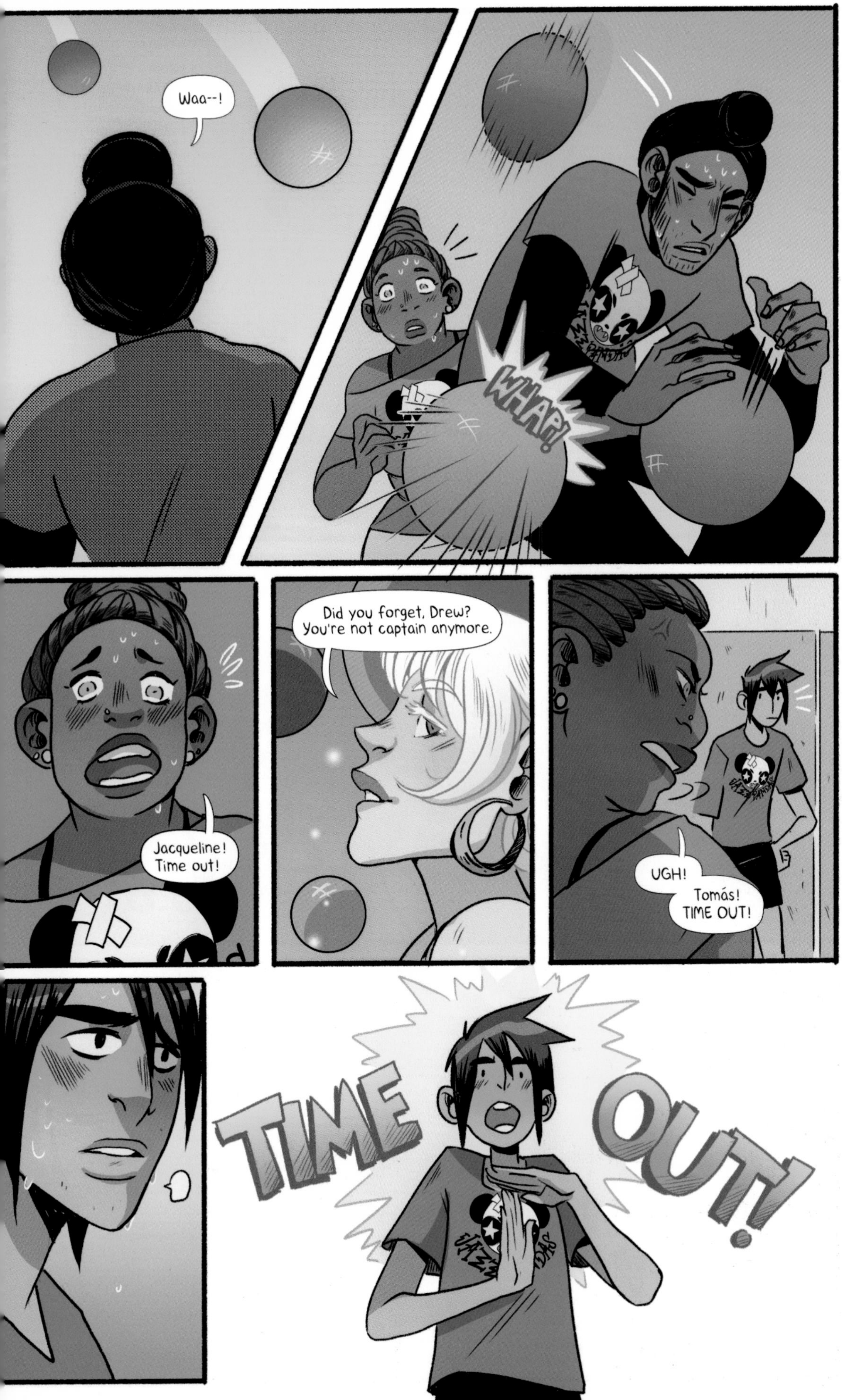
Waa--!
WHAP!
Jacqueline! Time out!
Did you forget, Drew? You're not captain anymore.
UGH!
Tomás! TIME OUT!
TIME OUT!

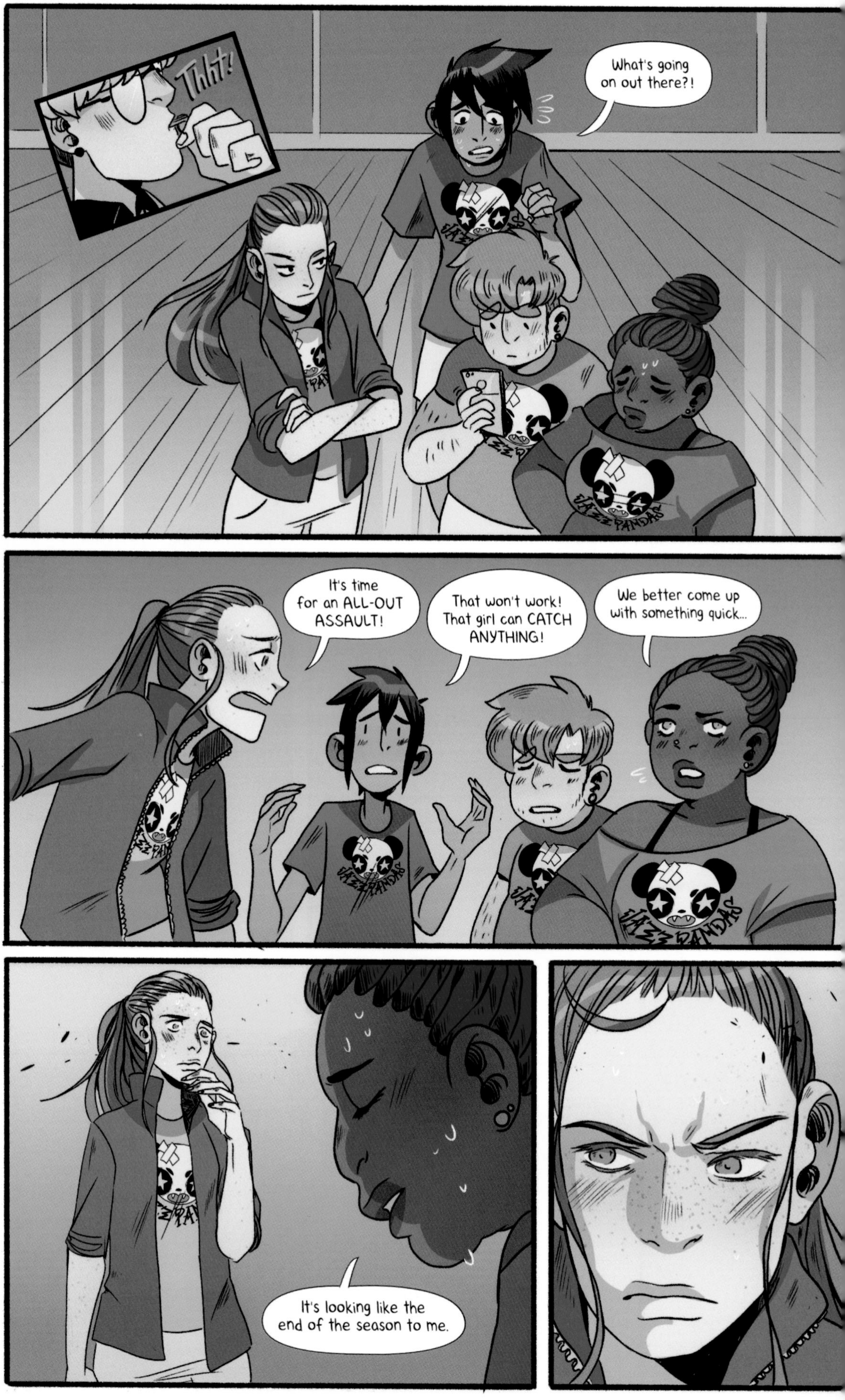
Thht!
What's going on out there?!
It's time for an ALL-OUT ASSAULT!
That won't work! That girl can CATCH ANYTHING!
We better come up with something quick...
It's looking like the end of the season to me.

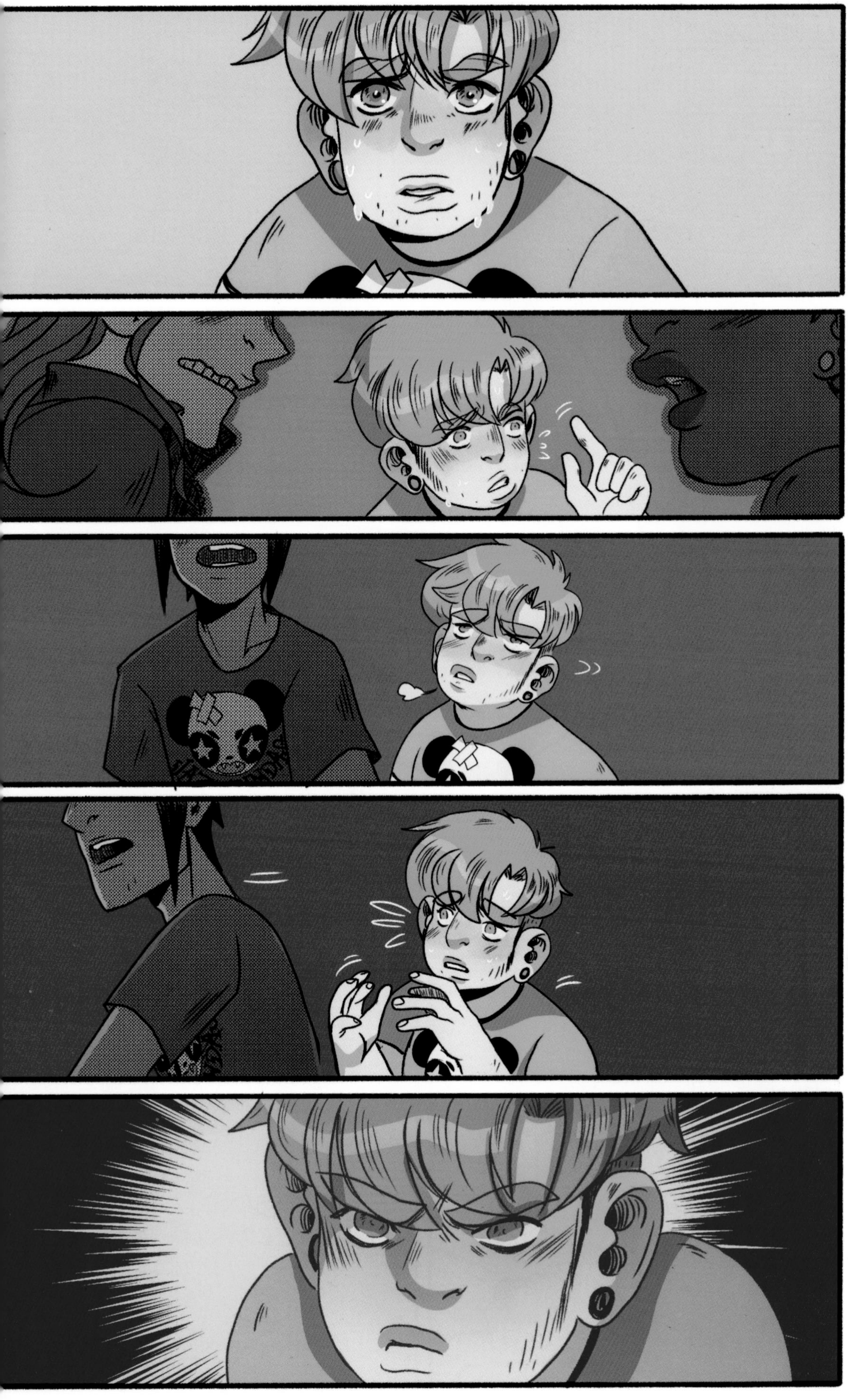

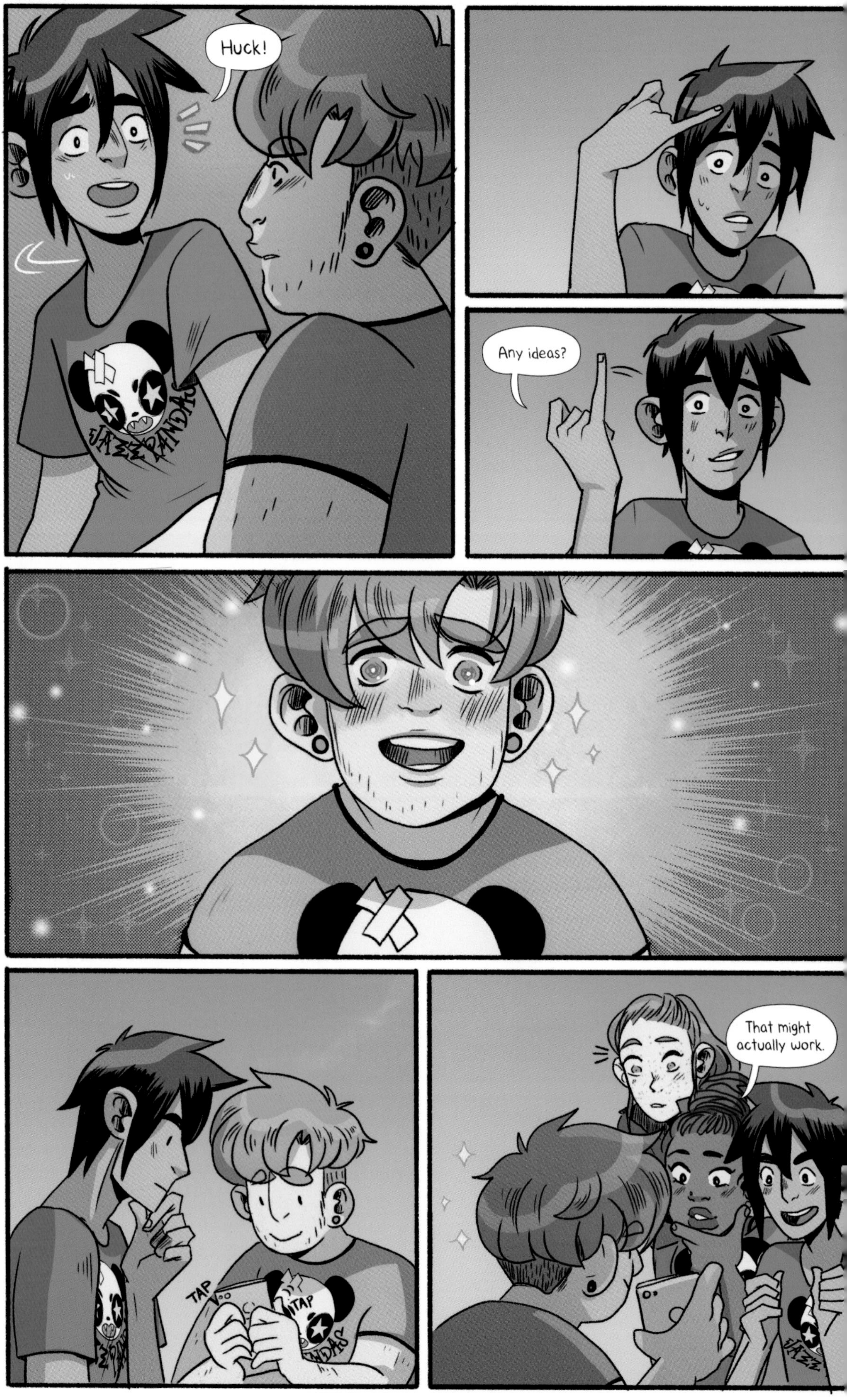
Huck!
Any ideas?
TAP
TAP
That might actually work.

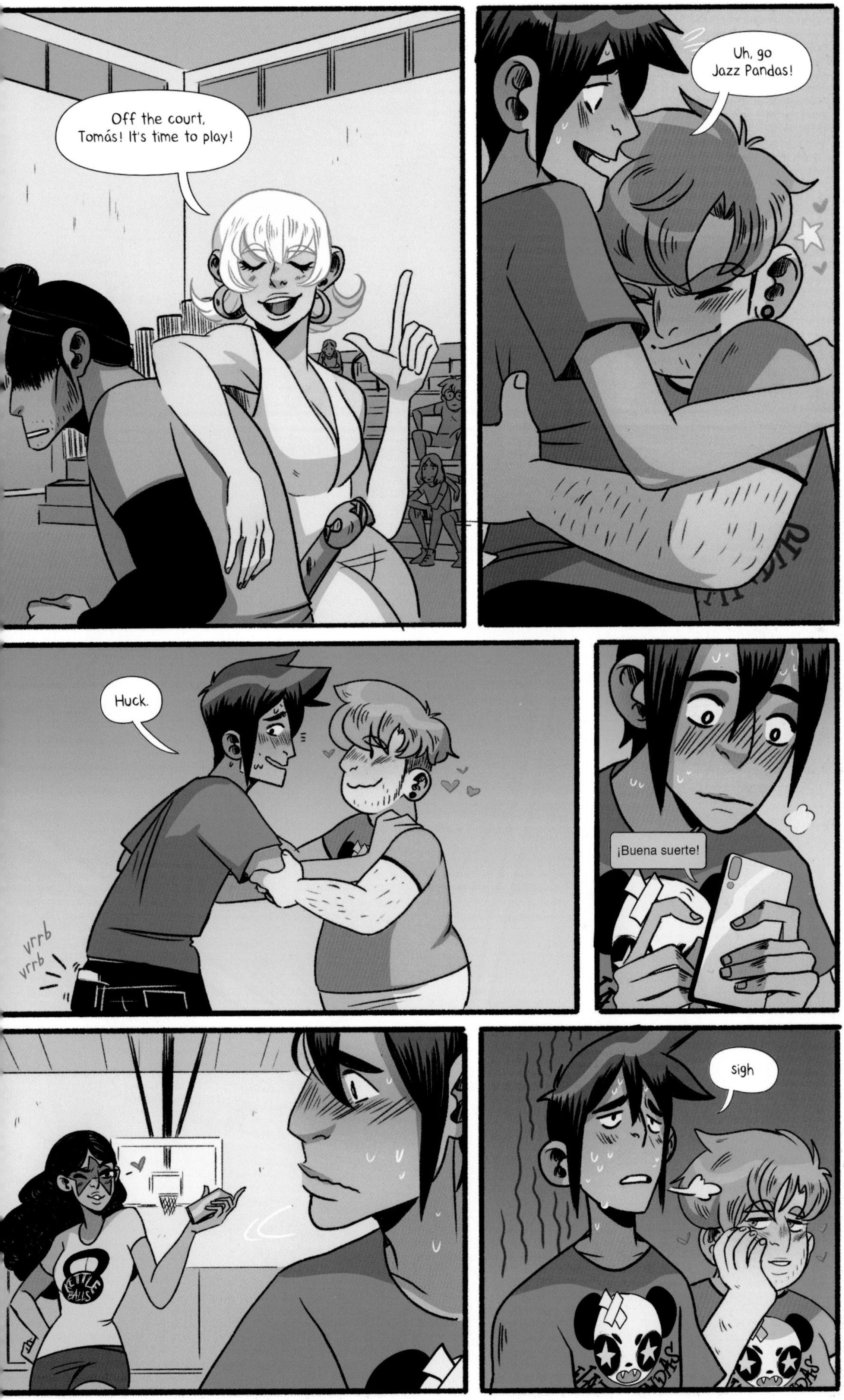
Off the court, Tomás! It's time to play!
Uh, go Jazz Pandas!
Huck.
vrrb vrrb
¡Buena suerte!
sigh

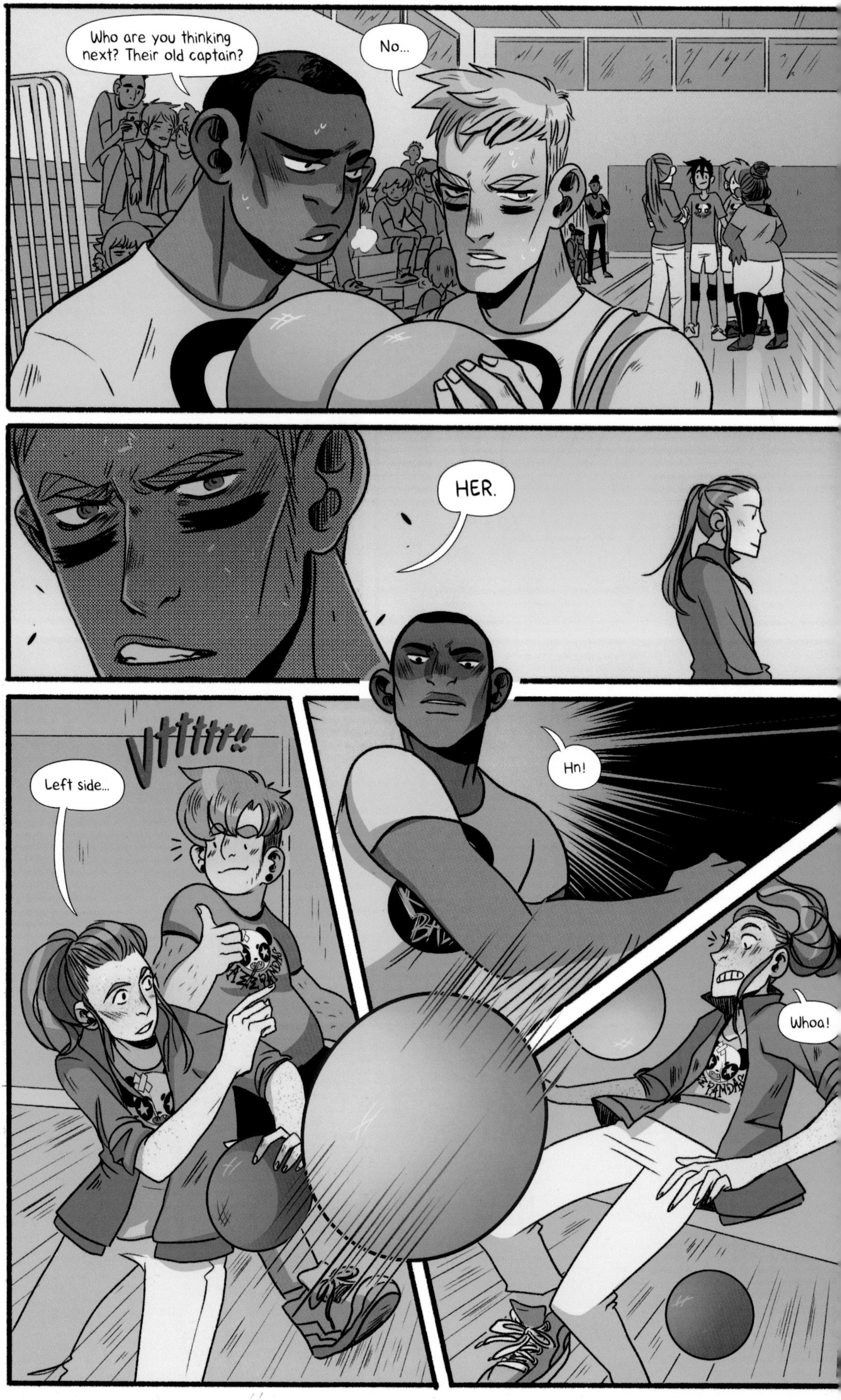

Who are you thinking next? Their old captain?
No...
HER.
VTTTTTT!!
Left side...
Hn!
Whoa!

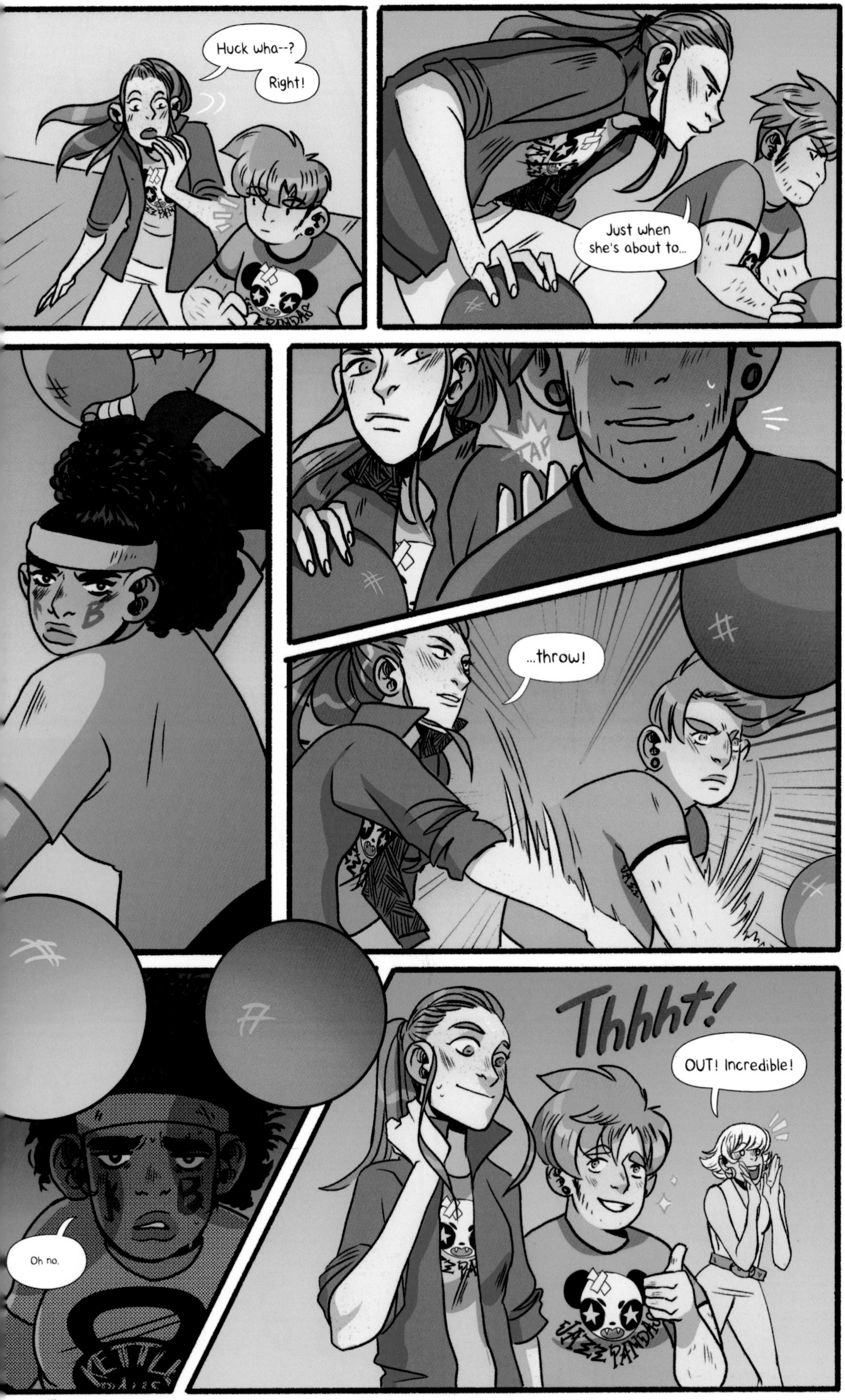
Huck wha--?
Right!
Just when she's about to...
TAP
...throw!
Oh no.
Thhht!
OUT! Incredible!

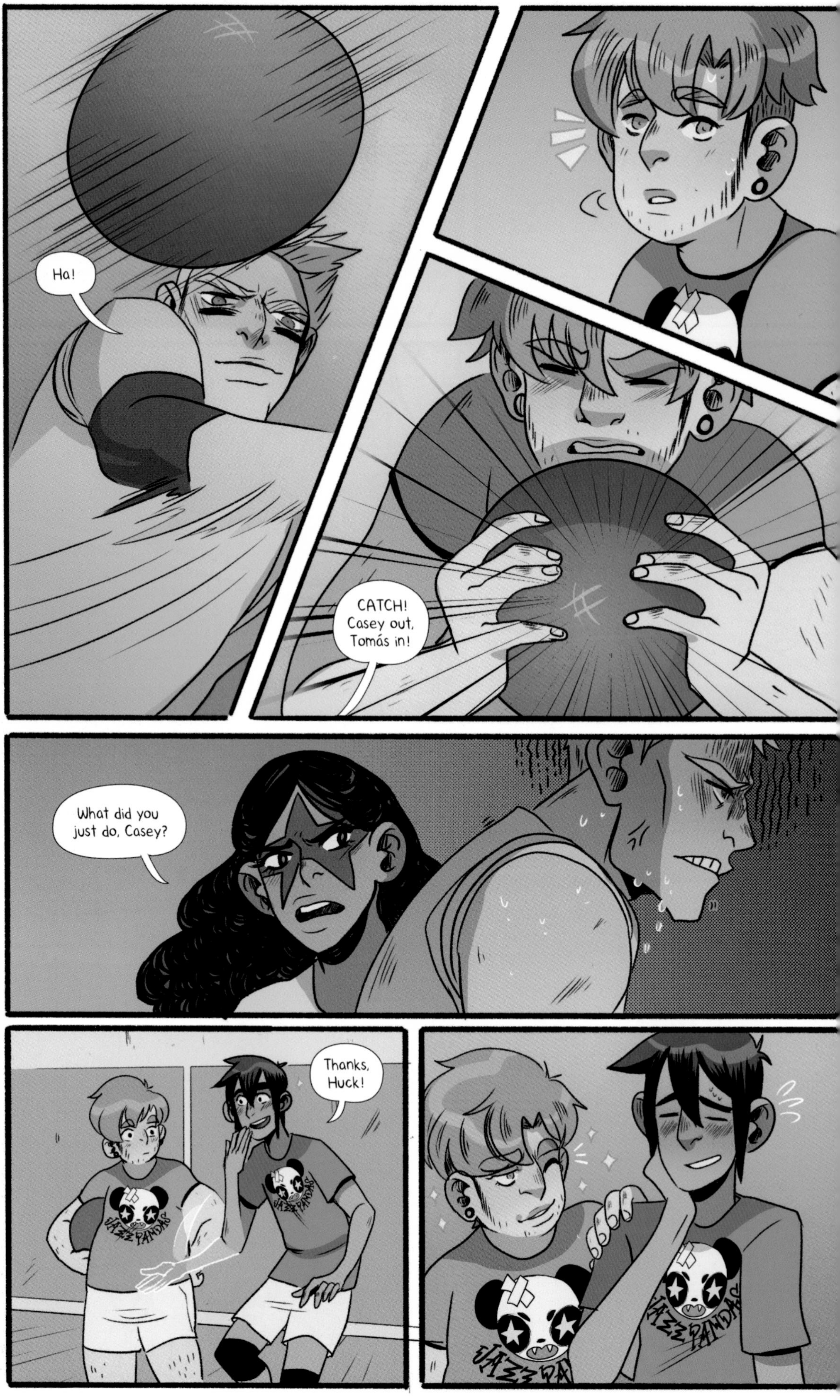
Ha!
CATCH! Casey out, Tomás in!
What did you just do, Casey?
Thanks, Huck!
JAZZ PANDAS

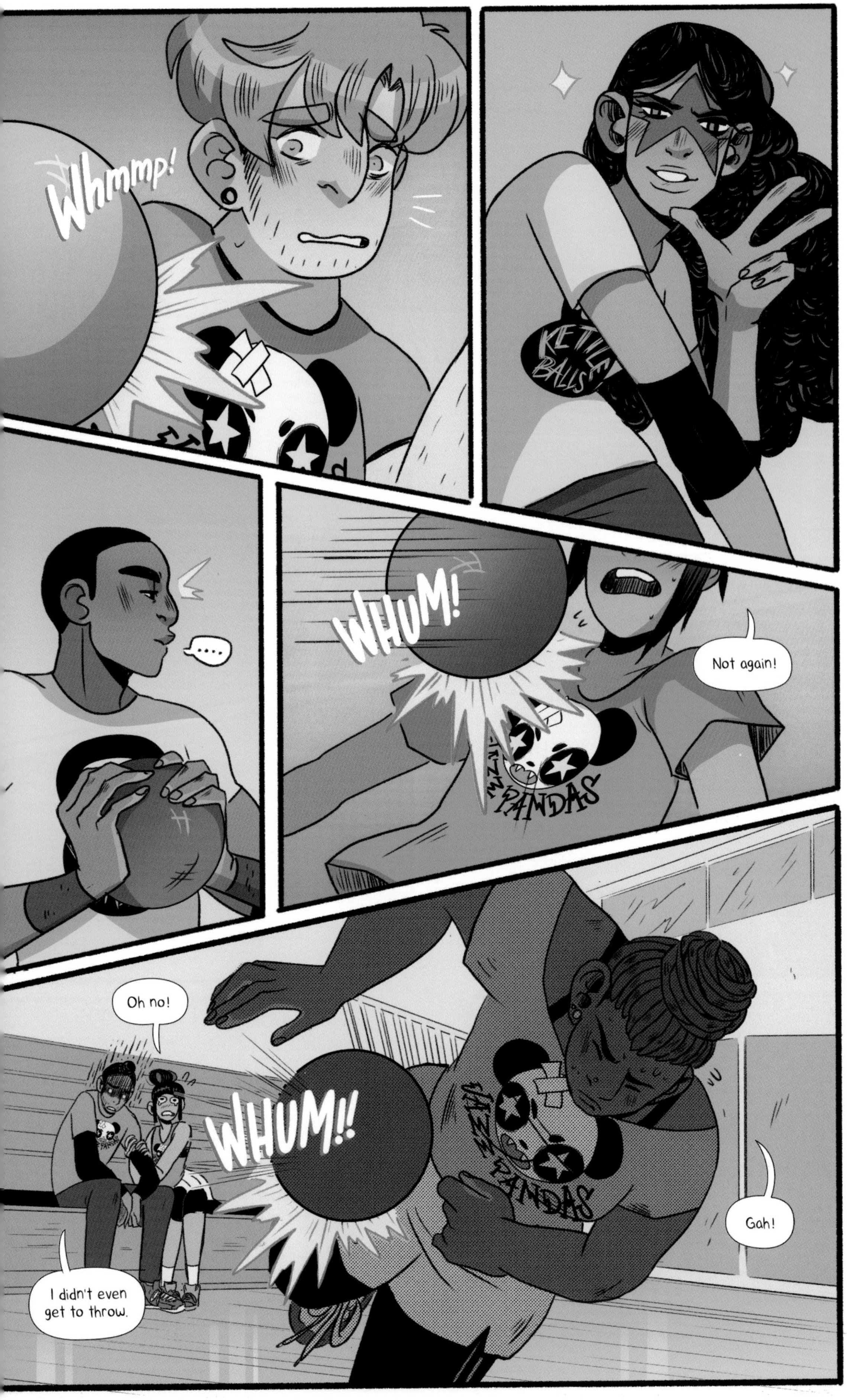
Whmmp!
....
WHUM!
Not again!
Oh no!
WHUM!!
I didn't even get to throw.
Gah!

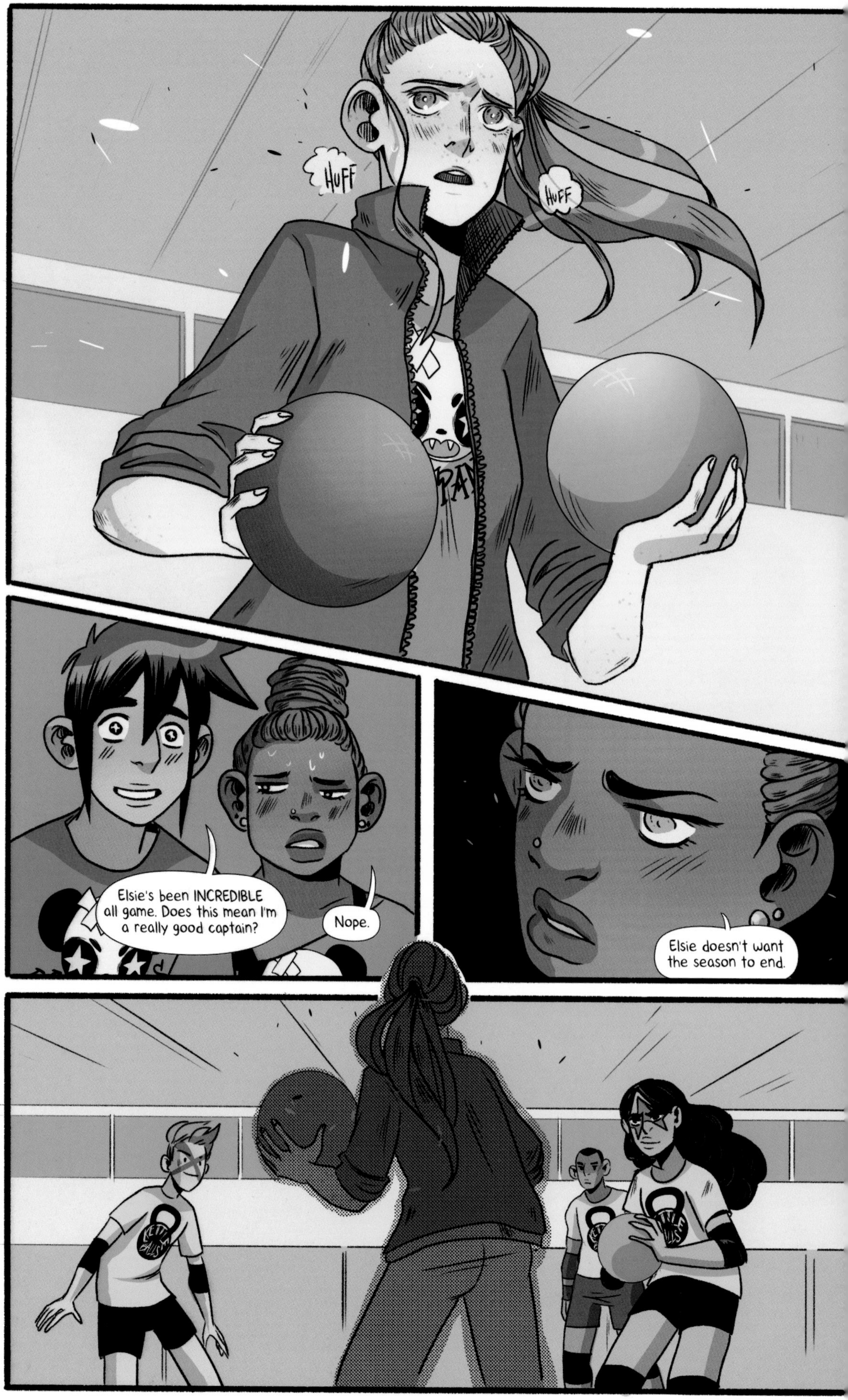
HUFF
HUFF
Elsie's been INCREDIBLE all game. Does this mean I'm a really good captain?
Nope.
Elsie doesn't want the season to end.

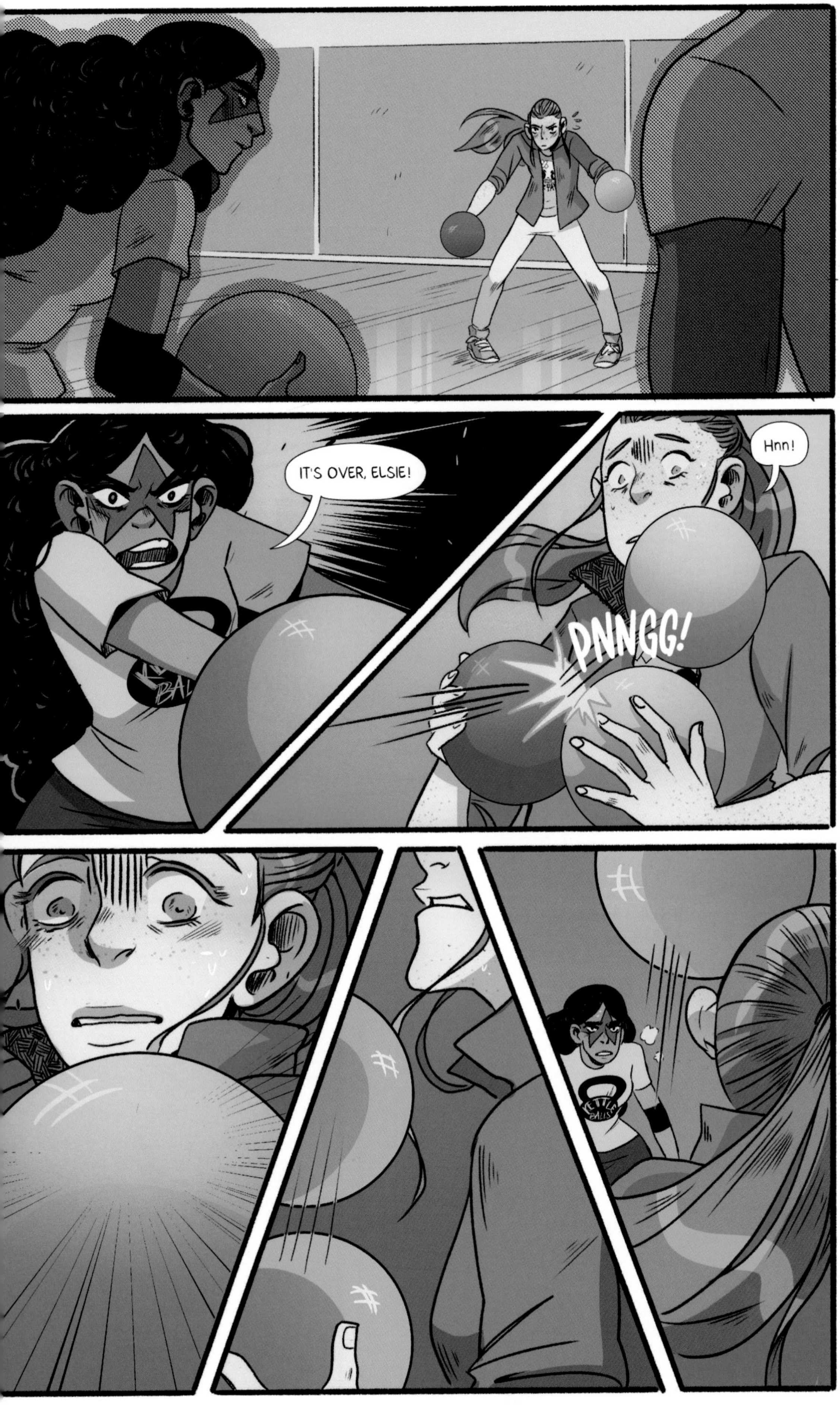
IT'S OVER, ELSIE!
Hnn!
PNNGG!

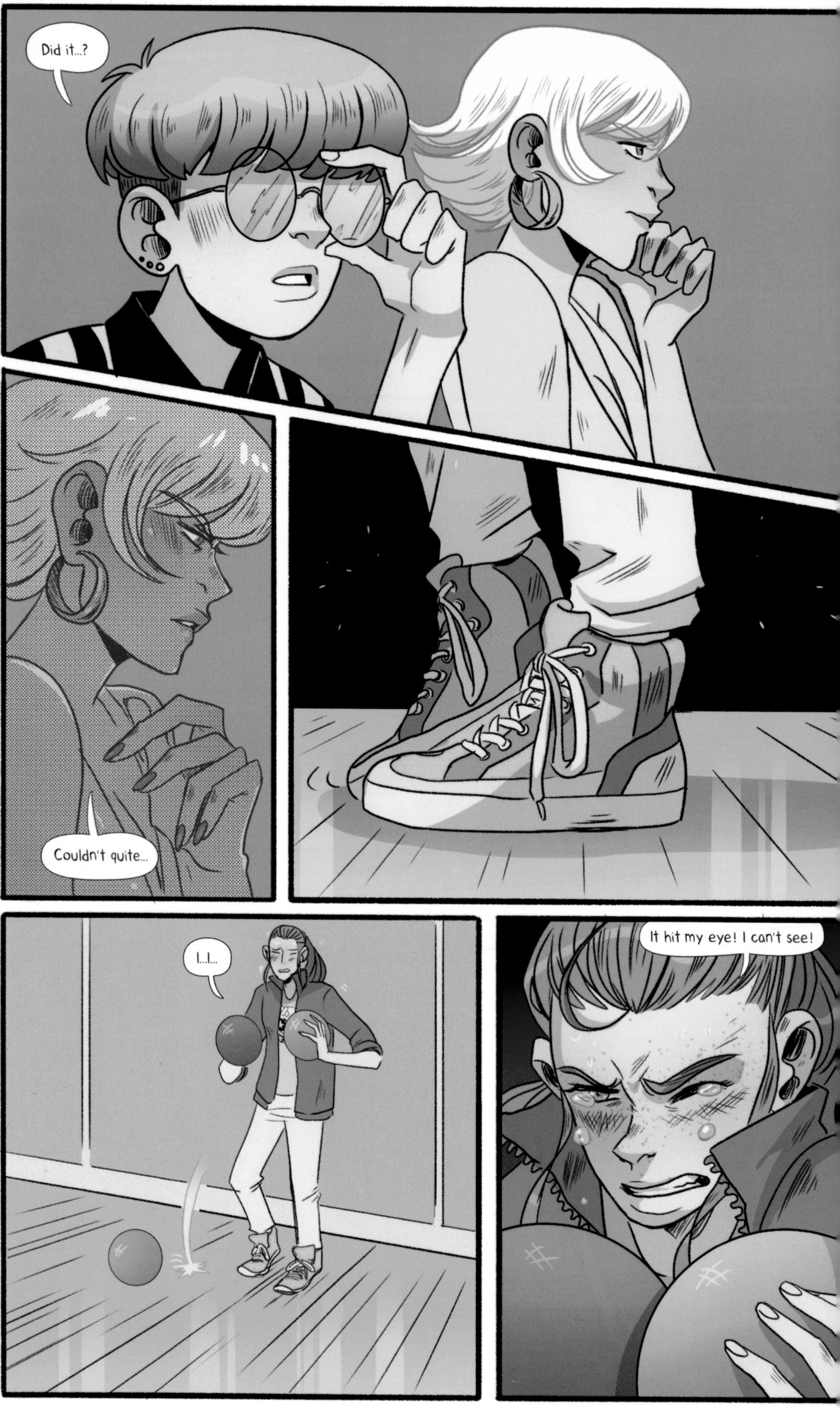
Did it...?
Couldn't quite...
I...I...
It hit my eye! I can't see!

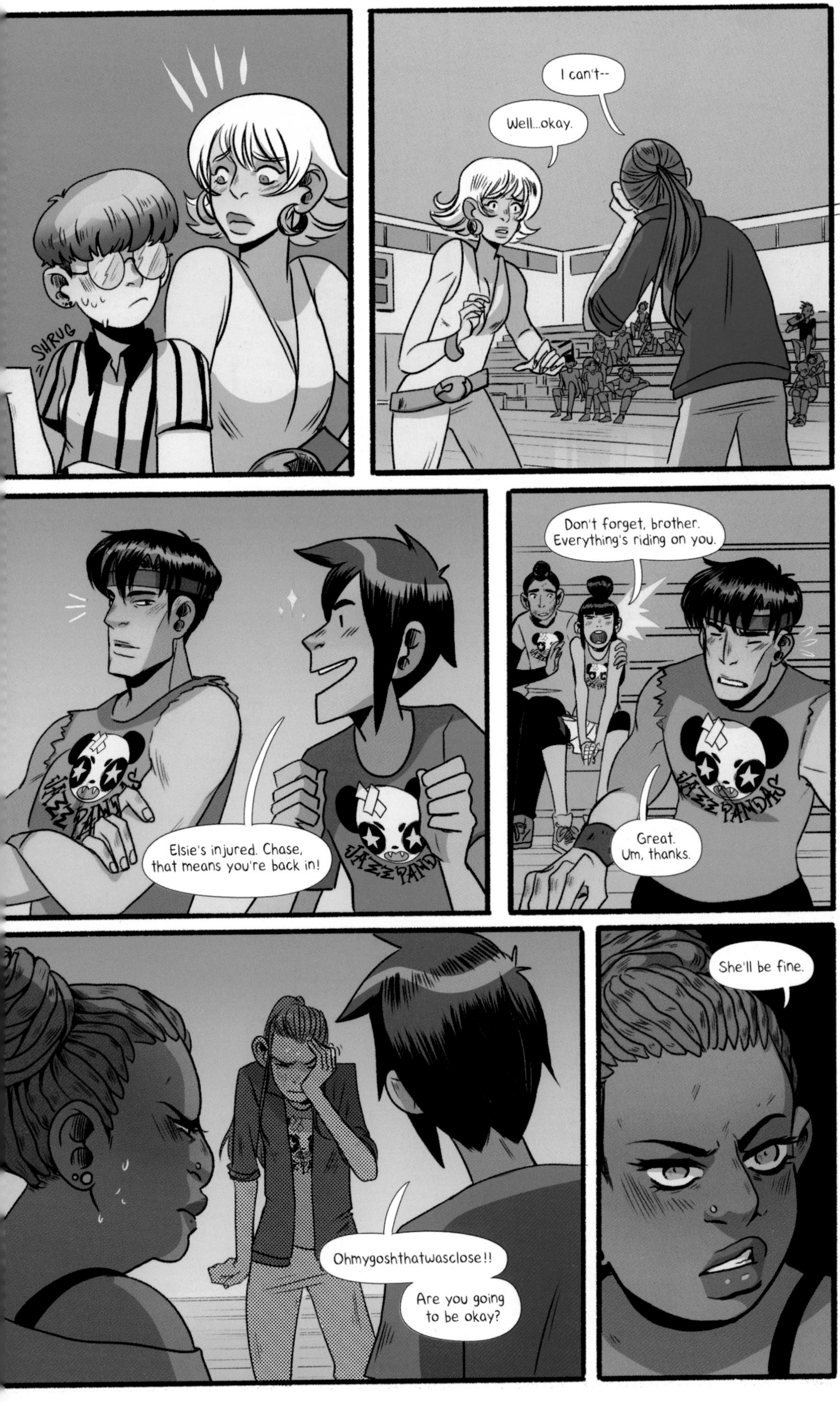
SHRUG
I can't--
Well...okay.
Elsie's injured. Chase, that means you're back in!
Don't forget, brother. Everything's riding on you.
Great. Um, thanks.
Ohmygoshthatwasclose!!
Are you going to be okay?
She'll be fine.

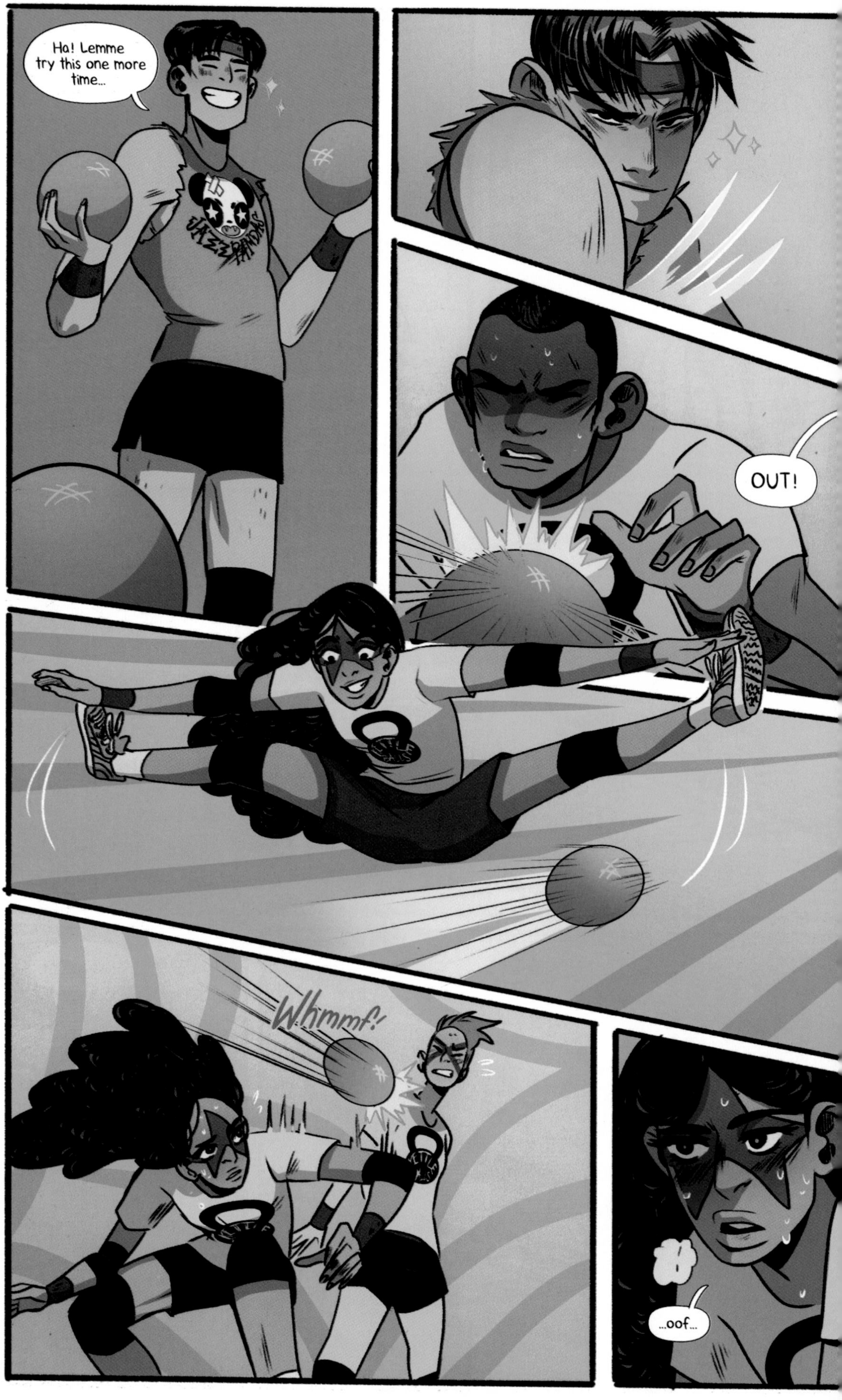
Ha! Lemme try this one more time...
JAZZ BANDITS
OUT!
Whmmf!
...oof...

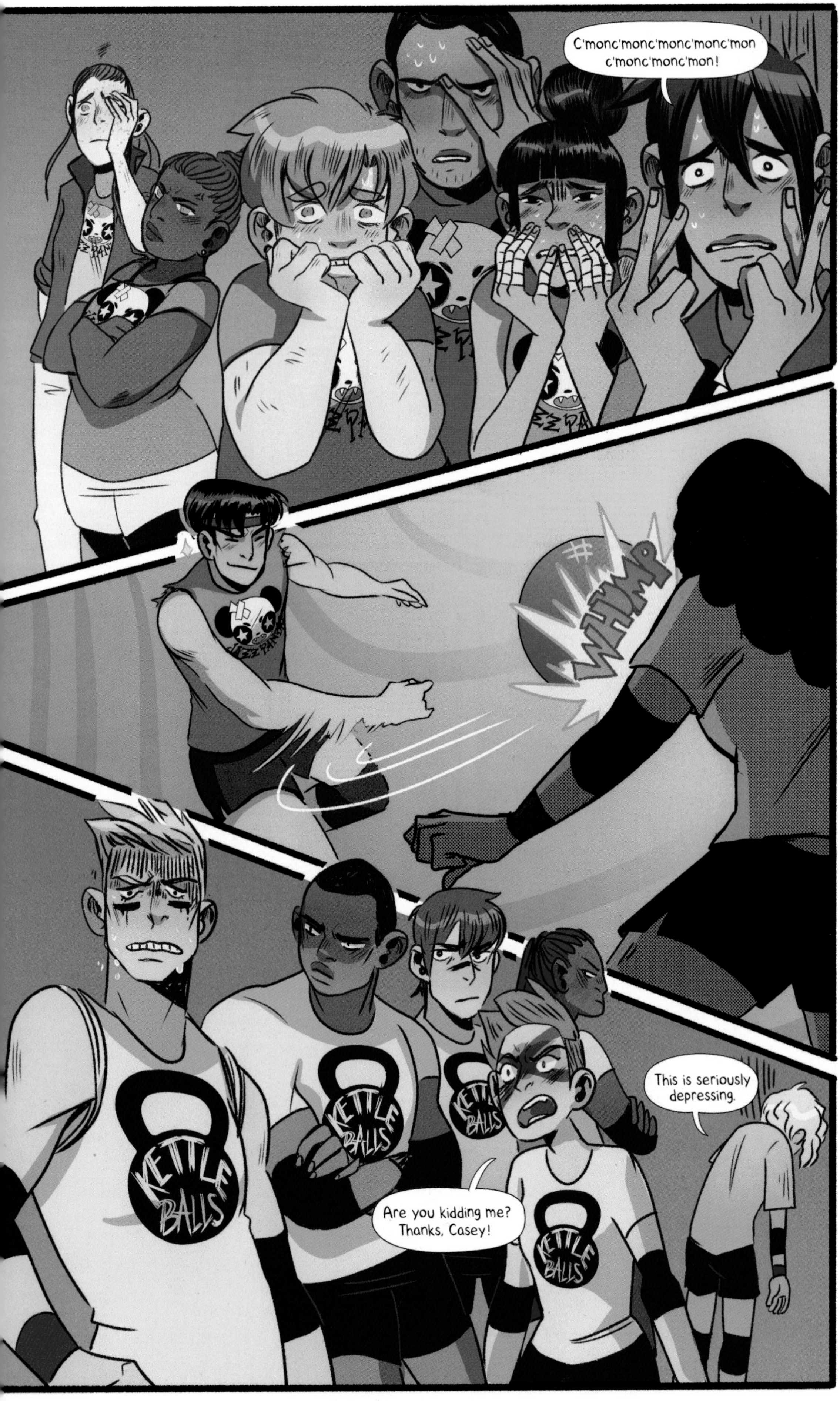
C'monc'monc'monc'monc'mon c'monc'monc'mon!
WHUMP
This is seriously depressing.
Are you kidding me? Thanks, Casey!

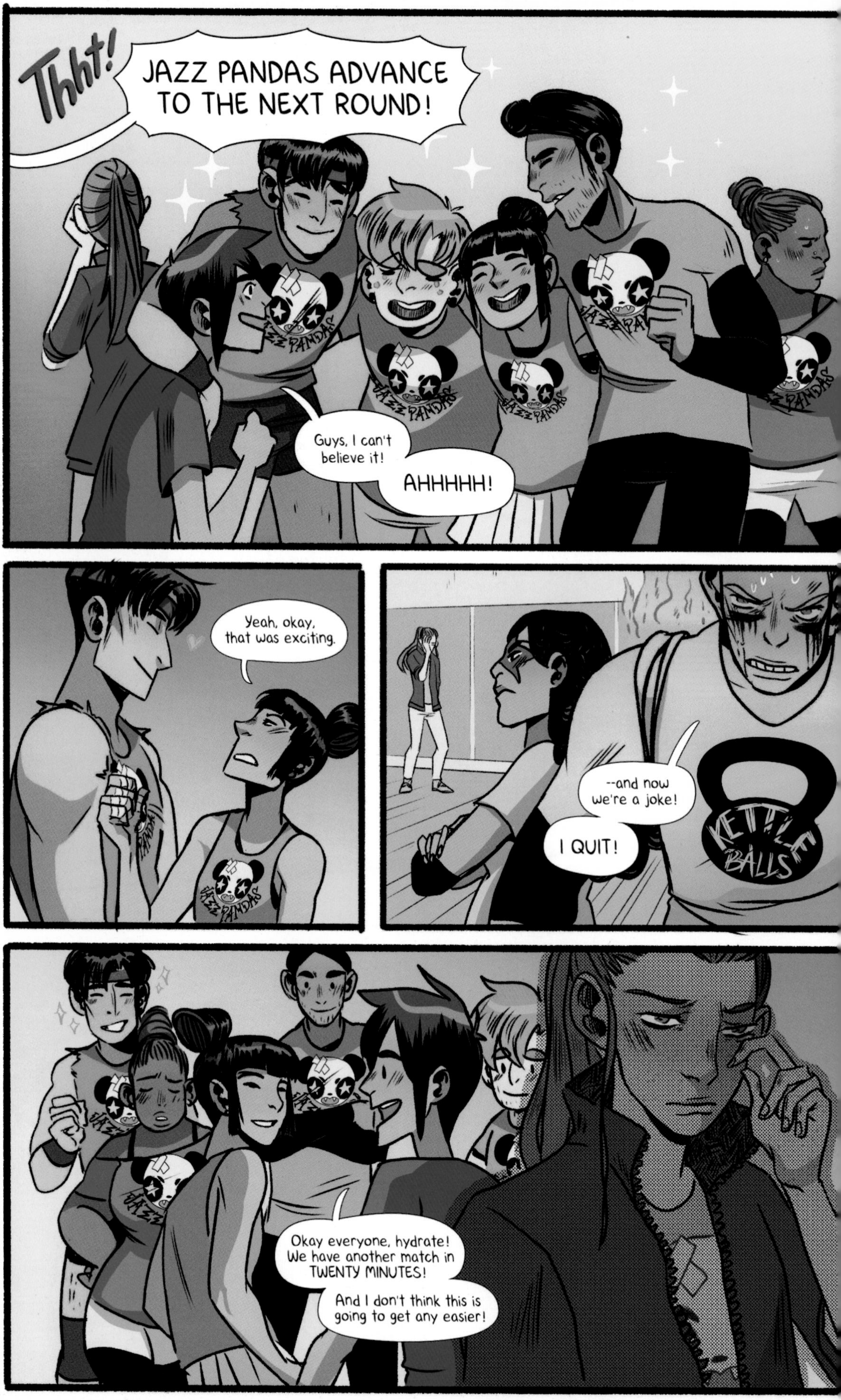
Thht!
JAZZ PANDAS ADVANCE TO THE NEXT ROUND!
JAZZ PANDAS
Guys, I can't believe it!
AHHHHH!
Yeah, okay, that was exciting.
--and now we're a joke!
I QUIT!
KETTLE BALLS
Okay everyone, hydrate! We have another match in TWENTY MINUTES!
And I don't think this is going to get any easier!

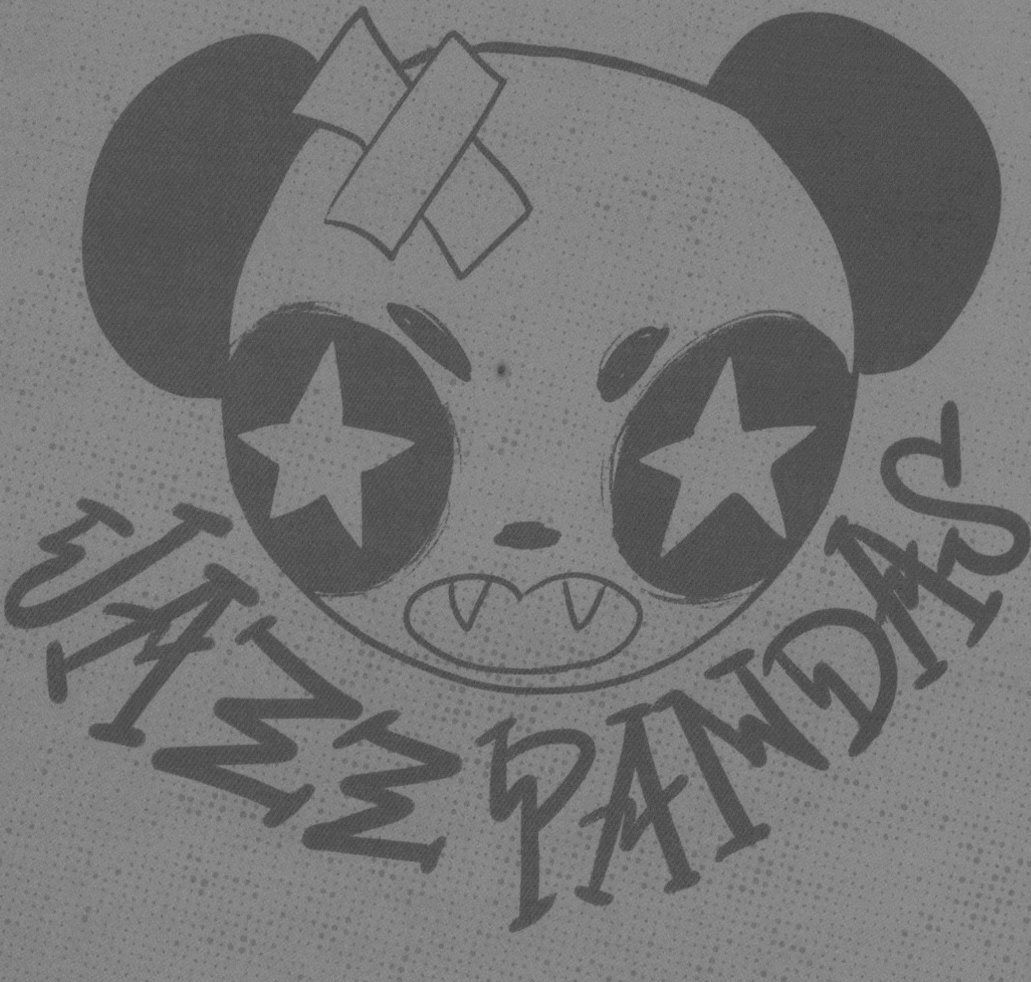
JAZZ PANDAS

FOUR!

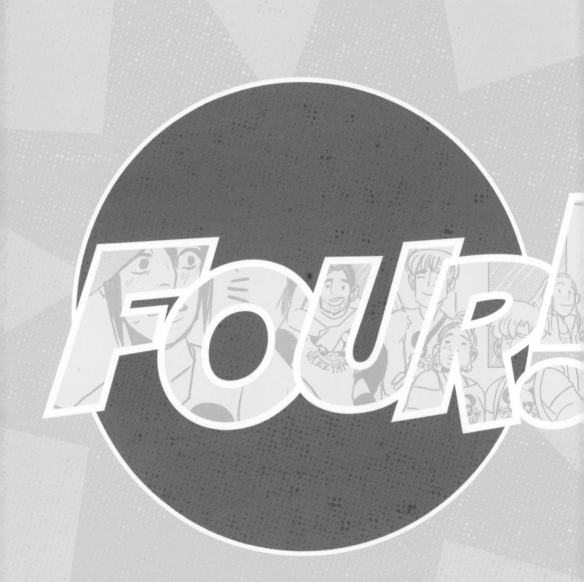

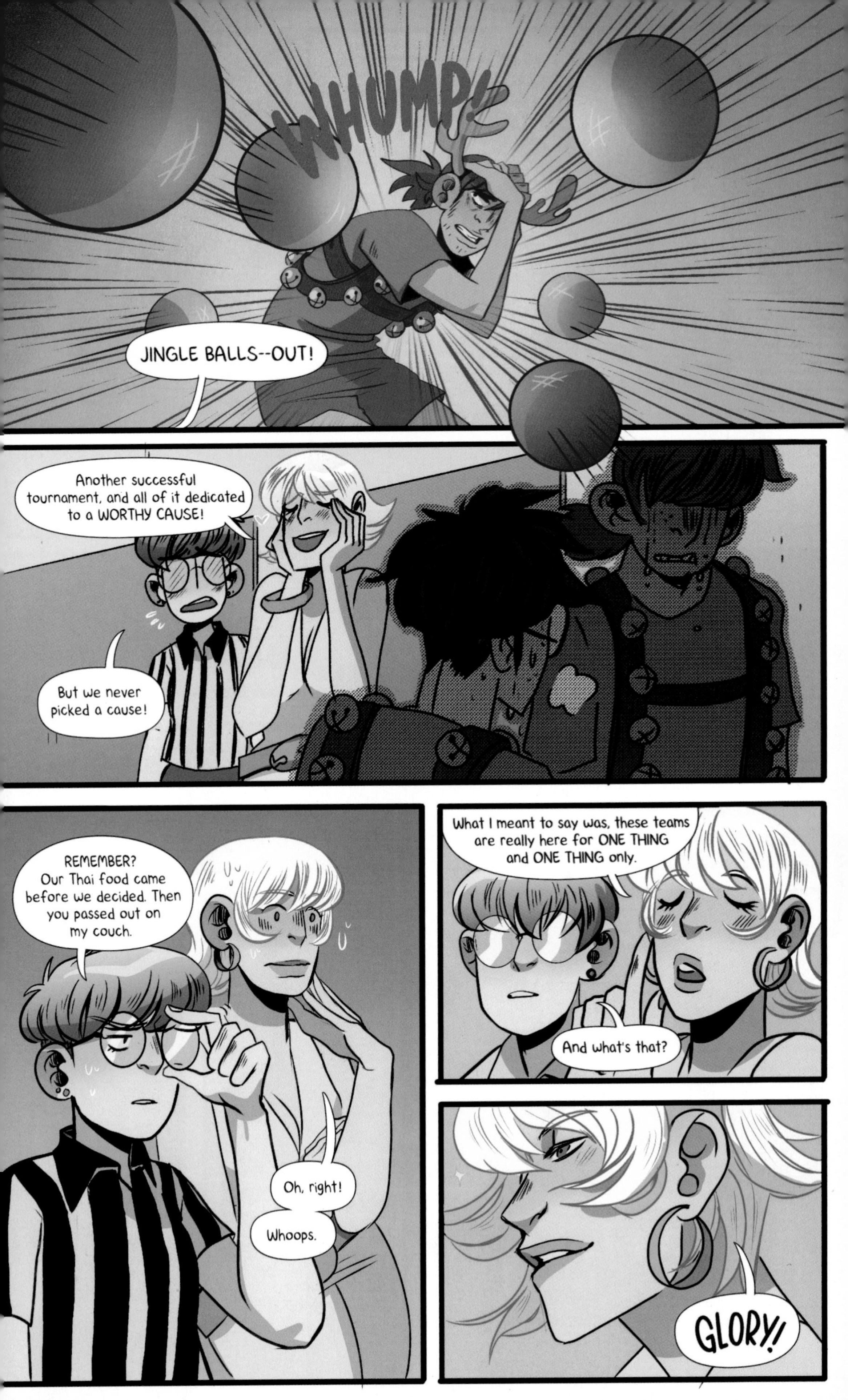
WHUMP!
JINGLE BALLS--OUT!
Another successful tournament, and all of it dedicated to a WORTHY CAUSE!
But we never picked a cause!
REMEMBER? Our Thai food came before we decided. Then you passed out on my couch.
Oh, right!
Whoops.
What I meant to say was, these teams are really here for ONE THING and ONE THING only.
And what's that?
GLORY!

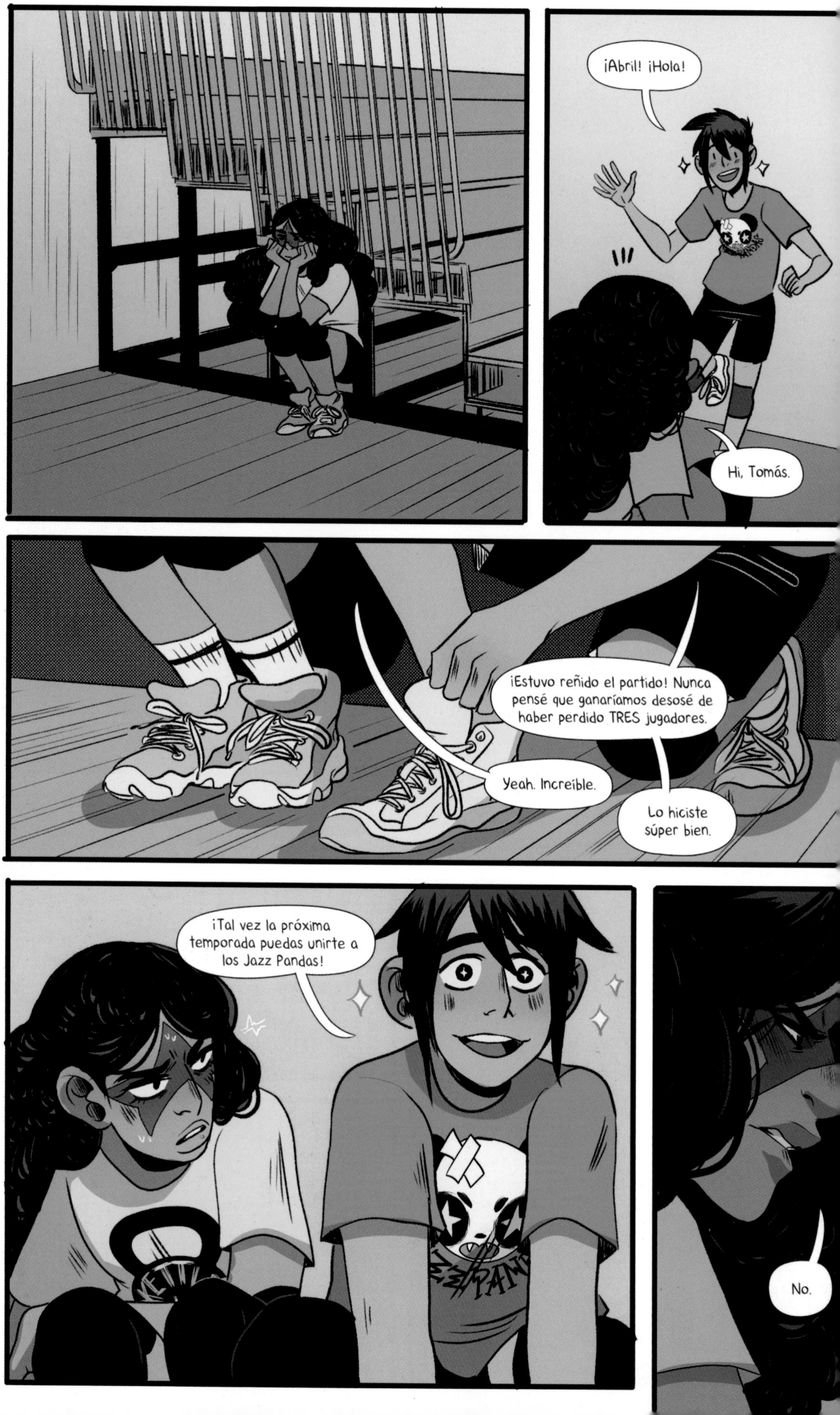
¡Abril! ¡Hola!
Hi, Tomás.
¡Estuvo reñido el partido! Nunca pensé que ganaríamos desosé de haber perdido TRES jugadores.
Yeah. Increíble.
Lo hiciste súper bien.
¡Tal vez la próxima temporada puedas unirte a los Jazz Pandas!
No.

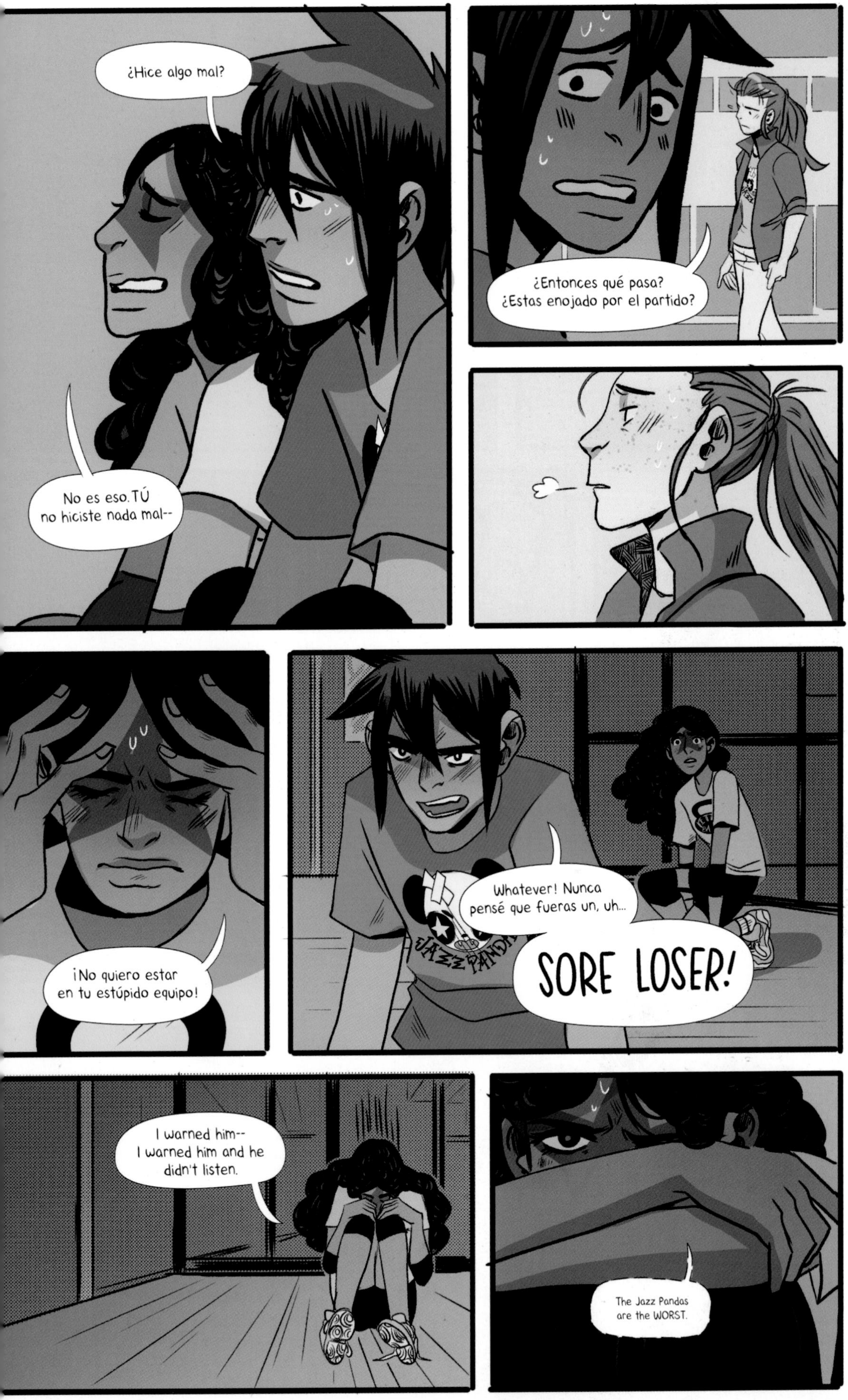
¿Hice algo mal?
No es eso. TÚ no hiciste nada mal--
¿Entonces qué pasa? ¿Estas enojado por el partido?
¡No quiero estar en tu estúpido equipo!
Whatever! Nunca pensé que fueras un, uh...
SORE LOSER!
I warned him-- I warned him and he didn't listen.
The Jazz Pandas are the WORST.

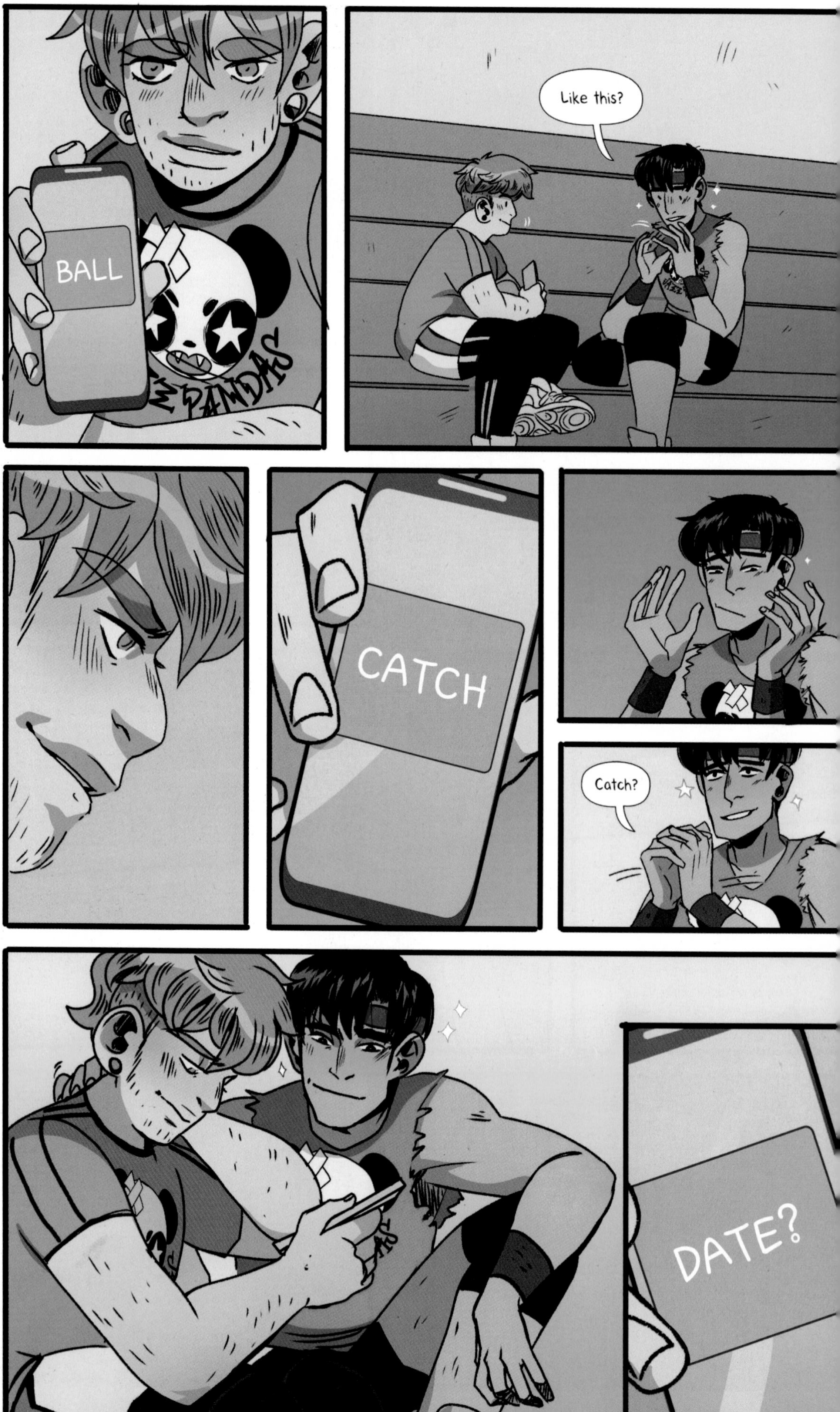

BALL
PANDAS
Like this?
CATCH
Catch?
DATE?

AGHGHHG!

This dang ankle is REALLY FLAMIN' HOT right now!

There we go. Sweet relief!

Get out of there!

Casey! I thought you dramatically stormed off!

I WANTED A SODA!

You still can. They're in BOTTLES.

But it's GROSS.

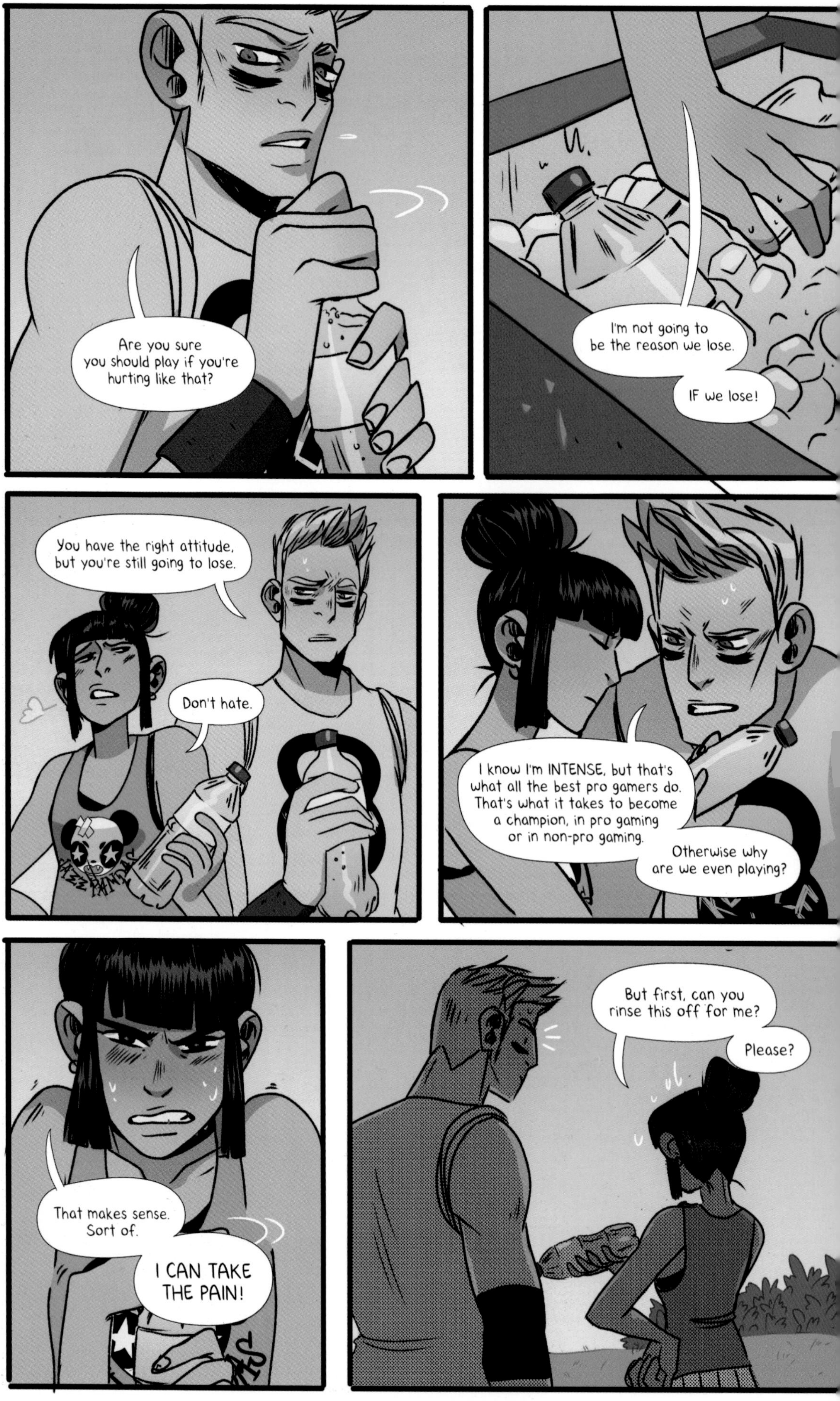

Are you sure you should play if you're hurting like that?
I'm not going to be the reason we lose.
IF we lose!
You have the right attitude, but you're still going to lose.
Don't hate.
I know I'm INTENSE, but that's what all the best pro gamers do. That's what it takes to become a champion, in pro gaming or in non-pro gaming.
Otherwise why are we even playing?
That makes sense. Sort of.
I CAN TAKE THE PAIN!
But first, can you rinse this off for me?
Please?

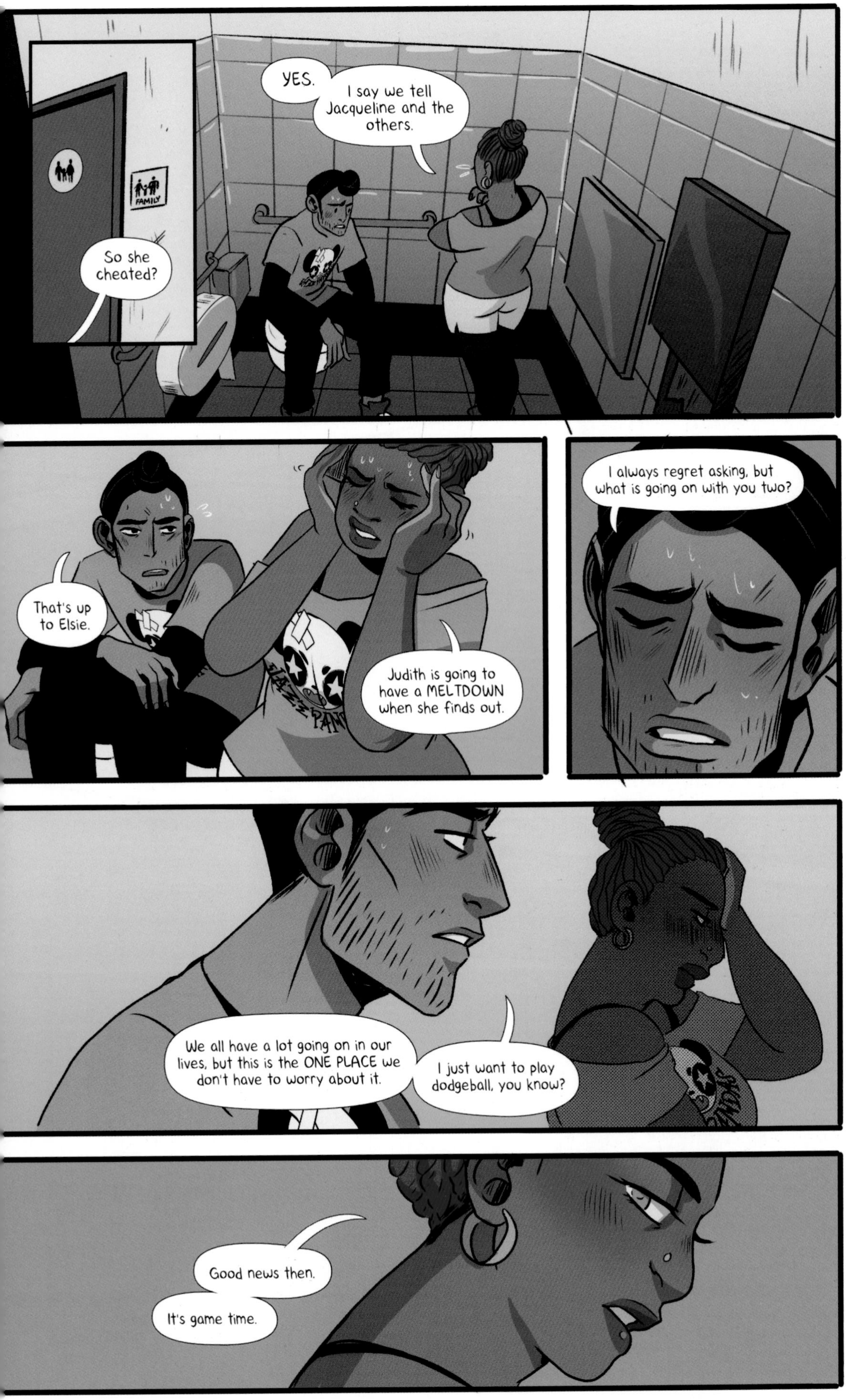
FAMILY
So she cheated?
YES.
I say we tell Jacqueline and the others.
That's up to Elsie.
Judith is going to have a MELTDOWN when she finds out.
I always regret asking, but what is going on with you two?
We all have a lot going on in our lives, but this is the ONE PLACE we don't have to worry about it.
I just want to play dodgeball, you know?
Good news then.
It's game time.

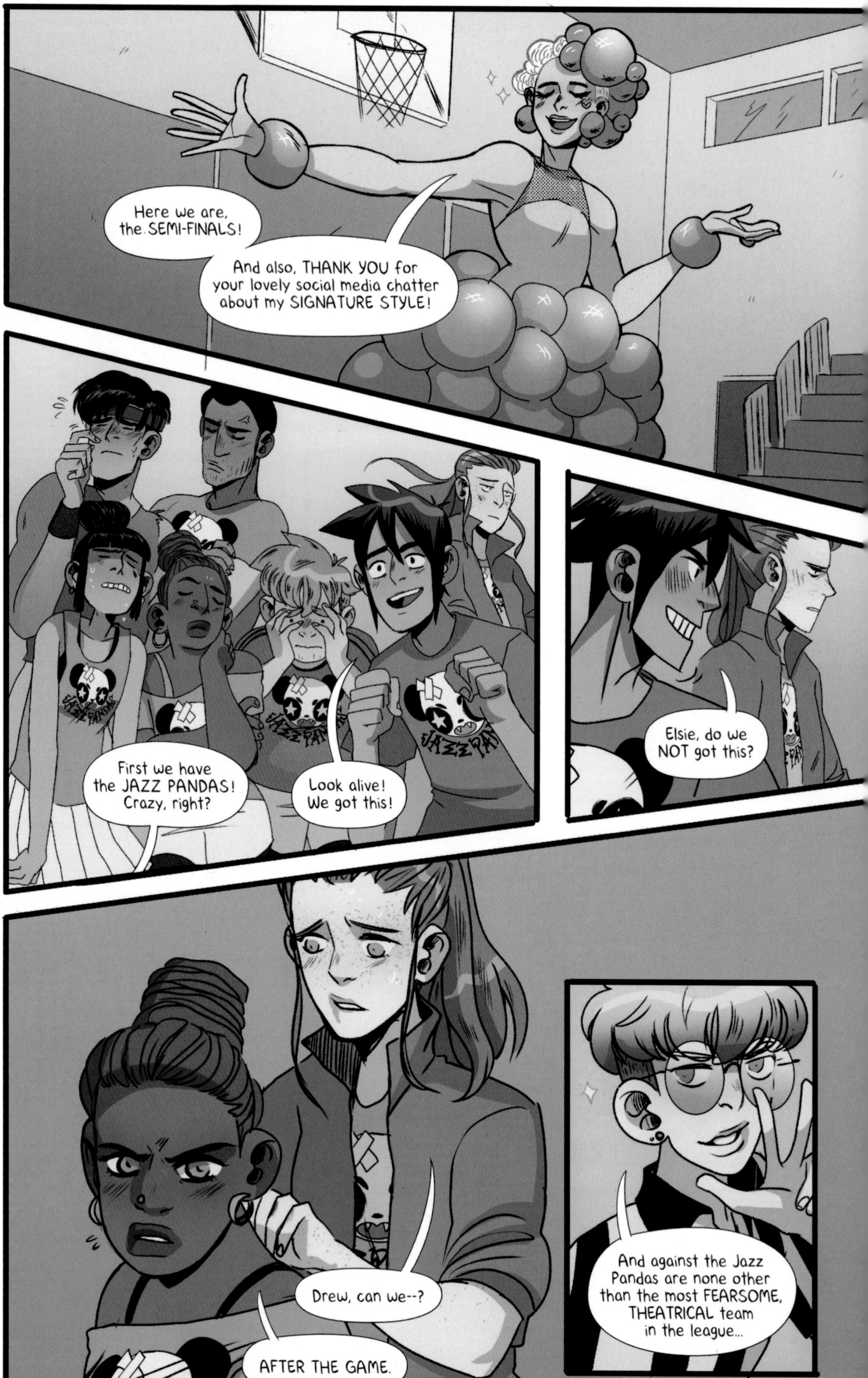

Here we are, the SEMI-FINALS!
And also, THANK YOU for your lovely social media chatter about my SIGNATURE STYLE!
First we have the JAZZ PANDAS! Crazy, right?
Look alive! We got this!
Elsie, do we NOT got this?
Drew, can we--?
AFTER THE GAME.
And against the Jazz Pandas are none other than the most FEARSOME, THEATRICAL team in the league...

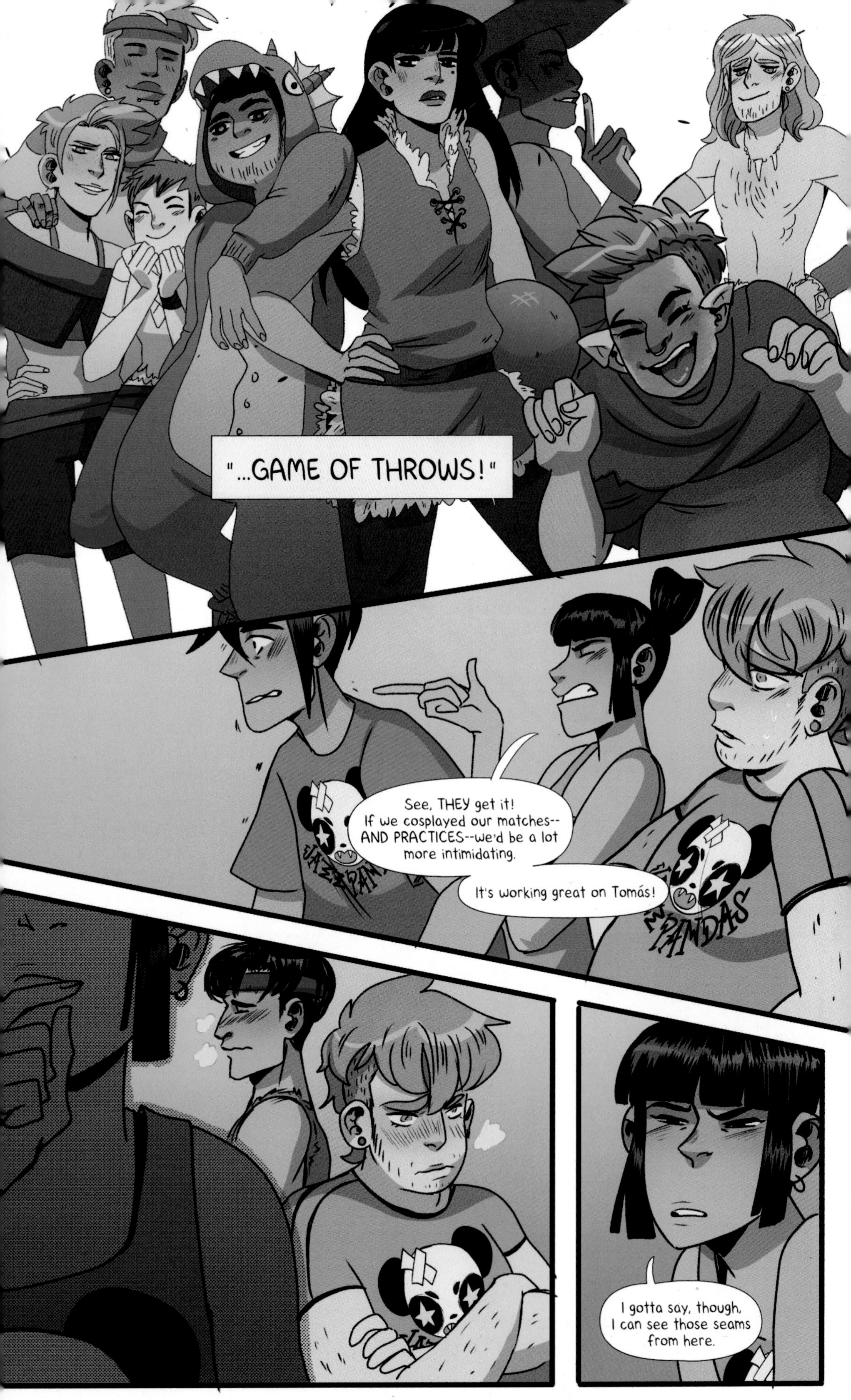
"...GAME OF THROWS!"
See, THEY get it! If we cosplayed our matches--AND PRACTICES--we'd be a lot more intimidating.
It's working great on Tomás!
I gotta say, though, I can see those seams from here.

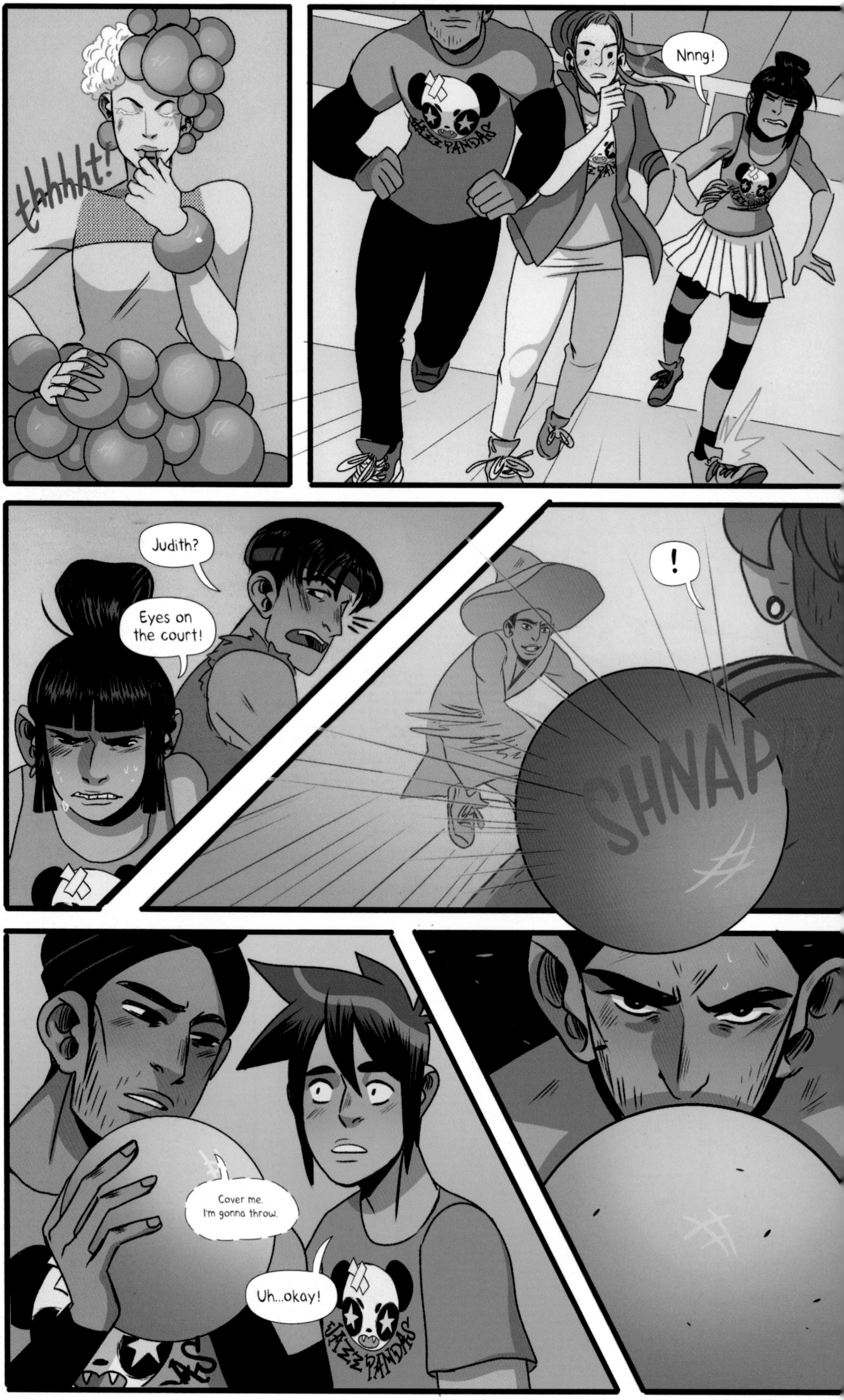
thhhht!
Nnng!
Judith?
Eyes on the court!
!
SHNAP!
Cover me. I'm gonna throw.
Uh...okay!

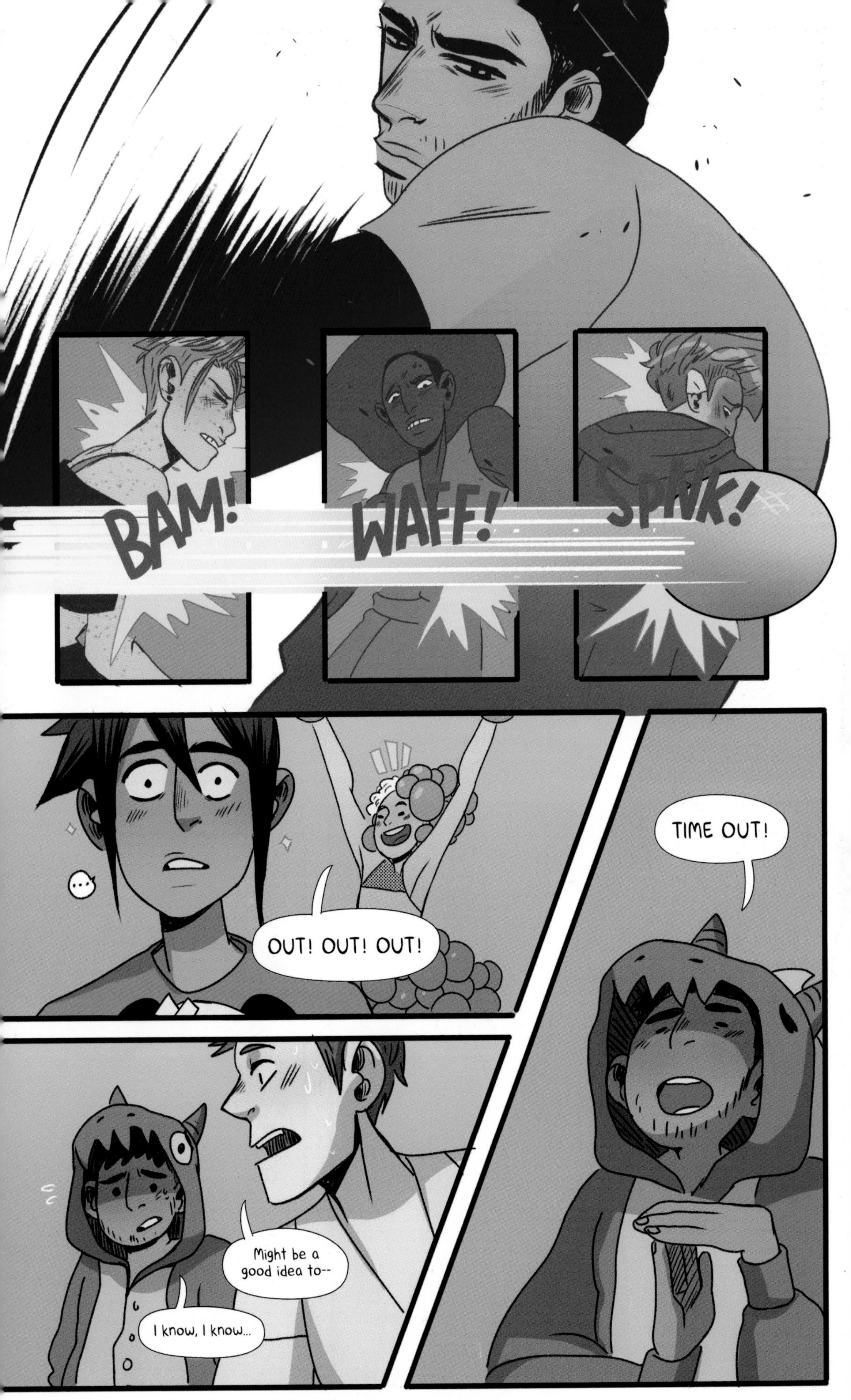
BAM!
WAFF!
SPNK!
...
OUT! OUT! OUT!
TIME OUT!
Might be a good idea to--
I know, I know...

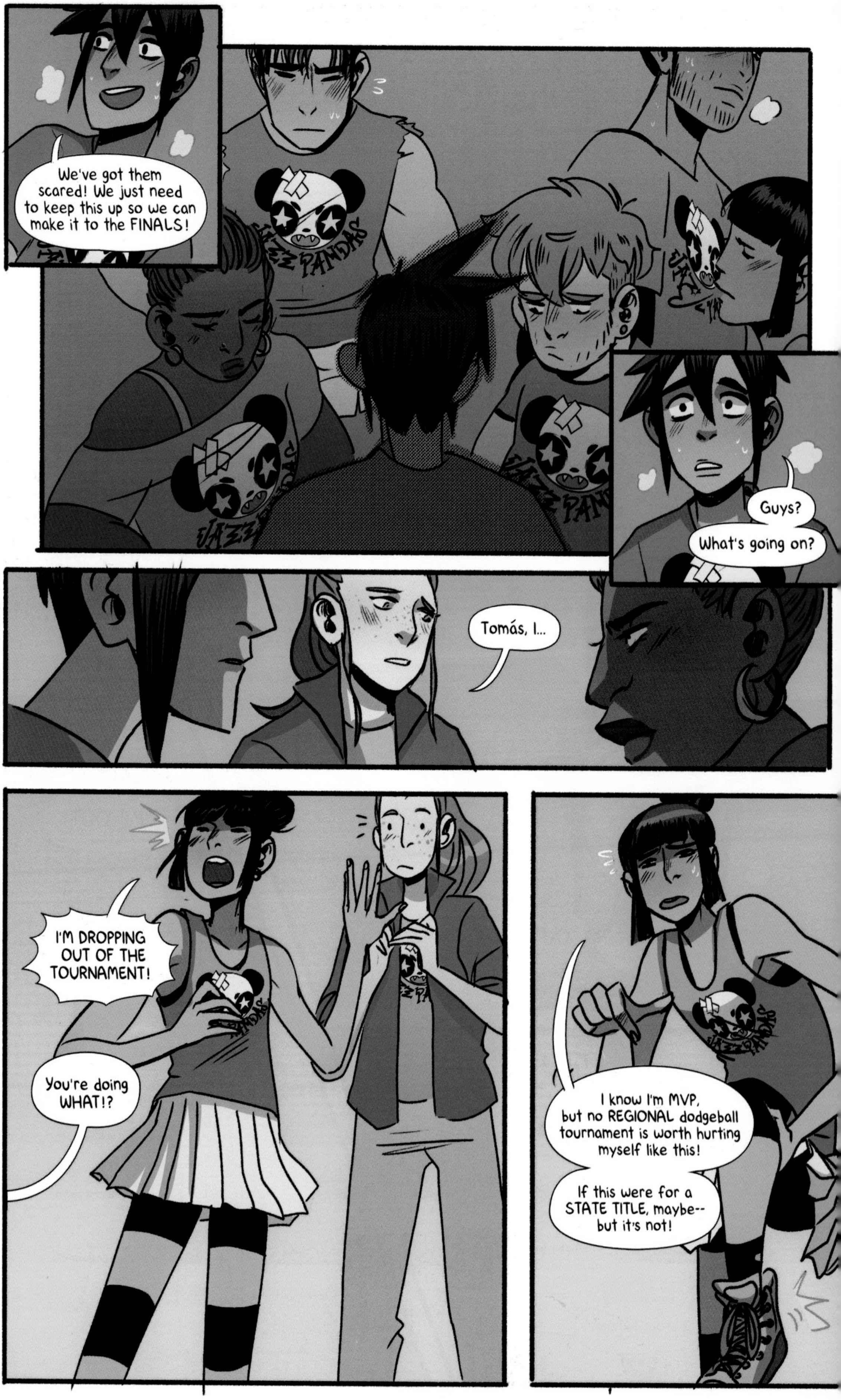
We've got them scared! We just need to keep this up so we can make it to the FINALS!
Guys?
What's going on?
Tomás, I...
I'M DROPPING OUT OF THE TOURNAMENT!
You're doing WHAT!?
I know I'm MVP, but no REGIONAL dodgeball tournament is worth hurting myself like this!
If this were for a STATE TITLE, maybe-- but it's not!

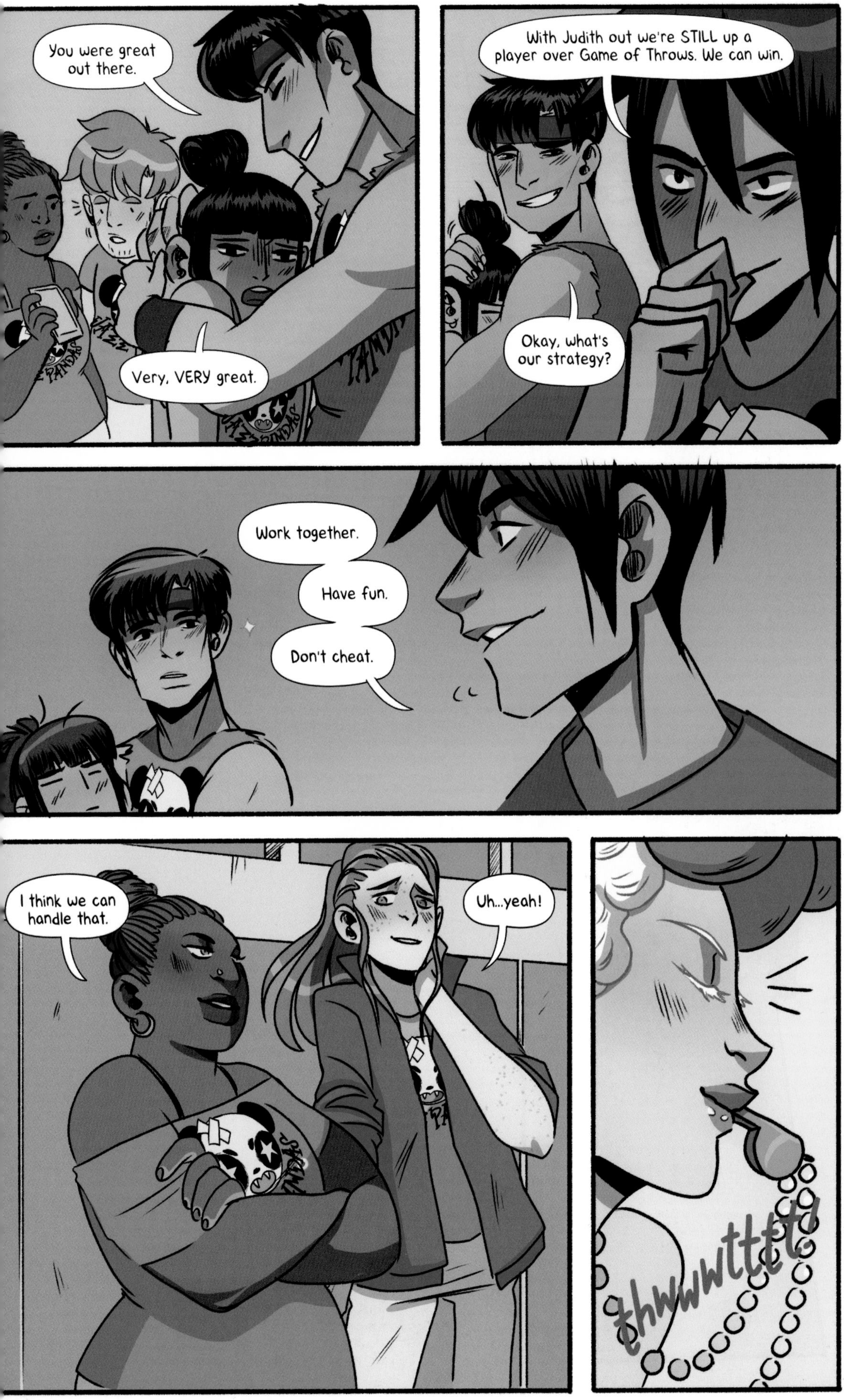
You were great out there.
Very, VERY great.
With Judith out we're STILL up a player over Game of Throws. We can win.
Okay, what's our strategy?
Work together.
Have fun.
Don't cheat.
I think we can handle that.
Uh...yeah!
thwwwttt!

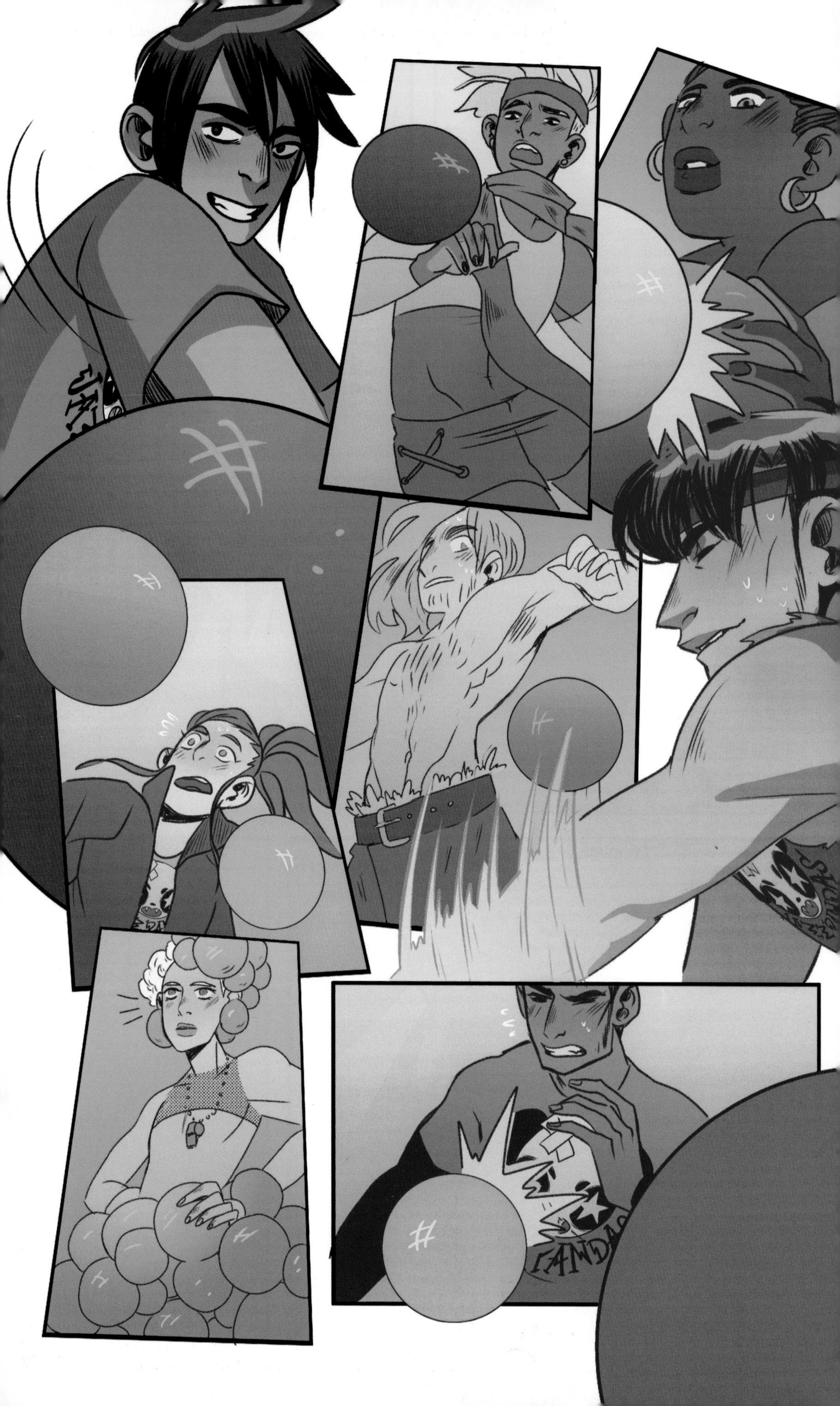

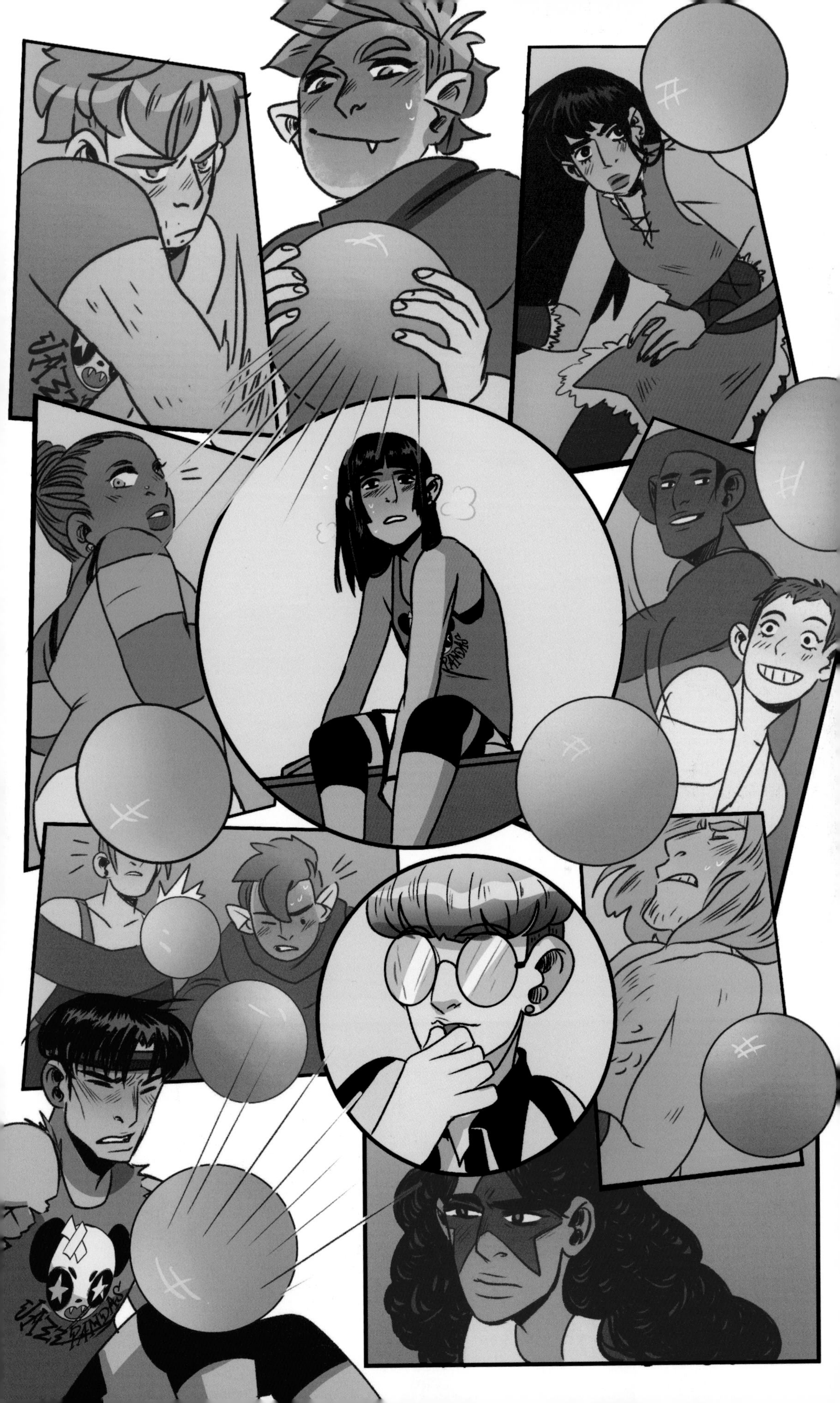
PANDAS

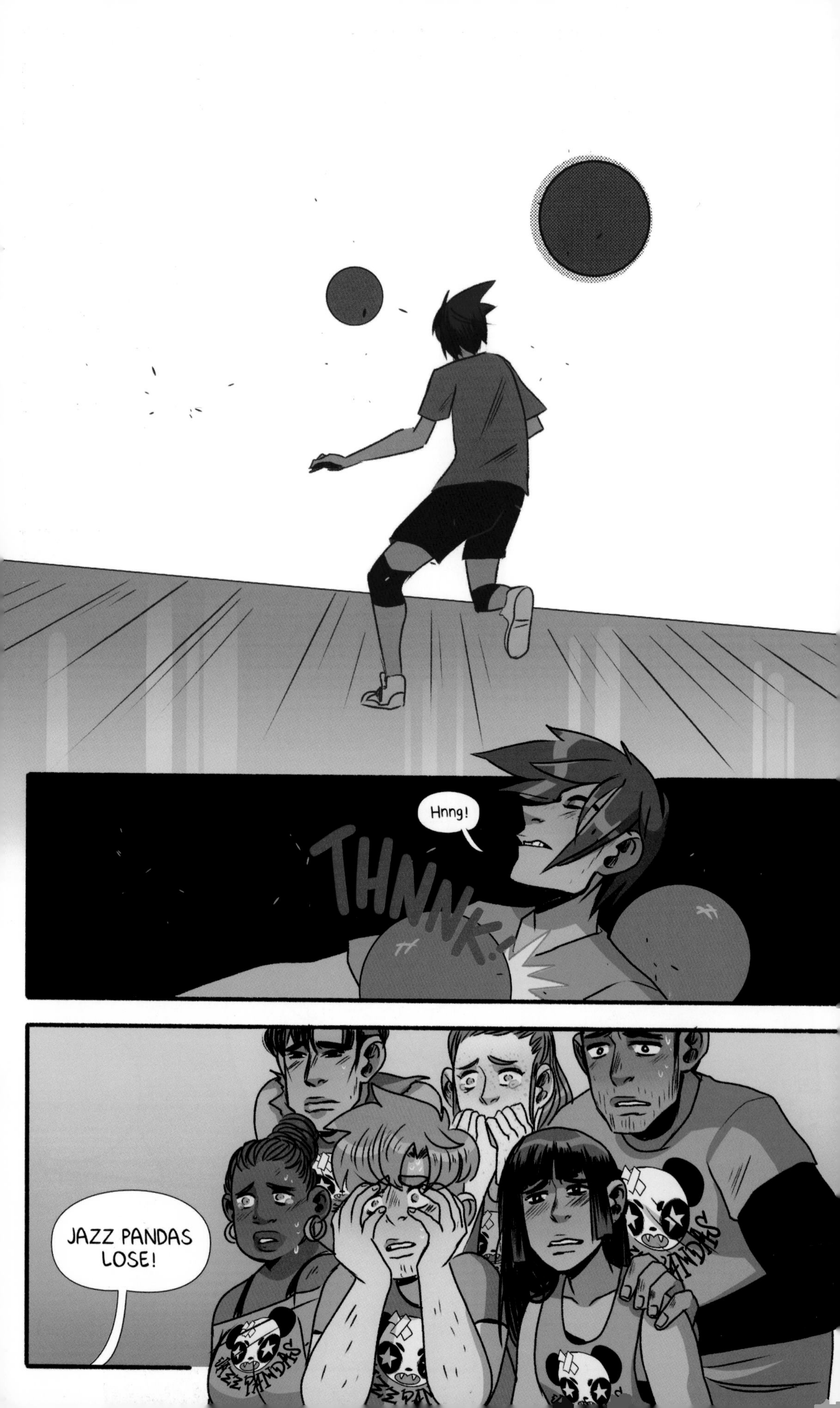
Hnng!
THNNK!
JAZZ PANDAS LOSE!

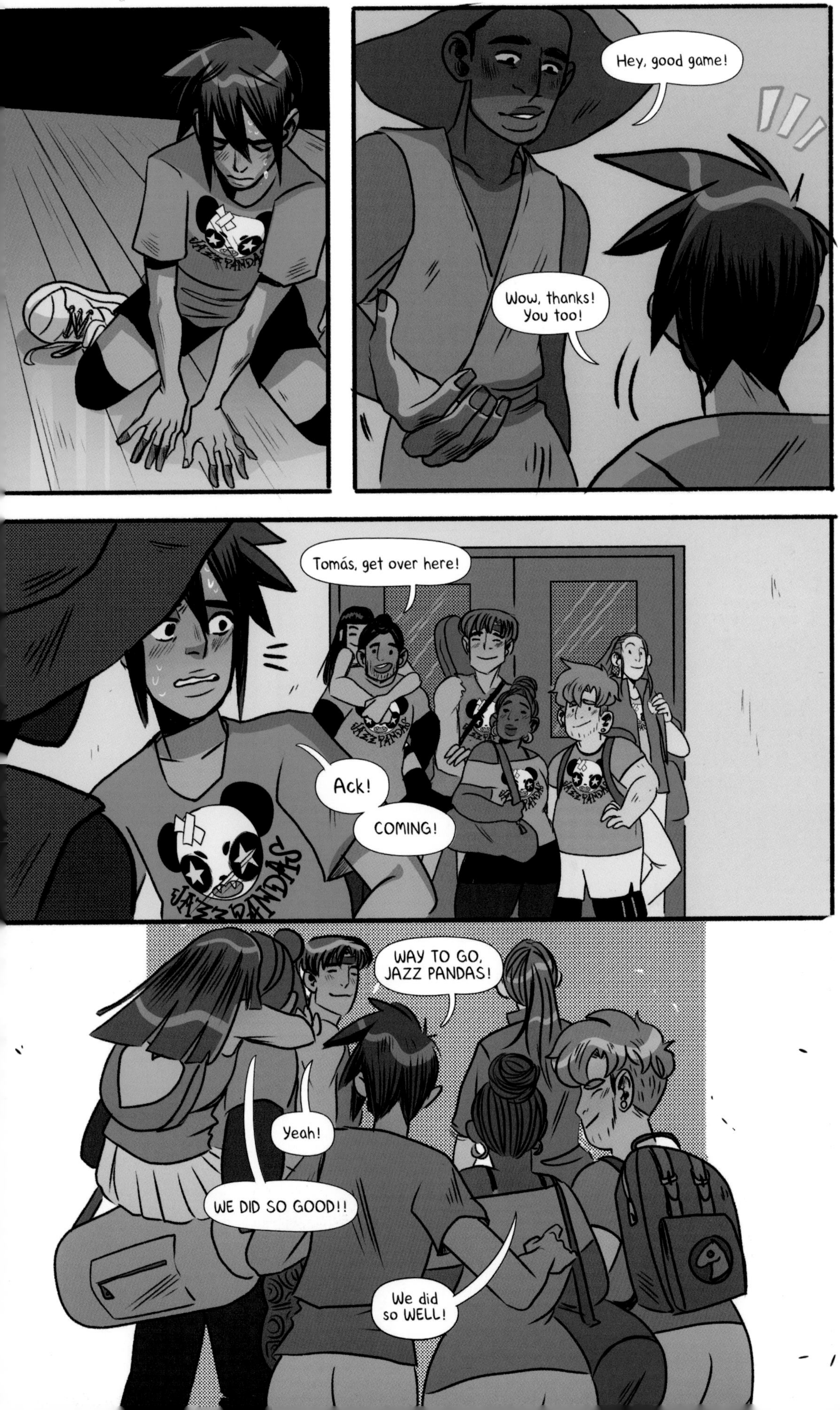
JAZZ PANDAS
Hey, good game!
Wow, thanks! You too!
Tomás, get over here!
Ack!
COMING!
JAZZ PANDAS
WAY TO GO, JAZZ PANDAS!
Yeah!
WE DID SO GOOD!!
We did so WELL!

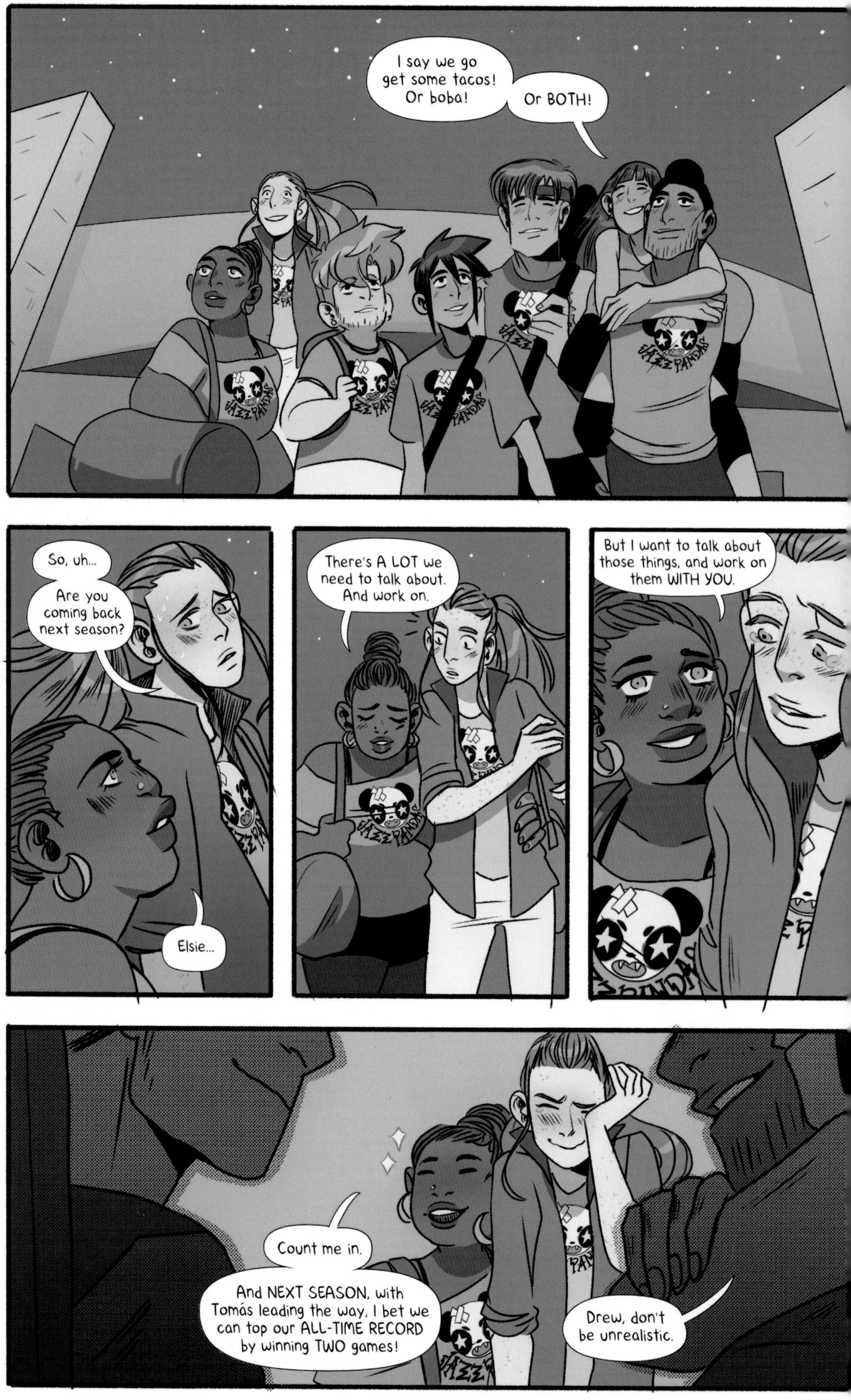
I say we go get some tacos! Or boba!
Or BOTH!
So, uh...
Are you coming back next season?
Elsie...
There's A LOT we need to talk about. And work on.
But I want to talk about those things, and work on them WITH YOU.
Count me in.
And NEXT SEASON, with Tomás leading the way, I bet we can top our ALL-TIME RECORD by winning TWO games!
Drew, don't be unrealistic.

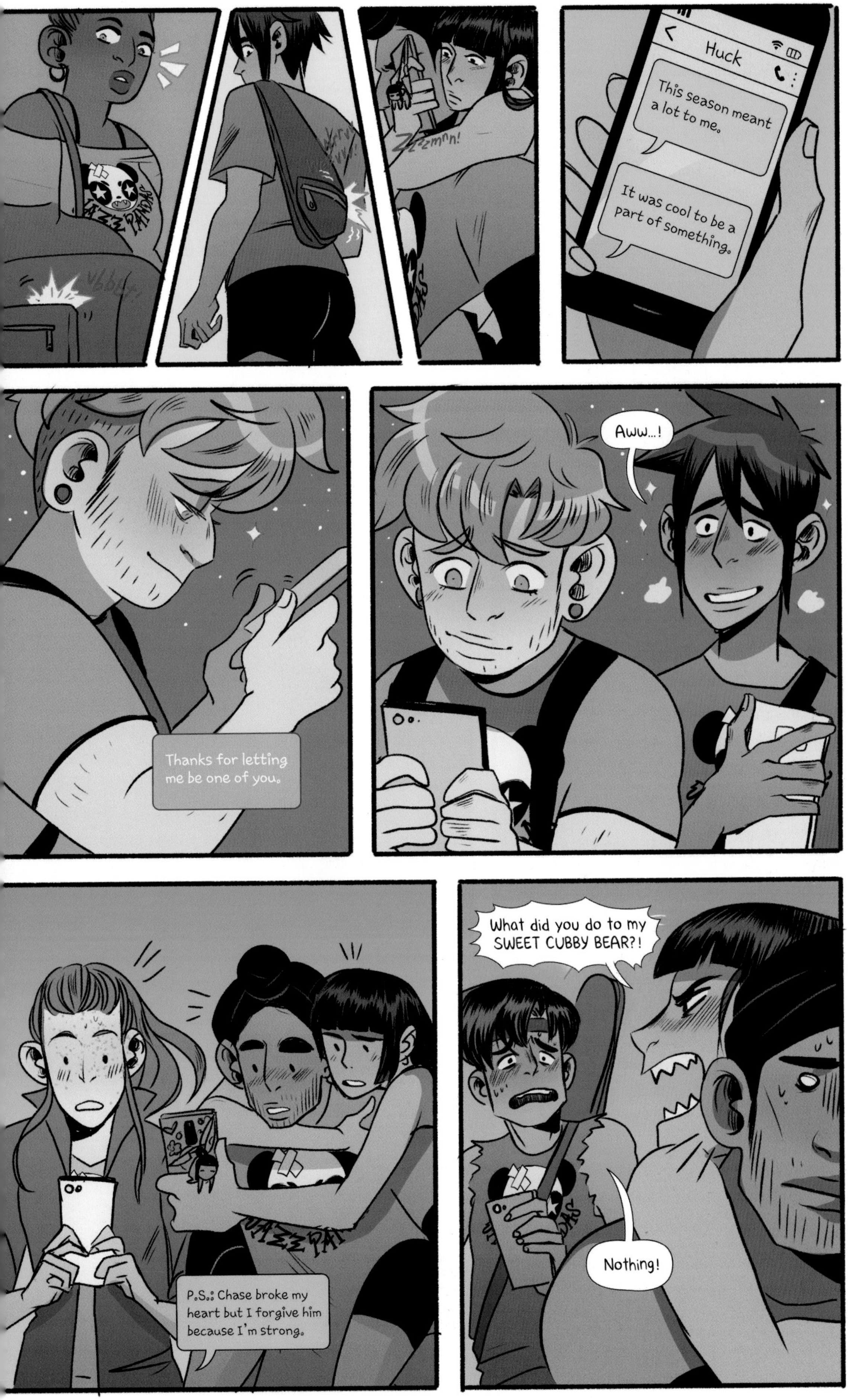

Huck
This season meant a lot to me.
It was cool to be a part of something.
Thanks for letting me be one of you.
Aww...!
P.S.: Chase broke my heart but I forgive him because I'm strong.
What did you do to my SWEET CUBBY BEAR?!
Nothing!

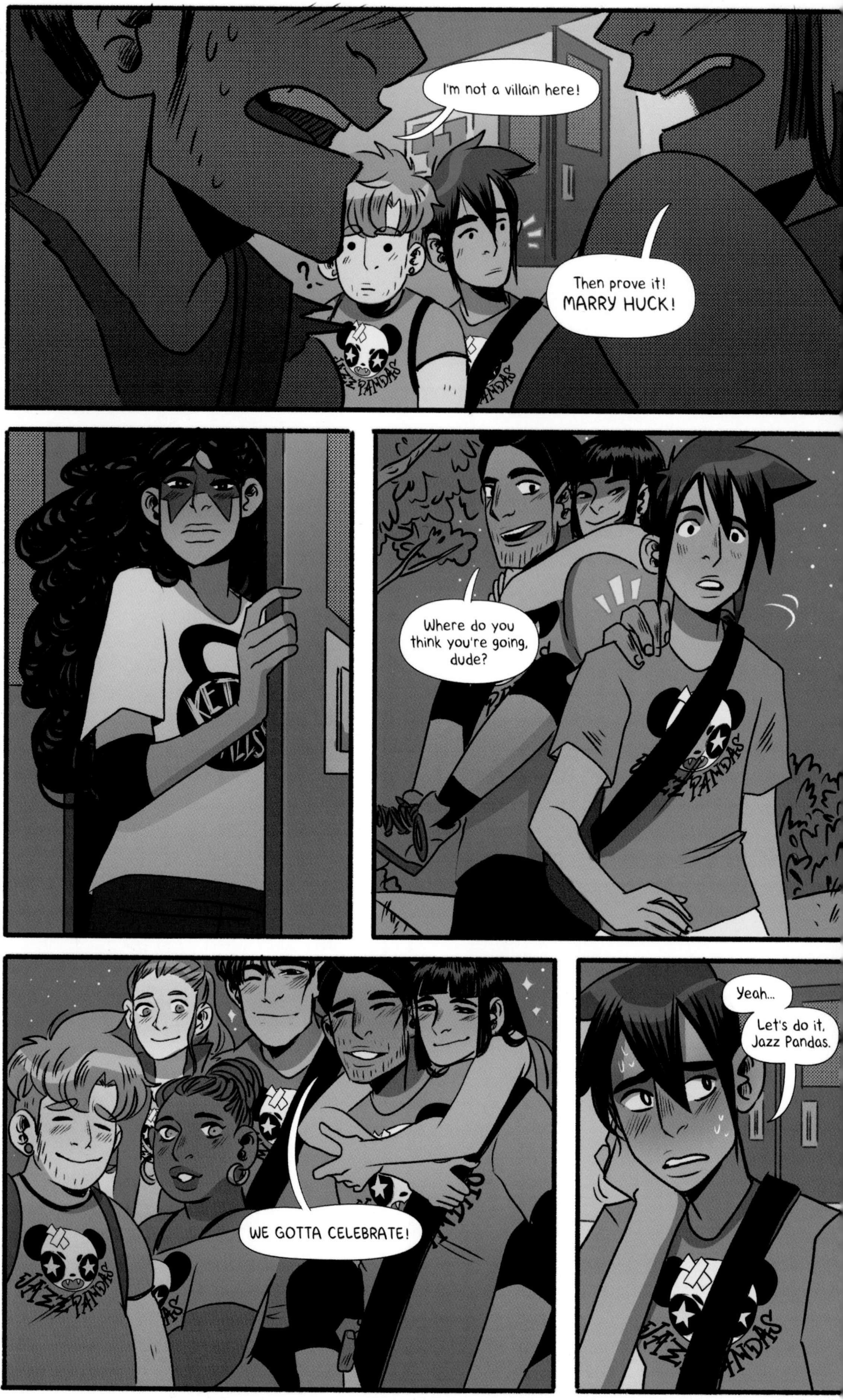
I'm not a villain here!
Then prove it! MARRY HUCK!
Where do you think you're going, dude?
WE GOTTA CELEBRATE!
Yeah...
Let's do it, Jazz Pandas.

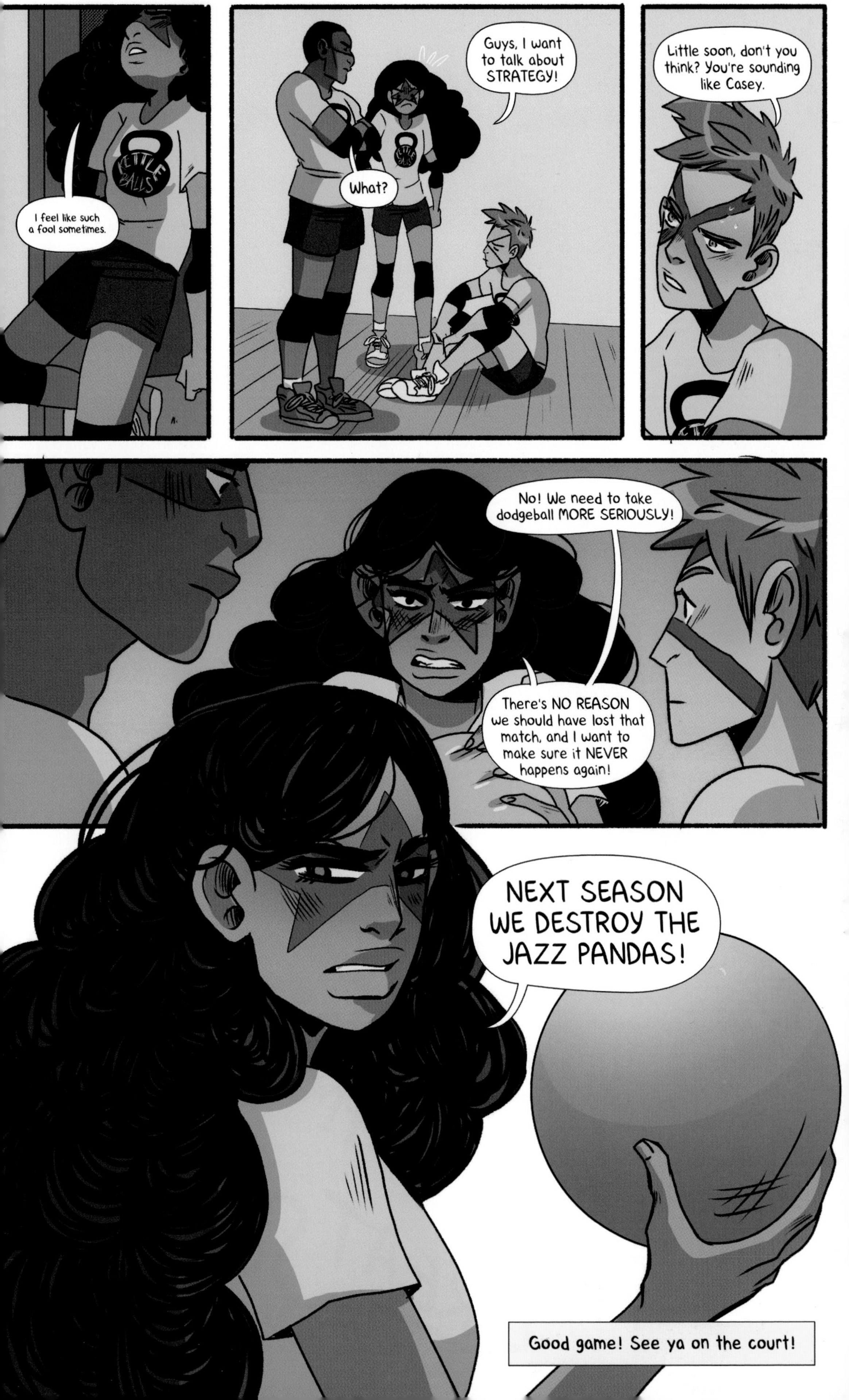
I feel like such a fool sometimes.
Guys, I want to talk about STRATEGY!
What?
Little soon, don't you think? You're sounding like Casey.
No! We need to take dodgeball MORE SERIOUSLY!
There's NO REASON we should have lost that match, and I want to make sure it NEVER happens again!
NEXT SEASON WE DESTROY THE JAZZ PANDAS!
Good game! See ya on the court!

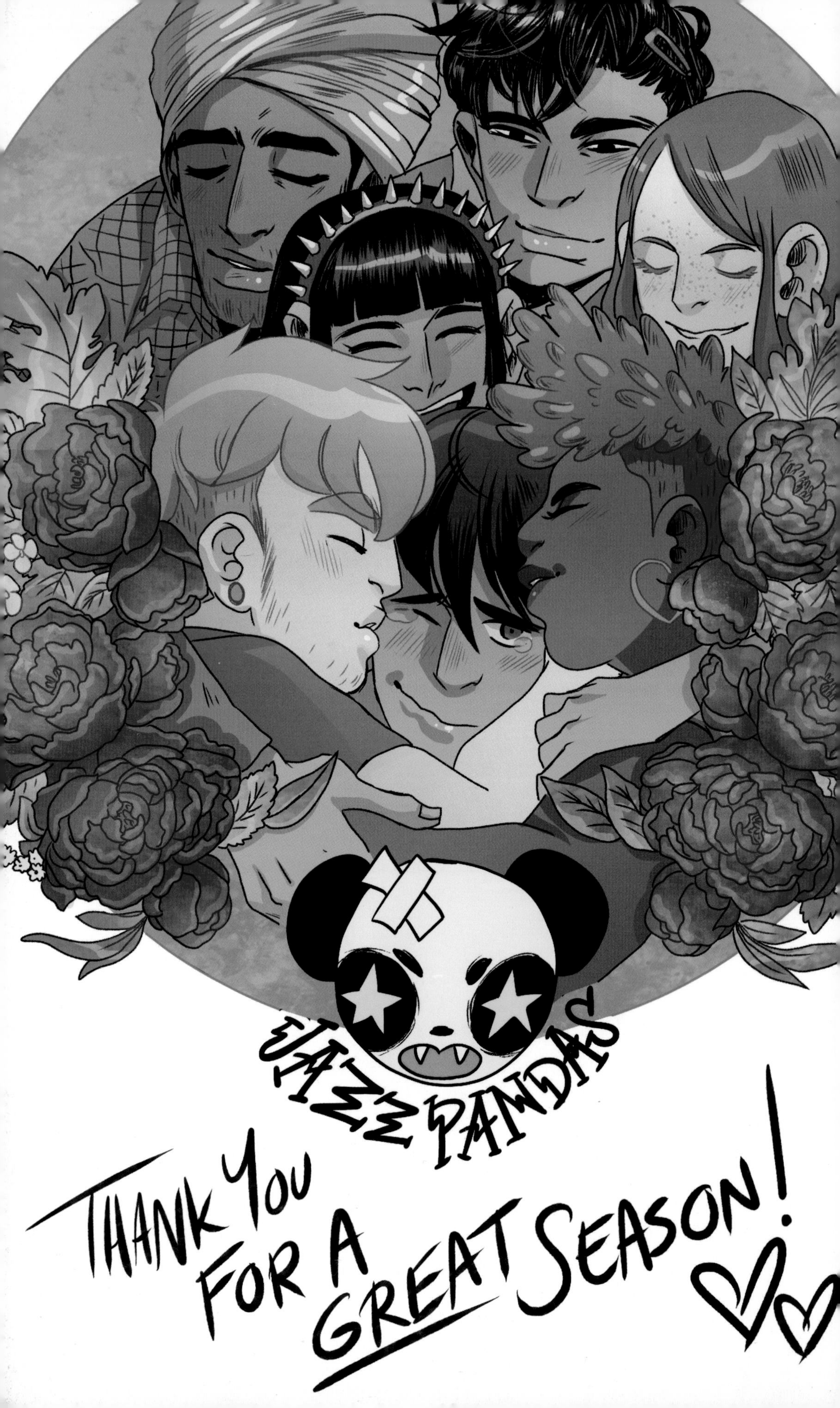
JAZZ PANDAS
THANK YOU FOR A GREAT SEASON!

JAZZ PANDAS

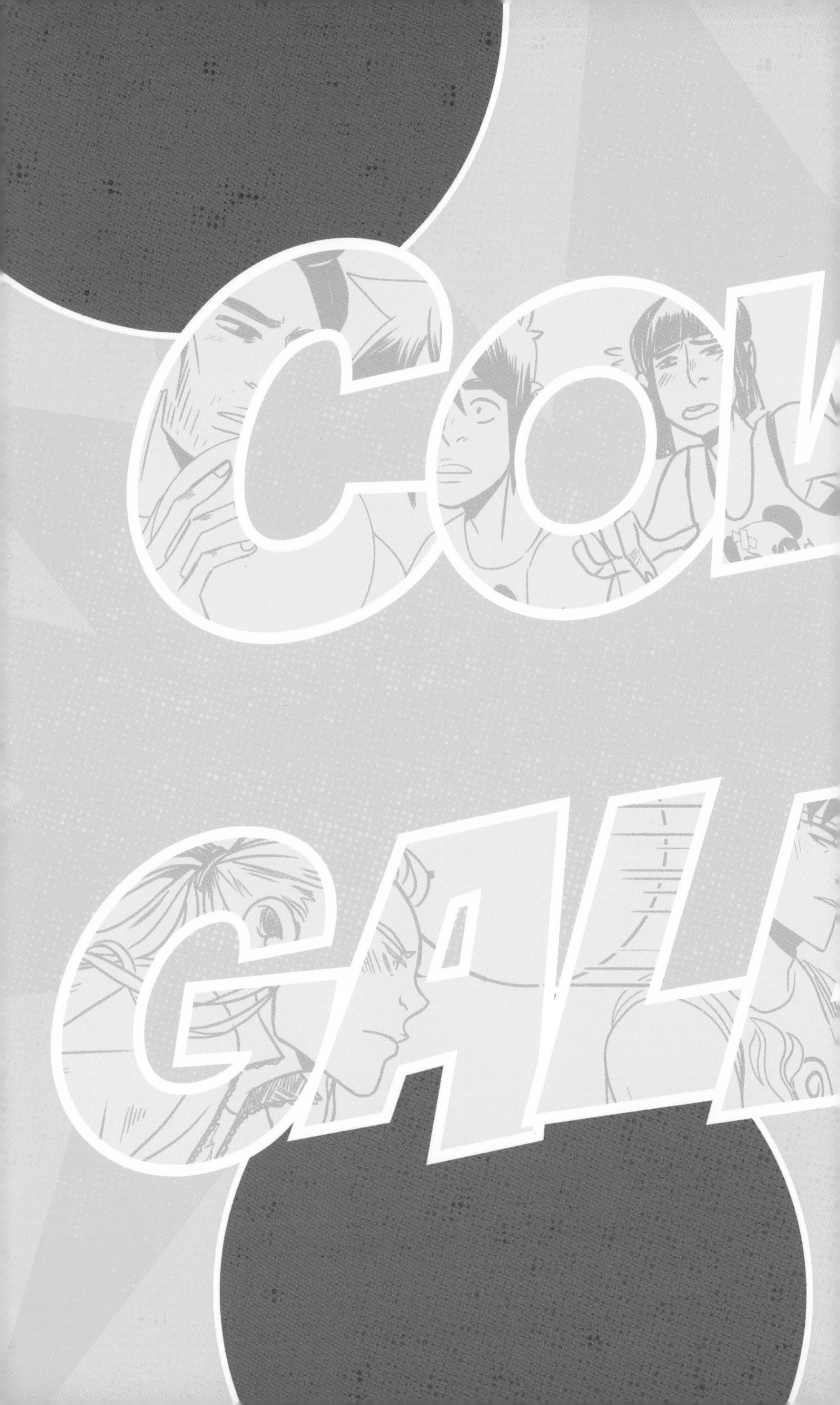

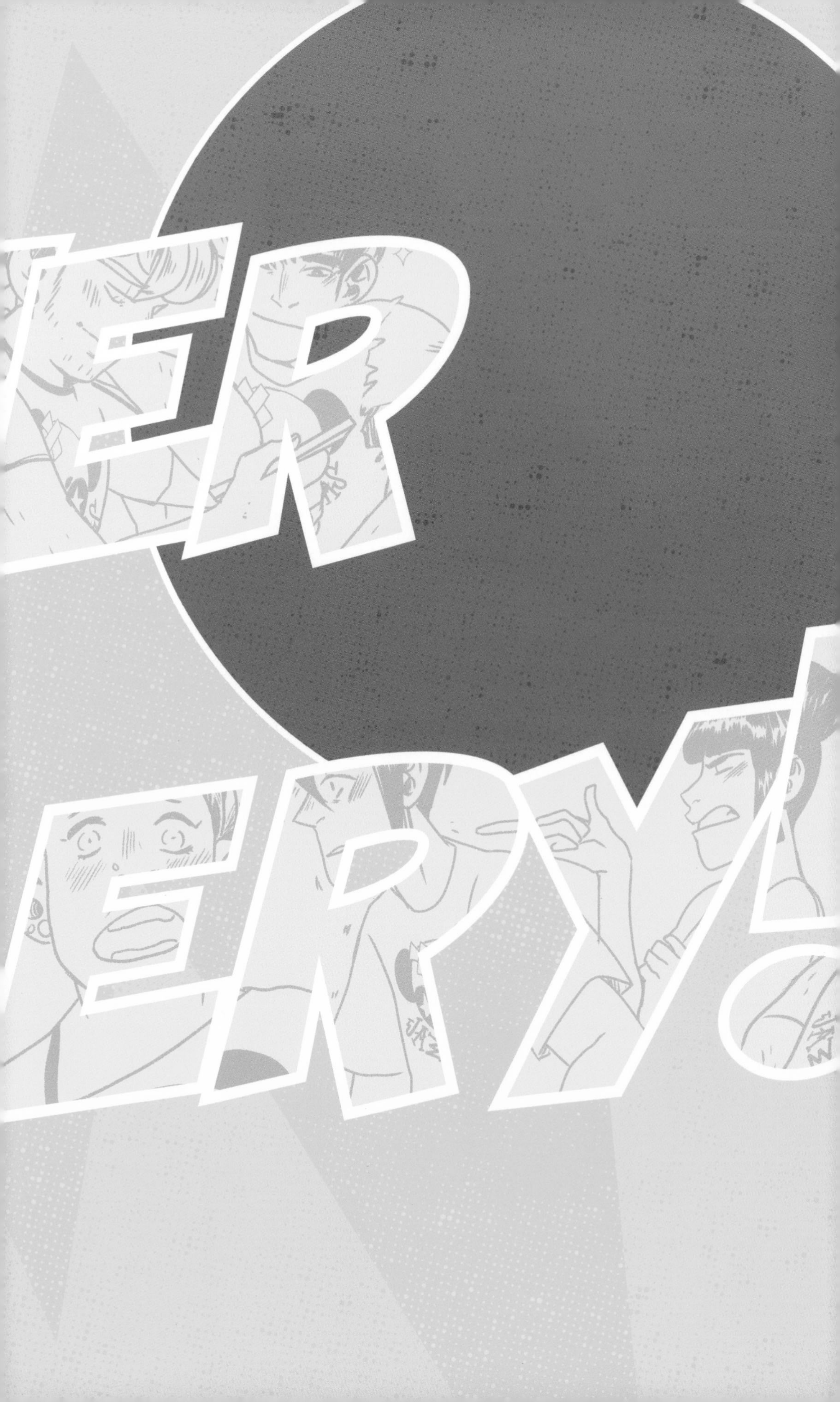
ER
ERY!

Issue One Cover by
CARA McGEE

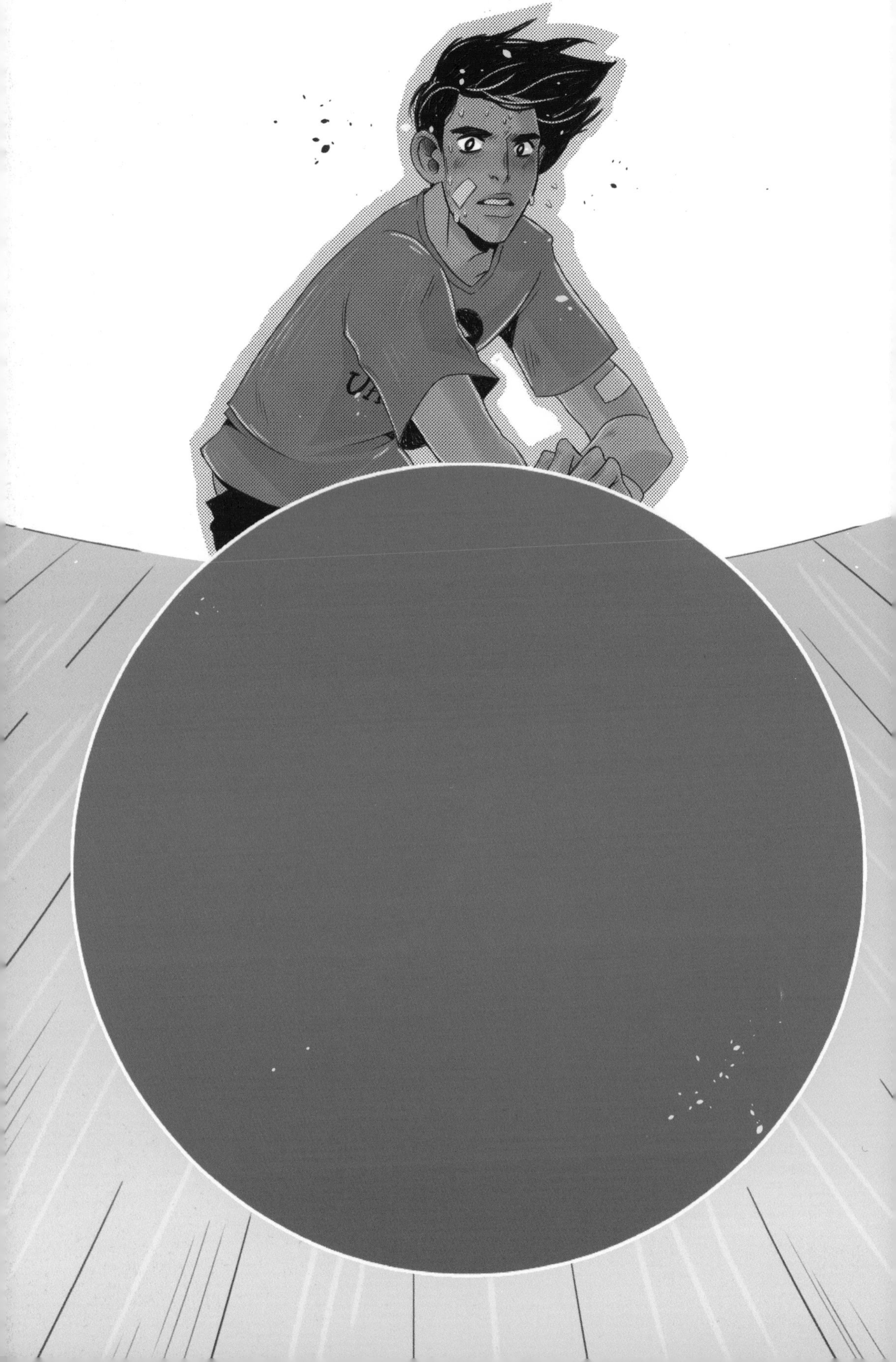

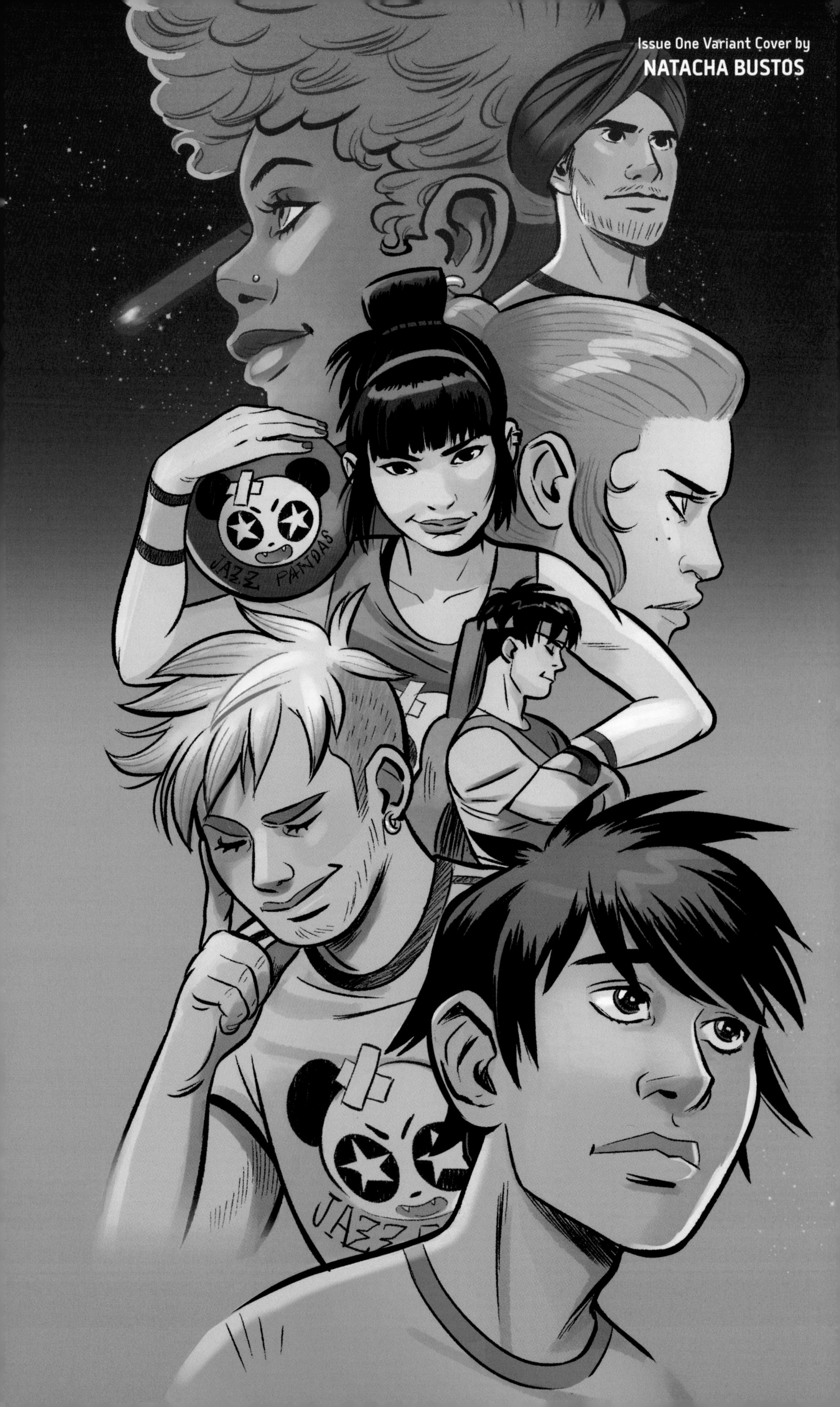
JAZZ PANDAS
JAZZ

Issue One Variant Cover by
NATACHA BUSTOS

Issue One Fried Pie Variant Cover by

CARA McGEE

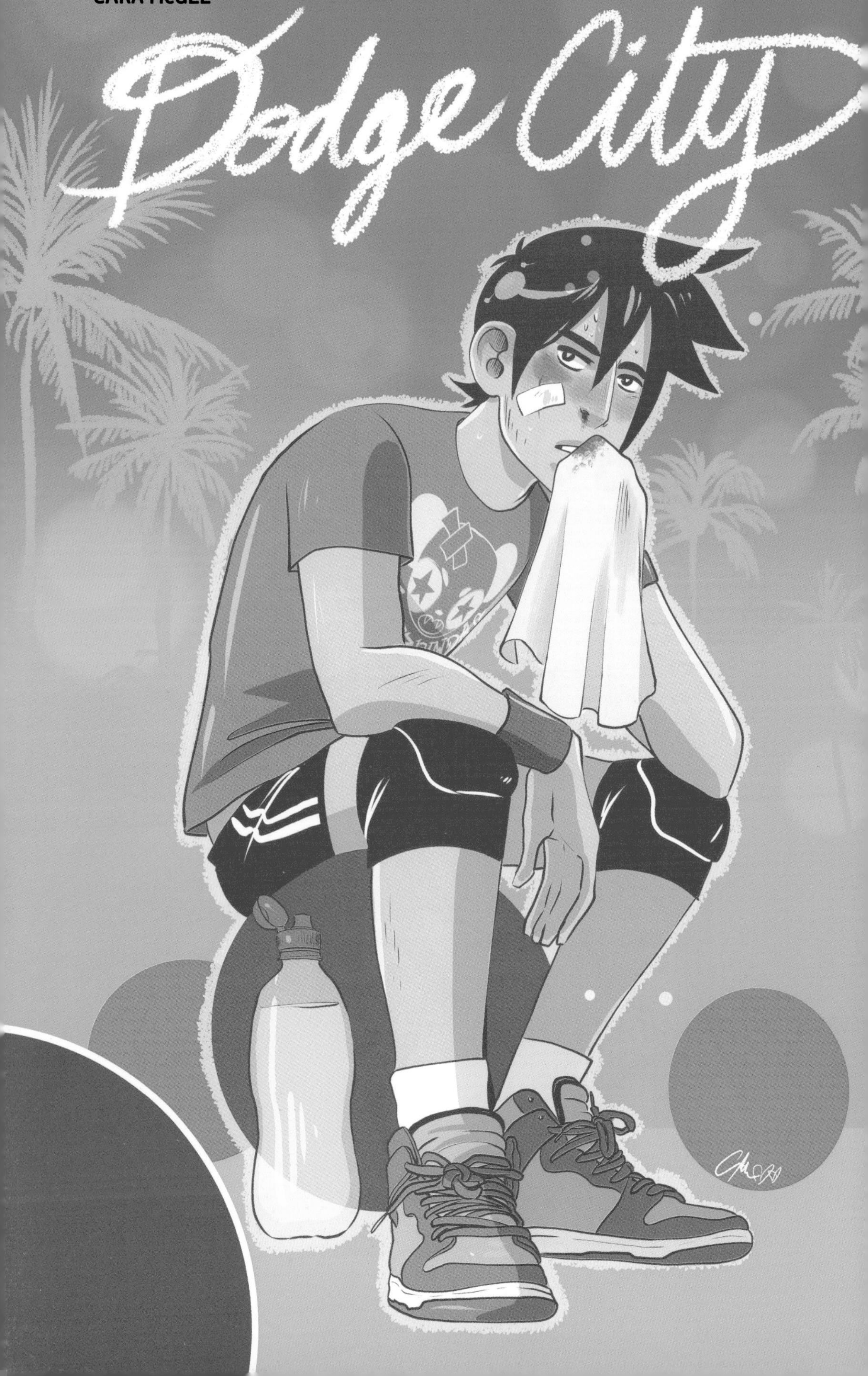

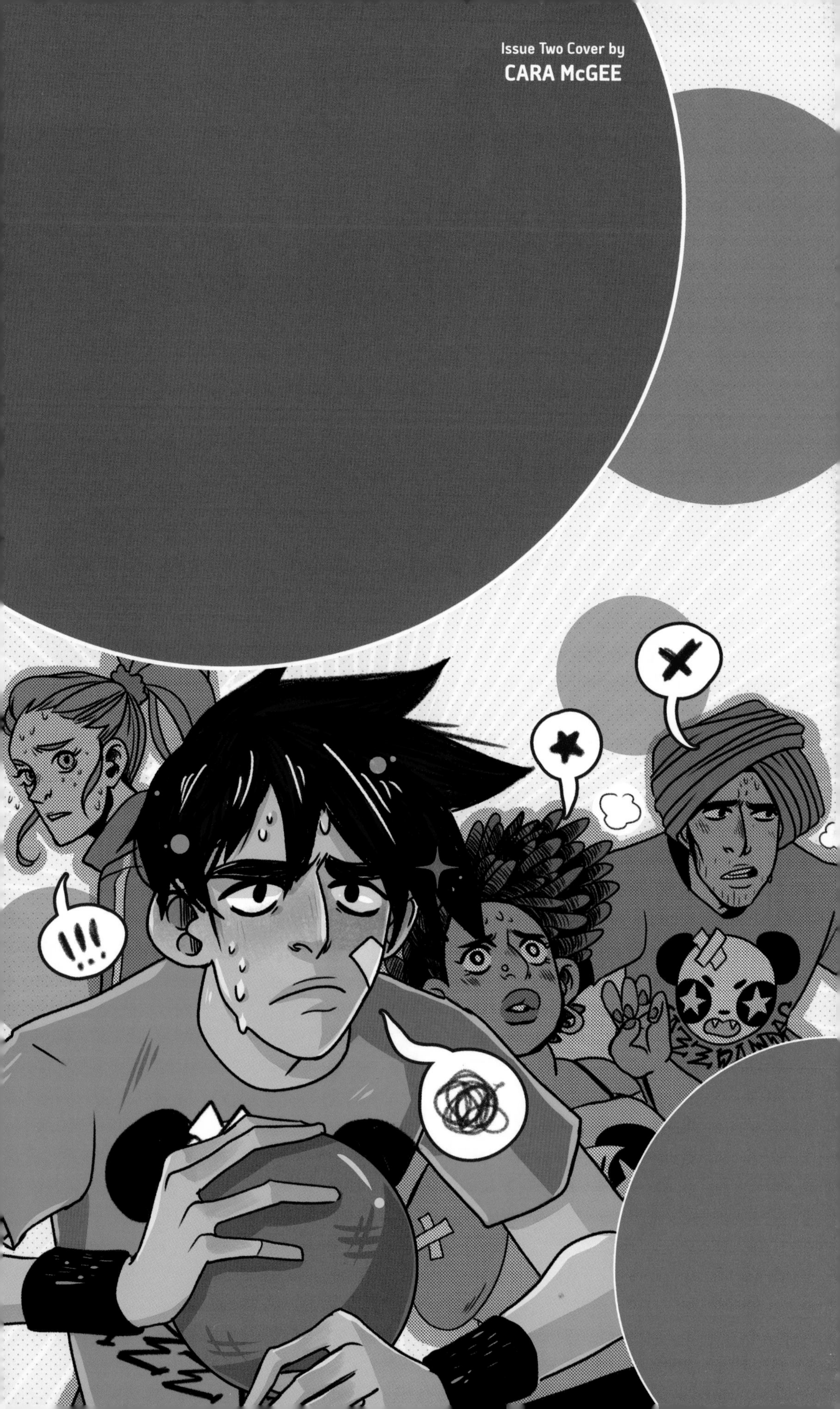
!!!

Issue Two Cover by
CARA McGEE

Issue Three Cover by

CARA McGEE

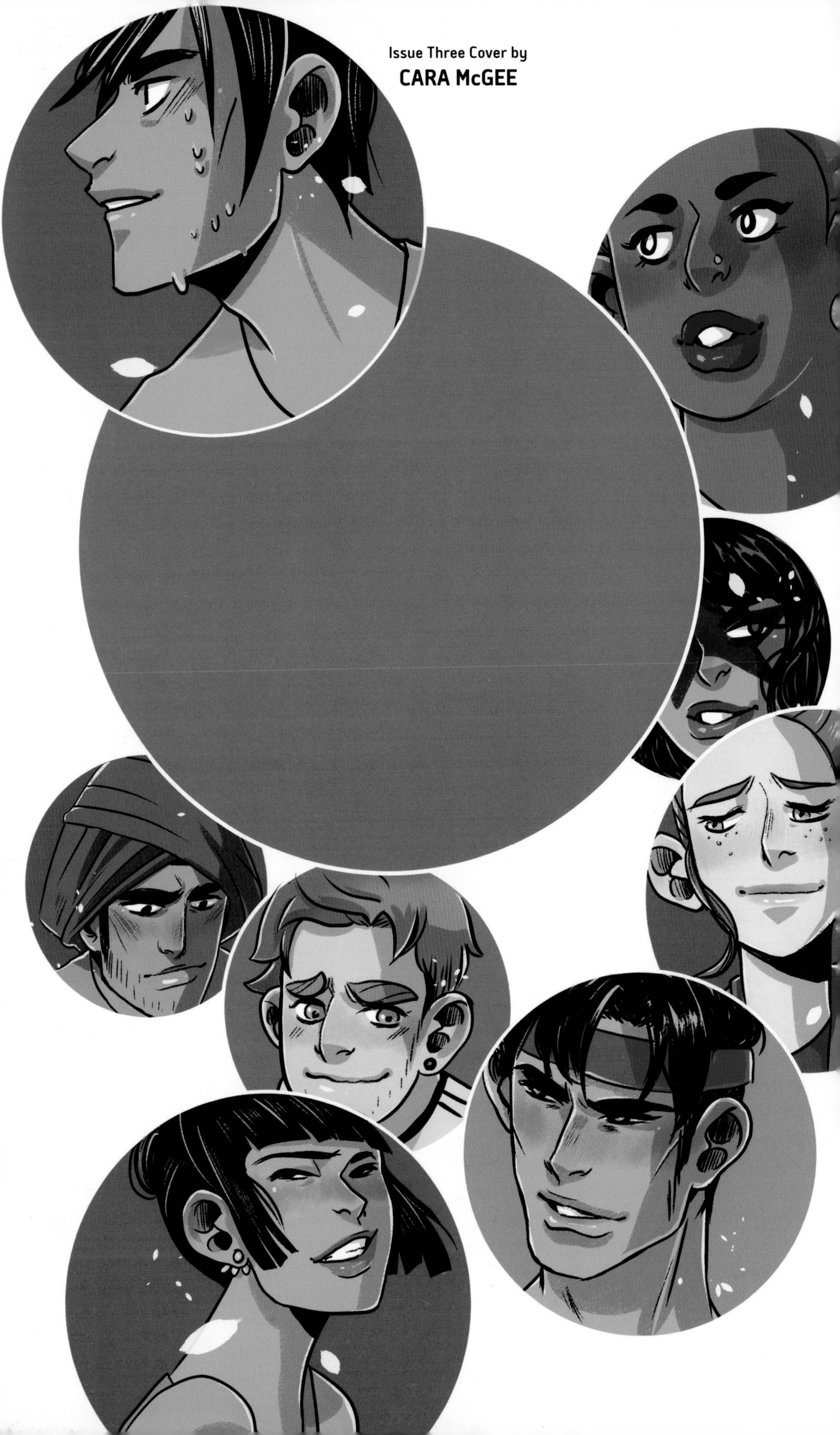

Issue Four Cover by
CARA McGEE

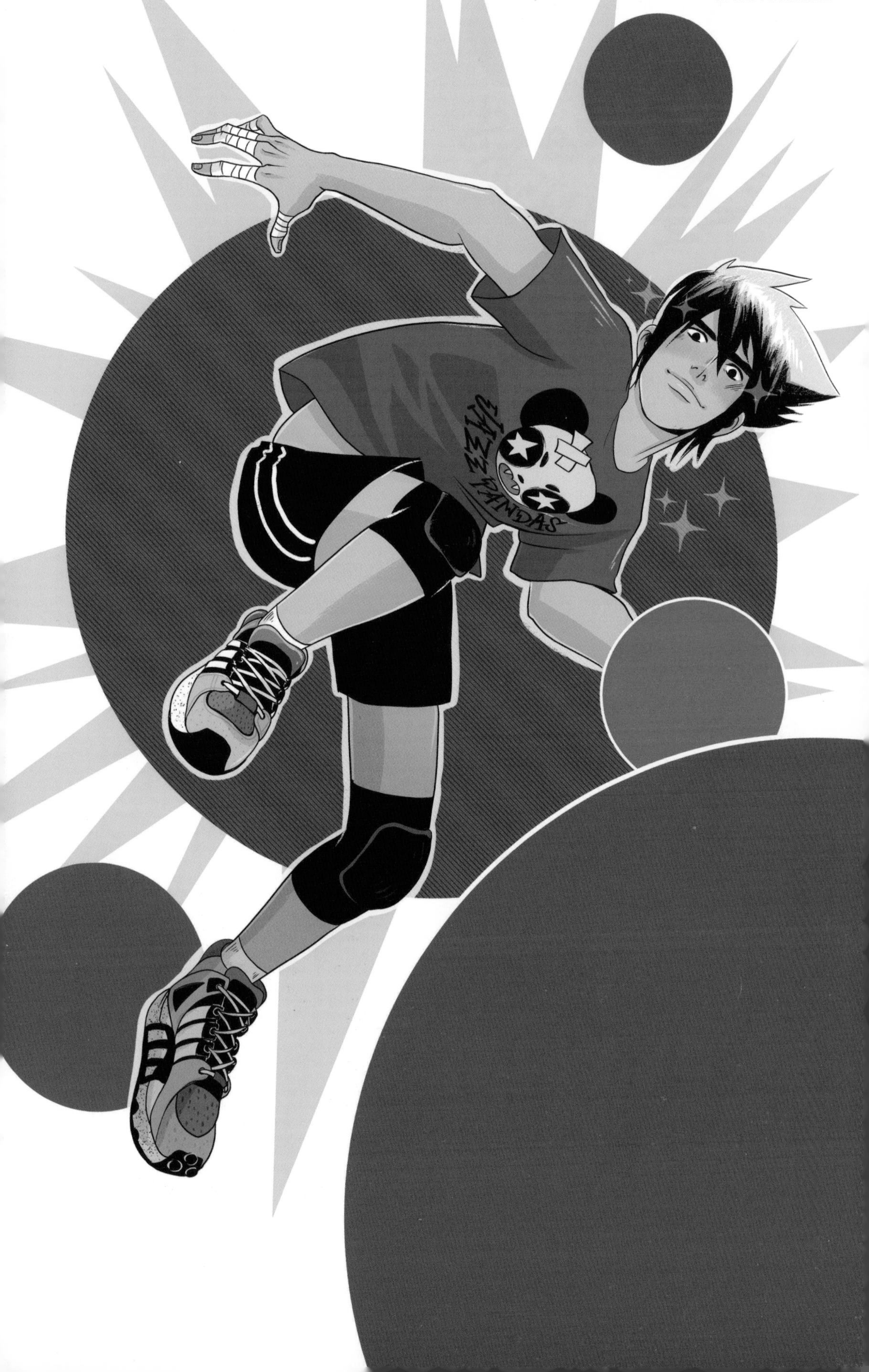

Original Character Designs by
CARA McGEE

Clockwise:

Tomás

Elsie

Drew

Huck

Judith

Chase

Amardeep

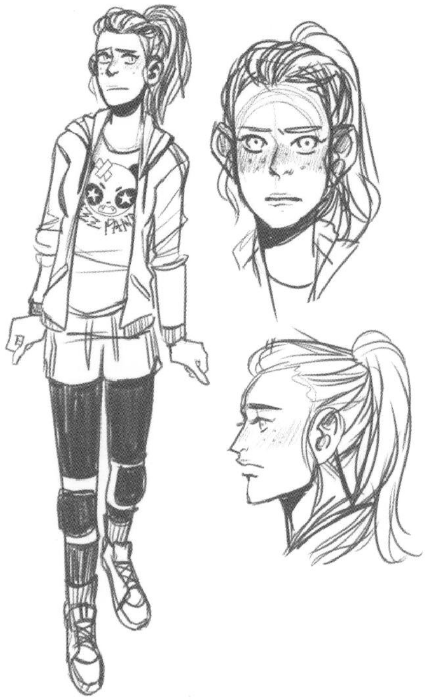

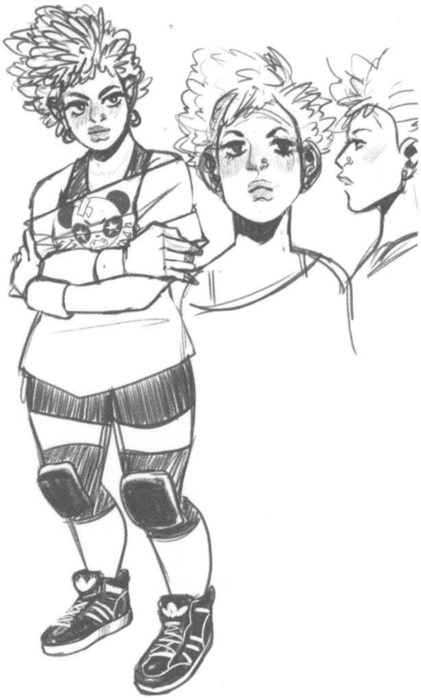

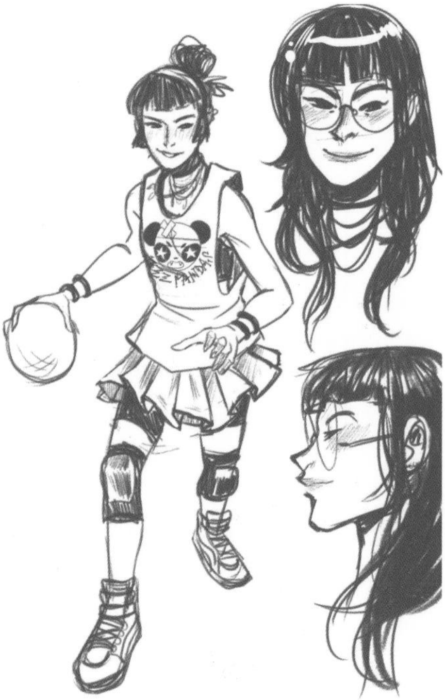

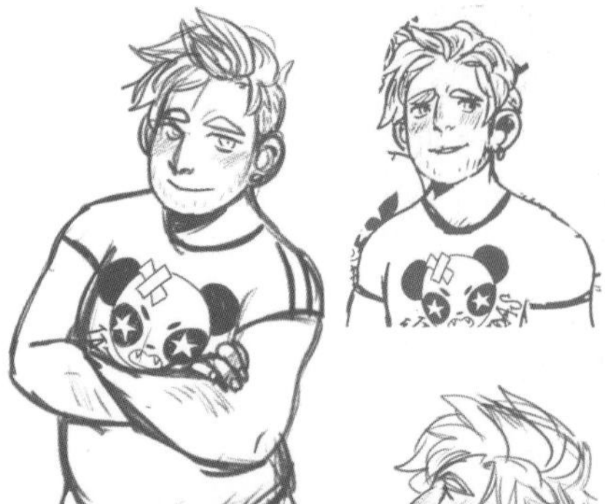

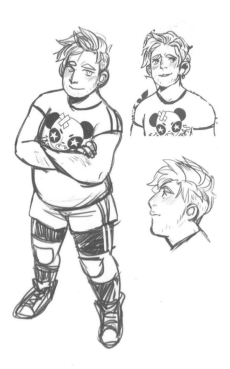

DISCOVER
ALL THE HITS

STEVENSON • ELLIS • WATTERS • ALLEN
LUMBERJANES
BEWARE THE KITTEN HOLY
NEW YORK TIMES BESTSELLING SERIES
WINNER

Allison + Treiman + Cogar
GIANT DAYS
VOLUME ONE

RIBON • FISH • PEER
SLAM!
VOLUME ONE

Hope Larson • Brittney Williams • Sarah Stern
GOLDIE VANCE
Volume One

THE BACKSTAGERS

TYSON HESSE'S
DIESEL
IGNITION
Graphic Policy

BOOM! BOX™

AVAILABLE AT YOUR LOCAL COMICS SHOP AND BOOKSTORE

WWW.**BOOM-STUDIOS**.COM

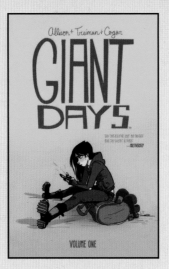

Lumberjanes
Noelle Stevenson, Shannon Watters, Grace Ellis, Brooklyn Allen, and Others
Volume 1: Beware the Kitten Holy
ISBN: 978-1-60886-687-8 | $14.99 US
Volume 2: Friendship to the Max
ISBN: 978-1-60886-737-0 | $14.99 US
Volume 3: A Terrible Plan
ISBN: 978-1-60886-803-2 | $14.99 US
Volume 4: Out of Time
ISBN: 978-1-60886-860-5 | $14.99 US
Volume 5: Band Together
ISBN: 978-1-60886-919-0 | $14.99 US

Giant Days
John Allison, Lissa Treiman, Max Sarin
Volume 1
ISBN: 978-1-60886-789-9 | $9.99 US
Volume 2
ISBN: 978-1-60886-804-9 | $14.99 US
Volume 3
ISBN: 978-1-60886-851-3 | $14.99 US

Jonesy
Sam Humphries, Caitlin Rose Boyle
Volume 1
ISBN: 978-1-60886-883-4 | $9.99 US
Volume 2
ISBN: 978-1-60886-999-2 | $14.99 US

Slam!
Pamela Ribon, Veronica Fish, Brittany Peer
Volume 1
ISBN: 978-1-68415-004-5 | $14.99 US

Goldie Vance
Hope Larson, Brittney Williams
Volume 1
ISBN: 978-1-60886-898-8 | $9.99 US
Volume 2
ISBN: 978-1-60886-974-9 | $14.99 US

The Backstagers
James Tynion IV, Rian Sygh
Volume 1
ISBN: 978-1-60886-993-0 | $14.99 US

Tyson Hesse's Diesel: Ignition
Tyson Hesse
ISBN: 978-1-60886-907-7 | $14.99 US

Coady & The Creepies
Liz Prince, Amanda Kirk, Hannah Fisher
ISBN: 978-1-68415-029-8 | $14.99 US